Of GRACE *and* CHOCOLATE

Of GRACE and CHOCOLATE

a novel

KRISTA LYNNE JENSEN

Covenant Communications, Inc.

Cover image: *Girl with Chocolate* © Izusek, courtesy iStockphoto.com.

Cover design copyright © 2012 by Covenant Communications, Inc.

Published by Covenant Communications, Inc.
American Fork, Utah

Printed in the United States of America
First Printing: January 2012

18 17 16 15 14 13 12   10 9 8 7 6 5 4 3 2 1

ISBN-13: 978-1-60861-865-1

For my brave mom, who taught her children how to fight to remember who we are and who we are meant to become.

For my dad, who is so obviously in love with my mom—and her homemade hot fudge sauce.

For all those who struggle against and overcome the widespread, devastating effects of substance abuse, you have my deepest respect.

Though this story was inspired by my mother's courage, it is in no way biographical—except that a howler monkey really did throw a mango pit at me. It hit my shoe.

Acknowledgments

I am grateful to so many people who helped bring this book into existence, so I'll start at the beginning.

Thanks cannot be expressed enough to my parents, Mike and Debby Anglesey. There was never a time that I felt you doubt my capability to do anything. Anything at all. I'm sure I still don't realize how much that single fact has influenced my life. And thanks for the reverse psychology. It worked. Love you both. Don't smile.

Thank you, Shelli Larson, the best sister and friend and cheering section I could have. Thanks to my not-so-little brothers, Michael Scott, and Craig. You guys are pretty good too. Mike, I kind of borrowed you for this book. Just a little. Hope that's okay.

I need to thank my parents-in-law, Bernie and Virginia Jensen, for your enthusiastic support. To you and all my brothers- and sisters-in-law, thanks for continually asking how the writing is going and not looking bored when I tell you. I love you all.

Thanks to my critique group, Writing Friendzy. Carla Parsons and Norma Rudolph, without you, there would be no book. Carla, thank you for challenging me to write fiction; thank you for teaching me everything you know about writing it. And thank you for being my dear, dear friend. Norma, thank you for encouraging me to submit to Covenant. Thank you for reading so voraciously, and thank you for being quick to laugh and quick to rise to my defense. Leah Berry, you were part of us for all the chaos of getting this book out, and we loved having you. Thank you for being fresh eyes for *Of Grace and Chocolate*, and thank you for your enthusiasm and joy. We will miss your face in the Wapiti Room. I am so fortunate to be surrounded by talent, encouragement, and intelligence every week.

Many thanks go to my alpha readers, Carla, Norma, Rebecca Sorensen, Andy Mogle, and Kimberly Vanderhorst. Your invaluable feedback helped get this story past my editor. To my beta readers, Annette Lyon, Josi Kilpack, Luann Staheli, Shanda Cottam, Mindy Holt, Melanie Jacobson, Sherrie Burt, and Leah Berry, your feedback put me and this story through the refiner's fire. I am so fortunate. To Officer Chris Wallace, thanks for answering my crazy questions at the Church Halloween party or Christmas party or whatever that was. To Annette, Josi, Sarah Eden, and Robison Wells, thanks for giving me some backbone.

To my editor, Samantha Van Walraven, thank you for making me work harder than I ever thought I would to make this book the best it could be. And thank you for always looking so happy to see me. It makes me breathe easier.

To Kathryn Jenkins and everyone at Covenant Communications, thank you for giving my stories a chance; thank you for your part in creating something that will forever be a part of who I am.

To my Twitter Tweeps and Facebook Friends, my bloggers and the LDS writing community, you are so, so terribly fun. To my amazing girlfriends, thanks for cheering me on. To my amusing guy friends, you rock.

I would like to thank my two youngest children, Maren and Jacob, for thinking it is pretty dang awesome that their mom is a writer. For my two oldest children, Braeden and Chelsea, thank you for stopping short of telling people I traded you for my laptop. I love you all so much. You are the best, most astounding part of me. Leftovers are in the fridge.

Thank you, Brandon Jensen, for patiently wondering what happened to your wife for the last three years; thank you for finally seeing what all this means to me; and thank you for taking me to Costa Rica twelve years ago with a bunch of high school, third-year Spanish students. Thank you for your story suggestions—some of them real—and for telling me I need more hobbits. You've made me stronger, braver, and a little funnier. I love you. Hope the kids left you something to eat.

Grace. Divine means of help or strength,
given through the bounteous mercy and love of the Lord.

Chocolate. (See *Grace*)

CHAPTER 1

The harsh scrape of chair against linoleum jerked Jill out of her daydream, and the dripping, moss-hung trees of an ancient forest dissipated into the bland meeting room of the offices of Brasher Books Publishing. She blinked as she heard more chairs push away from the conference table. They had been dismissed.

It wasn't like her to lose focus like that.

She looked over the notes she'd taken, circling the number she was to call the minute she returned to her desk, where she'd absently left her phone on a pile of paper. Again, out of character. People filed out of the room, murmuring about trends, clients, and the Labor Day weekend they had planned.

"Is this a manuscript?"

Jill's gaze jumped to the manicured fingertips pressed on the stack of documents next to her. "Uh . . ." Her gaze then climbed to the face belonging to the red lacquered nails. "Ms. Martin. Yes. I mean, no. I mean . . . I was just cleaning out my desk before the meeting, and it was tucked in my—"

Rowena Martin, managing editor of Brasher Books Publishing, pointed to the name under the title. "This is you?"

"Yes."

"What is it about?"

"Umm . . ." Jill swallowed. She had just read somewhere that an author should have two really good sentences at the ready, a hook, so she can answer that exact question. She hadn't taken the time to think of any. "It's a novel . . . based on a woman's faith . . . and overcoming obstacles against all odds." Jill cringed at how boring that sounded. "It's a romance."

"What faith, if I may ask?"

She took a deep breath. "I'm LDS." She paused, wondering if that statement meant anything to Rowena Martin—but the woman only watched her, waiting. "It's a Mormon novel."

Ms. Martin's sharp eyebrows rose. "And this is the title?"

"Yes. Tentatively."

In a quick movement, Jill's manuscript was in the woman's arms. "Are you any good?" She lifted the top page as she asked.

What kind of question was that?

But Ms. Martin didn't seem to expect an answer. "I'll take a look. We're exploring a new division, as you heard. Faith-based fiction. Ripley and Grosskopf have already approached me with their own ideas."

Jill thought to argue that Ripley and Grosskopf were slush-pile editors, given the mind-bending task of sorting through doubtful first submissions and were only above mere secretaries on the publishing ladder, but held her tongue.

The woman perused the unbound pages. "This falls into that category, does it not?"

Jill nodded numbly, her voice receding somewhere deep inside her abdomen, not to be found. The woman turned on her heels and walked away.

Jill blinked, then panic slapped her in the gut, dislodging her voice. "Ms. Martin!"

The woman turned, looking over her rectangular glasses.

Jill stood and steadied herself, eyeing the manuscript in such powerful hands. "I'm sorry, Ms. Martin, but I can't let you take that."

The woman stared, disbelieving.

"I mean . . . that's only the second draft, a partial. It's a mess. Since then I've cut two characters, an aimless subplot, and thirty pages off the ending. That's not the copy you want." She swallowed and tried to stop grasping at her hands. She pulled them behind her back. Jill lowered her eyes but then blew out a breath and stepped forward, lifting her chin. "I can get you a copy of the finished revision though. It's on my flash drive."

Ms. Martin snapped her wrist over and glanced at her watch then at the title page in her grasp. She handed the manuscript back.

Jill's voice fled back to its hiding place, along with any hopes this encounter had conjured.

"I'll be in Bob Brasher's office until two. Get the copy to me before I leave, Miss Parish."

Jill's heart leapt. "Yes. Thank you. I will."

The glass door closed soundlessly behind Rowena Martin.

Jill stood, magnetized in place, trembling hand holding the partial manuscript. She had nearly thrown it out while cleaning her desk but had decided at the last minute to hang on to it with the crazy notion that it might, just might, be valuable someday. It was sheer luck that she'd mistakenly grabbed it with her notebook in her haste to get to the meeting.

"I would get on that if I were you."

Jill jumped at the soft voice next to her ear. A shiver dispelled any lock the moment had on her. It was not pleasant.

"Not so close, Ortiz. I've got your wife's cell phone on speed dial."

He put his hands up defensively, his dark eyes wide in feigned innocence. "Hey, hey. Just sayin' you shouldn't waste time, that's all."

Jill cut him a sharp look, ignoring his smoldering grin and heady cologne, and gathered her things.

He chuckled. "I love it when you call me by my last name."

Ugh. She pushed through the door. She could think of a few things she'd rather call him. She made her way to her cubicle.

Marci popped up over the partition, her red hair bouncing above her shoulders. "Hey, how'd it go?"

"You mean besides the visual groping I just received from Ortiz?" Marci's grimace told her she didn't have to explain, so she said, "Ask me in twenty minutes."

"Right-o." Marci dropped back down.

Jill liked that about Marci—not too pushy. She opened the top drawer of her desk. "Keys, keys, keys . . ." They weren't there. She began again, methodically this time.

"My keys are gone. My keys are gone . . . Marci?"

Marci popped up. "Yes?"

"Have you seen my keys? You know, four keys, library card, very important flash drive?"

Marci was nodding her head as she searched the unusually littered desktop over the partition. "Yeah, with the silver palm tree. No, I haven't seen them. Wow, I've never seen your desk this messy."

Jill spoke from below the desk. "I was cleaning it out."

"Why are you cleaning your desk *now*?"

"I wanted it done before the long weekend." Jill blew out an exasperated breath and scanned her desk from a kneeling position. She attacked the drawer where she kept her keys once more. "Wait a minute." Her eyes came up, searching. "Where's my phone?" She stood. "I left it here on top of this pile." She glanced around the office. "Has anyone been at my cubicle?"

"I didn't see anyone while I was here. But I've been down in editing for the last hour."

Jill sat down hard on her chair and rubbed her hand over her forehead. "Okay, okay, I've got it at home." She checked the time. She'd never make it. And her keys were missing. She dropped her elbows on the manuscript. "Why would this happen right now?"

Abruptly, music started playing, and she jumped at the sound.

"Is that your phone?" Marci asked.

"No," she answered, aware of the knot forming in her stomach. "I don't have that ringtone."

"Well, it's coming from your desk."

It was definitely coming from her desk. Jill sorted under some files and wrapped her fingers around the slim phone. She pulled it up. 3 Doors Down played "Away from the Sun." The song instantly triggered a distant memory, and Jill froze for a moment. The image of a lost young girl caught in the clutches of something too monstrous to fight clawed at Jill's heart. She sucked in a breath and brushed it away. The effort was one of survival. "This isn't my phone, but the call is from my number."

"Well, answer it."

"Don't you think this is odd?"

Marci shrugged, her blue eyes unquestioning.

Jill lifted the phone to her ear. "Hello?"

"Hey, I believe you have my phone."

"Who is this?"

"Stand up."

She didn't have time for this. "Why should I? Do you have my phone?" She winced. Of course he had her phone. "Who is this?"

"Relax, Sister Parish, and the phone won't get hurt." His voice was friendly. "Stand up . . . please."

Carefully, she stood.

"Now, walk to the east windows."

Marci followed her as Jill canvassed the east windows beyond the next row of cubicles. She entered the empty conference room she had just left and stood facing the next glass building on their block. Cape & Moore Publishing occupied the same floor in that building as her company did in this one. They were a smaller company, new.

"Is something going to blow up?" she asked, only half joking. Marci widened her eyes and stepped back, twirling a short lock of red hair in her fingers.

The voice chuckled. "No. Well, maybe your temper, but I hope not."

Jill took a deep breath and folded her arms. "Who is this, and how did you get my phone?"

"Fourth window from your right, straight across."

She counted and then spotted him. "Wave."

He did. He placed his hand in his pocket. Scott Gentry.

Marci peered forward. "Ooh, do you know him?"

Jill covered the phone and steadied her breathing. She did know him. A little. She doubted he remembered. "He moved here a couple of weeks ago . . . goes to my church."

"Hm. Churchgoing and bold. And cute. At least from here. Well, what does he want? Not to blow us up, I hope."

Jill's sense of the minutes ticking away dulled her curiosity. She glanced over her shoulder at a wall clock.

His voice came across again. "Do you have a key to that drawer in your desk?"

Jill took a deep breath. "Yes." She pictured it in the tray, next to the place her keys should have been.

"Hm. You should use it. By the way, your desk is a mess."

"How dare you. Listen, I—"

She stopped at his soft laugh and watched him as he paced casually behind the window. "Please, the front desk was busy, so I asked someone where I could find you. I only wanted to get your attention."

Her heart flopped unpleasantly. "Why would you want to do that?" If he remembered anything at all, he would say so now. Eight years was a long time, true, and yes, she'd lost weight, and yes, her hair was different, and yes, she was wearing makeup, but still—

"I don't know." He floundered. "I was hoping we—"

Wrong answer. "So you stole my keys?"

"Well, I didn't want you driving off. And I *borrowed* them. They're ransom."

"My phone isn't?"

"Well, you have *my* phone."

"Not for long. You have my attention, Brother Gentry, but I don't think it's the kind you're after."

"See, you *do* know me. And it's Scott."

Her teeth ground at the clumsiness of her heartbeat. "Listen, *Scott*, I am in dire need of those keys. There is something on that flash drive, and if I don't get it in the next ten minutes, I could miss the opportunity of a lifetime. Do you understand me?" Did he understand anything?

She watched him fumble in his pocket then look at the drive in his hand.

"I'm sorry." The play in his voice was gone. "What do you want me to do?" He looked her way.

She thought. Elevators would take too long. Sprinting down the stairs in heels would be risky in more than a few ways. "Unless you have a high-powered slingshot, I suggest you stick that drive in the nearest computer and send me the file called Grace and Chocolate." She'd like to tell him where else he could stick it but hung on to what was left of her composure.

"You're serious?"

"Yes, Scott, I am. So serious my fingers are hovering over the number for the downtown Portland Police Bureau."

He disappeared from the window. "I'm uploading the file right now. Where do I send it?"

"jparish@brasherbooks.com." She shook her head at the ceiling and made her way back to her cubicle. "What were you thinking?"

"Is this a book?"

"Yes, and you are not to open the file, got that?"

"I didn't know you were an editor."

"I'm not."

"Then why would you have someone's manuscript on your flash drive—wait, is this your book? You're a writer?"

"Yes," she fired back. "I mean, no." She was losing it. "Aren't most of us?" She could name at least a dozen aspiring authors on her floor alone. "Please just send it." The *please* was difficult.

"There. It's sent."

She breathed a silent sigh of relief as she watched her inbox. "I hope it prints in time," she mumbled.

Marci leaned over her back. "Does somebody want it?"

"Maybe. Rowena Martin."

"Rowena Martin?" Jill heard through the phone.

She found herself annoyed that Scott Gentry was still on the line. "Yes, Scott, Rowena Martin, managing editor of Brasher Books. She gave me until two o'clock." His silence reminded her of her previous question. "Well, what were you thinking?"

"I . . . well, it's pretty lame now . . ."

"I'm thinking it was pretty lame before."

"I asked about you. I heard you were . . . well, that you were . . ."

"That I was what?"

"That you were difficult to . . . distract."

"Distract from what?"

"From your busy life."

The knot in her stomach tightened. Her busy life was her protection. Her stability. She clenched her fist. "Well, Scott, you've certainly succeeded in distracting me for several infuriating minutes, but now I have to get back to that busy life and see if I can make something of it. I have the file. You can pick up your phone at our front desk. I'll expect to find mine there too. And my keys. Good-bye."

She handed the phone to Marci. "Could you please take that down for me? Scott Gentry."

"Sure." Marci took the phone. "Mind if I wait around, have a peek when he brings yours in?"

"If you do, I don't want to hear about it."

Marci gave her a pout, turned her petite frame, and pranced away to the elevators. Jill sent the file to the high-speed printer in the copy room, and only then did she fold her arms over her messy desk and drop her head on top of them.

Difficult to distract? *Difficult to distract?* Compelling a man to theft? Whatever happened to a rose and a telegram, like in the old movies? Or a chance encounter . . . briefcases colliding and eyes meeting over the mess of papers. *That* is a distraction. Finding each other at sunset along a tropical shore . . . But *theft*? Who had he been talking to? And he certainly did not remember . . . It was a long time ago. A lifetime ago.

Jill groaned into her arms. "I have a *busy life*." She needed it that way. Keeping busy kept the hurt from eating her up.

Her eyes lifted to the computer screen. Printing: 85 percent complete.

She jumped out of her chair, stuffed her purse into the cabinet, and locked it with the key from the drawer. She hurried to the copy room, only then remembering the phone call she had been assigned to make as the meeting let out. Jill reached for her cell phone then pulled her hand back from her empty pocket. The call would have to wait until she got her phone back.

Jill snatched the papers off the printer and strode toward the desk in front of Robert Brasher's corner office, the manuscript feeling warm, thick, and new in her hands. She had wanted to slip it into one of the large copy envelopes, but the cupboard where they were kept was empty. She'd clamped a big jaw clip on the top edge and had headed for the supply room. She looked down again at the title page right out in the open.

Saved by Grace and Chocolate
Jillian Parish

"Whoa—"

Something heavy slammed against the book and her arms. She felt the pages fan out, and her fingers grappled to keep them together in that thickness she loved, but the clip had other ideas, slipping away and flinging to the floor, followed by the gentle fluttering of three hundred and twenty-eight newly printed pages of a faith-based fiction romance.

Scott Gentry's voice cut into her bewilderment. "Oh no."

Jill dropped to her knees as her gaze flew to the origin of that voice. He dropped down with her, tossing his own things aside and scrambling to pick up page after page after page . . .

It was all stuck. Stuck in her throat. All the things she wanted to say, ask, scream. She could only watch, her mouth slack, fighting back tears. Others gathered, and she heard quiet murmurs, counting, putting pages in order. She blinked and swallowed, remembering she was not helpless.

She gathered the pages around her feet and spied the clip near the corner of the desk. She crawled over, reached for it, and quickly wiped away the tear that had slipped down the side of her nose. She sat back on her heels, put the pages in her hands in order, then pushed herself up, afraid to turn around. But slowly, she did and found Scott Gentry standing, holding a growing stack of paper as coworkers added to the pile. Mr. Brasher's secretary squeezed Jill's arm and slipped quietly back behind her large desk.

Scott stood there a moment, looking miserable. He stepped forward and placed the stack on the desk, evening the pages as well as he could. He didn't raise his eyes but humbly gestured for the sheets in Jill's hands.

She hesitated but passed them on and gave him the clip when he had them in place.

He raised his eyes to meet hers and held the manuscript out between them just as Mr. Brasher's office door opened. They both turned their heads as people around them scattered.

"Thanks, Robert. Let me know about the contract on that thriller series. I'd like to get that going ASAP." Rowena Martin closed the door and turned. "Oh, Miss . . ."

"Parish," Jill cleared her throat. "Jillian Parish." She glanced at Scott. Her thrumming heart was somewhere in her throat. She wished it would slink away, hide in that place her voice had found before.

"Yes, Miss Parish. Is that the manuscript? Oh good." She reached for it but paused. "You know, it should be in an envelope."

Jill could only nod. Some sound came out of her mouth, but she had no idea what it was. She hoped it was polite.

"I'd hate to lose pages between here and Lake Oswego." The woman checked her watch again. "I'm late. Why don't you send it through submissions, and we'll see what happens, eh?" Rowena Martin smiled, nodded, and turned away. What had just happened? Disappointment cracked like an egg over Jill's head and ran down the sides.

"Excuse me, Ms. Martin?" Scott was speaking. Why he was speaking Jill couldn't guess, but she wished he'd stop.

"Yes?"

"Scott Gentry. Cape & Moore. I feel it only ethical to tell you—and it's why I came over here—that we have some interest in Miss Parish's novel, but since she is in-house, we'd like to extend the opportunity to Brasher to . . . have the chance to take her on."

Rowena considered Scott. "You've had a look at this manuscript?"

"I happened to stumble across the first pages, yes." He gave Jill the slightest glance.

Jill held her breath, wide-eyed, as Rowena looked back at her. Jill managed a weak smile and shrugged.

Scott continued. "It's strong, well written. Fresh. If Jill weren't an employee of Brasher, I'd push this along to Reid."

Rowena turned back to Scott. "You work with Cal Reid?"

"Yes."

"I don't recognize you, do I?"

"No, Ms. Martin. I've just started in submissions inquiries." He handed her a business card.

"Mmm." She held her hand back toward Jill. "Well, Miss Parish, let's have a look."

Before Jill could hand over the manuscript, Mr. Brasher's secretary deftly slipped it into an envelope, already labeled with her name and contact information. She gave Jill a hidden wink and stepped back out of the way.

"Thank you for the heads-up, Mr. Gentry. Would hate to lose one of our own to the competitors." She turned to Jill. "You know the process. We'll let you know." Then she was gone, down the hall and into the elevator.

Jill finally let out the breath she'd been holding and glanced around for a place to sit. Chairs, against a window near the secretary's desk.

Out of the corner of her eye, she saw Scott moving that way too, but she brushed her concern aside as she concentrated on keeping her knees from buckling. She did not need another scene today. She sat quickly, closing her eyes and pressing her fingers to her temples. The second chair over creaked as he sat down.

"That wasn't true," she said quietly.

"Well, we only had time to graze over the first few pages, but we liked what we saw."

She groaned. "I told you not to open it. Who's *we*?"

"Well, *me*. But it's a good thing I did look it over, or I would have had to lie and that's against my religion."

"No, you wouldn't have." She turned to him and shot out, "And why would that concern *you* after *stealing* from my desk?"

The secretary gently cleared her throat and raised her eyebrows, looking busy. Jill lowered her voice.

"Which is worse? Stealing? Or lying to cover the mess you made by stealing?"

Her eyes met his. Blue with gold flecks. Stupid flecks.

"I have nothing to say. No defense. I only have this."

He set the small black gift bag he'd tossed aside earlier along with a slightly trampled rose onto the seat between them. "I apologize. I . . ." He shook his head.

She swallowed, eyeing the items in the chair. "You didn't need—"

He stopped her. "The bag has your things in it. And I did need. Sorry for all the trouble. Good luck with the book. It does look promising. That wasn't a lie."

She held the rose in her fingers. The head drooped. "Thank you."

He stood. "Don't thank me. I'm going to go wallow in self-pity and humiliation. See you at church."

"Yeah."

He walked away, running his hand over his blond head. She heard the first few notes of "Away from the Sun." Scott answered his phone, and the elevator doors closed.

Scott Gentry. You've said my name over and over again, and you still don't know who I am. You still don't remember. You big jerk.

She grappled with whether or not she even wanted him to remember those couple of weeks so many years ago. After a few moments of trying to clear her wandering thoughts, she peeked into the black bag. Her phone, her keys . . . and a thick, foil-wrapped square of chocolate.

"You make that phone call yet, Jill?" Her boss hurried past her.

She jumped up. "Right away, ma'am."

She unwrapped the chocolate as she walked back to her desk . . . distracted.

* * *

Scott shook the rain off his umbrella and opened the door to his apartment building, quickly stepping aside for a couple just leaving. He'd been given flack at the office for using an umbrella—few of the natives did—but the last thing he needed was a lukewarm drenching. Stomping up the narrow flight of stairs, he frowned at the door to the apartment he now shared with his brother, stabbed his keys in the lock, and turned the doorknob. The smell of bacon hit him in the face.

"Bro! How'd it go? You sweep her off her feet?"

Scott watched his younger brother sink his teeth into a thick BLT and kick his feet with a leap over the back of the sofa, landing perfectly against a pillow leaning on the arm. He settled in with his plate.

"Are you takin' her out? Hope you don't mind, but I made myfelf fome dinna."

"Don't talk with your mouth full."

"Forry, Mom." Trey swallowed and smiled. "So?"

Scott felt that same block that had prevented him from calling Trey after the disaster. It may have been the fear that if he told his younger brother what had happened, he'd lose it and kill the kid.

Trey's smile faded. "Didn't it work?"

Scott took in a breath to say something but stopped and instead turned to throw his wet coat and umbrella on the rack and slide his briefcase toward the hall. He loosened his tie and then removed it entirely, unbuttoning his shirt at the collar.

"That bad, huh?"

Scott could hear the apprehension in Trey's voice. The kid was catching on. Maybe Scott wouldn't have to say anything. He turned for the kitchen, opened the fridge when he got there, looked for a minute, and then shut the door harder than he'd intended. He saw Trey wince.

"Well . . . what happened?"

Scott shook his head, giving his brother a warning look. He went to the cupboard and grabbed a bag of chips then threw them back in and shut the door.

"I can fry up some more bacon."

"*Why?*" Scott threw his hands in the air and asked the ceiling. "*Why* would I take advice from *you?*" He looked at his brother. "When was the last time you even had a date?"

"Saturday."

Scott glared at him. "Well, I bet you won't get a second one, will you?"

"We're going to a movie tomorrow night." Trey's mouth was full again. "And fee brought me cookief at work."

Scott breathed through his nose. "And tell me, little brother, did she bring you cookies at work because she thinks you are a felon?"

Trey swallowed and shook his head.

"Or a liar?"

"No, I don't think so."

"No. No." Scott gripped the counter to keep his hands from reaching for Trey's throat. "Thus, the *date*." He dropped his head and took a deep, slow breath. "You know what?" He brought his head up. "It's my fault. I deserved the humiliation . . . the assault on my ego. I did. I listened to you, true, but I didn't stop there. No. I had to *fix* it. Well, at least I tried. I didn't even know her, anyway, right? So no loss. *Right?*"

"Right, no loss." Trey watched him warily.

Scott bit his lip and released the counter. "No loss." He turned and headed for his room, slapping the wall on his way around the corner. Then why was it affecting him this way?

Her eyes still haunted him, and the words she'd spoken got to him. Something about her gave him an itch to know what lay behind those deep brown eyes—and he really wanted to scratch it. He had been at the desk in his bedroom for a while, trying to concentrate on the queries he was supposed to review, when he heard a careful knock on the door.

"Hm." The kid could take that however he wanted.

The door opened. Bacon.

"I made you a BLT. There's some Barq's here too."

Scott looked at Trey. His little brother had been off his mission a little more than a year. His hair had long grown out and was wavier than Scott's. He'd also grown out of his awkward, lanky look. His ears were still big, but the goatee looked pretty good on his face. Aside from his immature, harebrained ideas, his younger brother was becoming a man. Scott cleared a space on his desk, and Trey, encouraged, brought the plate and soda over. Trey set them down and stepped back.

The sandwich was piled with bacon and tomatoes. "Thanks."

"Yeah. Sorry about . . ."

Scott waved it away. "You warned me."

"Yeah. But still . . . I could see it happening, you know?"

Scott let out a chuckle and ran his hands over his face. "You wanna know what happened? Fine. I'll tell you what happened." He related everything to his brother, from the phone call to the flower.

Trey stared. Still he asked, "You don't think she would consider—"

"No. No, it's all right." He picked up the sandwich. "What do I need a woman for if I've got you?" He took a large bite. "Befides, there'f plenty of fif in the ofean." He swallowed. "At least that's what I've been told." Several times.

"There are, you know. I know why you don't try harder, but it's gotta be worth it."

Scott turned back to the computer screen. "Look who thinks he knows so much. Mr. 'Just-Steal-Her-Phone-It'll-Be-Great.'"

Trey folded his arms. "Yeah, well, you know what? I think you'd rather believe *every* woman is going to shut you down, just so you don't have to put yourself out there again."

"It's easy to believe with you hosting the show."

Trey shrugged. "Maybe it was a stupid idea, but I bet she's thinking about you right now."

"Yeah—about how fast she can get a restraining order against me. You done, Dr. Phil?"

"Yeah, I'm done." He turned. "I'm watching the game out here if you need something to do besides work."

"I'm busy. Maybe tomorrow we can rob a bank and I can ask out the teller." He took another bite of his sandwich.

Trey nodded, suppressing a smile. "Humor's good. Ladies love that."

"You would know." He took another big bite so he wouldn't have to talk anymore.

Trey smiled then, shaking his head as he closed the door. Scott reached for the soda and closed his eyes as the sweet fizz ran down his throat. He stared at the monitor in front of him and clicked open the file.

Grace and Chocolate. He scrolled to the place he had left off and read, feeling like it was some sort of penance.

* * *

Running up the steps to her brownstone apartment, Jill fumbled through her keys under the wide hood of her raincoat. How could it be dark already?

She would have to talk to Mrs. Holbrook about the broken front porch light. She turned the handle, shoved the sticky door open, switched on the hall light, and closed the door on the rain behind her. Dropping the mail on a small table, she turned to the sound of pattering feet on the old wood floor.

"Hobbes. Come here. Did you miss me?" She scooped up the scruffy brown mutt and let him lick her chin. "We're going to have to walk in the rain, pup. Let me get changed."

Hobbes jumped as she let him go. She hung up her coat and crossed the room.

"You hungry? I'm hungry. But first things first."

She yanked open the back door, and Hobbes scooted past her and out to the tiny enclosed patch of grass. Thick hedge surrounded the space, sheltering it from the neighbors and the unsightly alley. At times she missed the openness of a small town, but that patch of grass was why she'd chosen this apartment when she'd moved to Portland, and it had made the decision to get a dog an easy one.

When Hobbes finished his business and was back inside, she tossed him a biscuit from the ceramic jar on the counter and began preparations for a hot meal.

The kitchen was clean. Spotless. She assembled a simple chicken and rice dish, covered it with foil and shoved it into the oven, then checked the clock because the oven timer didn't work. She made her way to her bedroom, Hobbes at her heels.

As she changed, she found her thoughts drifting again, and her vacant eyes blinked back to life in the mirror next to the closet. "It was a very . . . strange day, Hobbes. I wish you could have been there. I needed someone with a level head."

Hobbes barked.

"Shh." She grabbed her walking shoes and sat down on the bed to tie the laces. "What if they like the book?" She was not as excited as she had imagined she would be. She sighed. "I feel like I cheated."

No. Ms. Martin had seen the book and had nearly stolen it before any of the other stuff had happened. Jill stood and folded her arms. "I didn't cheat. He just . . . fixed what he messed up, that's all." She left the bedroom. "A fraction of it, anyway," she murmured.

Scott's ringtone had been running through her head the entire afternoon, no matter how hard she tried to get it out. The song reminded her of home.

It reminded her of closed doors and of wondering why her family was so messed up and how she could change what seemed impossible to change . . .

Hobbes pulled at his leash as Jill tugged her raincoat on and pulled the door open. She gasped and hopped back. Hobbes barked and leapt forward.

"Hey, Jilly."

There on her front stoop, dripping wet and ragged, holding a bundle to her chest, was a young woman who looked far too old for her age, eyes rimmed in red, hollows under her cheekbones.

"Evie?"

The bundle in her sister's arms stirred.

CHAPTER 2

"Hobbes, hush." Jill pulled back on the leash, stunned. "Wha . . . what are you doing here?" She hadn't heard from her sister since . . . since Evie let her know she was taking off with that guy . . . that . . . Neil. Two summers ago. To Seattle. She had kept track of her for a couple months, but Evie had moved around a lot and stopped leaving forwarding information, stopped calling.

Evie peeked at the apartment over Jill's shoulder and began bouncing the bundle. "Oh, um, I . . . I needed somewhere to go, you know . . . so I looked you up, and here you are." Her eyebrows came up. "Look at you." She glanced at the dog that was sniffing her feet.

Jill pulled at Hobbes's leash. The drops of rain splatting on the small cement porch brought Jill out of her stupor. "Um, come in." She stepped back inside. "Come in out of the rain."

Her sister hesitated, looking at the leash. "I don't mean to interrupt. I mean, you're obviously about to leave."

Jill looked out at the street. She didn't see any unfamiliar car, no bags on the walk. Despite the cool air, Jill's pulse quickened and heat rose in her face. "No." She swallowed the tremor in her voice. "No, I can take Hobbes out later. Come inside."

She held the door open, and her sister hesitantly stepped forward. Hobbes barked again, wagging his tail. Jill removed his leash, trying to gather the calm she'd felt this morning, and he trotted back into the kitchen.

"When did you get a dog?"

It was such a normal question. "A couple years ago." Jill returned her raincoat to the closet. "When did you get a baby?" She turned to meet her little sister's eyes.

Evie bit her lip then broke into the widest smile the girl could have made on her thin face. "Eight months ago."

Jill had to smile in return. But eight months? Her sister had been a mother for almost a year, and Jill hadn't known, hadn't been there. Jill didn't know who the father was—though she could guess—or even what having a child was like. Eight months meant . . . the baby had been born in January. In January, Jill had bought a matching set of dishes and a writing desk. Evie had brought a human being into the world. She was little more than a child herself. The thought was staggering.

Jill gestured to the sofa, trying to remain composed. "Sit down, Evie."

Evie gazed around the small apartment, her eyes lingering on the kitchen as she walked to the sofa. She sat on the edge of the cushion, looking at the pictures on the walls and at the bookshelves. "You still read a lot?"

"Mm-hm, and write some." Jill found herself watching her sister's eyes, an old habit and one Jill hated. Though tired and strained, they weren't dilated. Jill breathed a little easier—but only a little.

The baby on Evie's lap stirred. Evie asked, "Do you want to see her?" She began to unwrap the dirty blankets from around the baby. Her hands trembled.

Jill sat down on the other end of the sofa, determined not to lose control of her emotions or her sister's trust. She knew how fragile it was. "What's her name?"

"Shiloh. Isn't that pretty?" The blankets revealed a head covered in dark, sweaty ringlets.

"Mm, she's got the Parish curls."

"I know, poor thing, but really, they're pretty on her, don't you think?" She turned the sleeping baby around.

Jill's swallow caught in her throat at the sight of this little person, this little girl so obviously a part of their family, no matter how messed up or broken it was.

"Shiloh," Evie whispered, "this is your aunt Jill."

The curls *were* pretty on her, falling around her face. Tight pink lips puckered under a little lump of a nose, and brown lashes rested on soft pale cheeks. Her little brows furrowed, and she brought a fist up to rest against her ear. Her shirt was too big, and she wasn't wearing any pants. Her diaper sagged, and her feet were bare. Jill reached to touch Shiloh's hair.

Her words came out hushed. "Where have you been, Evie?" From the looks of both of them, it hadn't been anywhere great.

Evie glanced back at the kitchen and bit her lip. Her fingers came up to brush her own dirty blonde hair out of her face, dull with neglect, most of it pulled back in a short ponytail. Her stained sweatshirt had a hole in the cuff. Underneath, her wrists were bruised. She turned to catch Jill's gaze and looked down at the sleeping baby, pulling her sleeves.

She lifted Shiloh onto the sofa between them and drew the rags back over her. "You're still straightening your hair."

Jill allowed the change of subject. She couldn't rush this. "Yes."

"It looks really good . . . makes you look all glamorous."

Jill nodded then tried again. "Where've you been, sis? For two years?"

Evie chewed on her lip again, glancing at the kitchen.

Jill followed her gaze and let the unanswered question go. "You must be hungry. I'll get you something to eat."

"Oh—" The eager look in her sister's eyes somehow angered Jill. "Okay. I guess I am a little hungry. We didn't eat much on the way here."

"I'll feed you, and then we can talk." Her voice held an edge Jill couldn't hide, and she regretted it as soon as she saw fear in her sister's eyes. She sighed. "What happened with Neil, Evie?"

The baby let out a cry, and Evie rushed to pick her up and quiet her. Big brown eyes looked up at Jill, and a bewildered pout formed on Shiloh's lips as she took in her strange surroundings. She pushed some fingers in her mouth as Evie bounced her.

Jill got up from the couch. "I'll make you some pancakes. That's quick." Evie peeked into the back of Shiloh's diaper and looked around as if a new one would appear on the sofa or end table. "Do you have any more diapers with you?" Jill asked.

Evie shook her head. "This was the last one I brought."

"Here." Jill grabbed a notepad and pen from her desk. She wrote her number down then handed the pad to Evie. "There's my number. Keep it, and make a list of things you need. When we take Hobbes for a walk, we can pick up the essentials. There's a Walgreens down a few blocks. It'll only take a few minutes." She went to the kitchen and studied the worn mother and child as she gathered ingredients. Evie pressed the pen against the paper; her brow furrowed as she wrote, reminding Jill of the countless hours she'd spent helping Evie with her homework. Five years separated the sisters in age, but even with Jill's help, even before the drugs, Evie had struggled in school.

Evie lifted an unsteady hand to her mouth and yawned.

"I could just go if you're too tired." Jill didn't want to leave her sister, but Evie appeared on the verge of physical collapse, and the smell of Shiloh's diaper was beginning to spread through the apartment. "I'll hurry."

Evie raised her head and nodded. "I'm sorry."

"It's all right. The chicken in the oven should be done in half an hour. If for some reason I'm not back yet, could you take it out of the oven?" She opened a kitchen cupboard and got out the box of pancake mix.

Evie said she would and hushed the baby while Jill made a small batch of pancakes. She set out the butter and syrup and a couple place settings.

"I don't have a bib or a highchair or anything."

"Oh, she's fine on my lap."

"You'll be all right while I'm gone?"

Evie nodded, eyes wide. Like a child. She held out the list, her hands still trembling. "Thanks, Jill," she whispered. She pulled out a bill from her sweatshirt pocket and timidly offered it.

One hundred dollars. With a glance, Jill saw the corners of a few more bills just like it before Evie tucked them back in her pocket.

Jill swallowed and took the list but passed over the money, confused and alarmed. If Evie had money, why were they in such a desperate state?

Surprising herself, Jill reached out her hand and brushed the stray hair out of Evie's eyes. The touch was the first between them in too many years. *What happened to you?* She studied the wear and sadness and fear there then turned. "I'll take the car. You'll be here when I get back?"

Evie nodded, her eyes on Shiloh.

"C'mon, Hobbes."

His eager patter lifted Jill somehow. She pulled her coat back on, hooked him with the leash, then grabbed her purse. "I'll be back as soon as I can," she repeated. "The bathroom is down the hall, first door on the right." With another look behind her, she pulled the door closed.

Jill stood a moment at the top of the stairs, clutching the handrail. Hobbes sat beside her, looking up, waiting for the go ahead. She stared out at the rain, the city street, the people walking around beneath umbrellas as if the world hadn't shifted in its rotation. Trees were still upright, and nobody ran crazily as they tried to escape the undoing of order and normalcy.

For years she had been haunted by a question, and it easily resurfaced now.

Should I have stayed?

Jill could have stayed home longer after high school—worked, continued at the community college. But Evie was already off the deep end by the time the choice was to be made. Her response to any help was to run to Neil and the relief he offered.

Her father had encouraged Jill to go to the university. She'd been prayerful. Would it have made a difference to this frightened young woman in her apartment? No matter how Jill searched, she could never find a solid answer.

Hobbes whimpered and shifted his front paws back and forth. She inhaled the cool, damp air and blew it out. "C'mon, boy."

At her step, he jumped down then paced himself alongside her as she made her way to the car. She didn't even pull her hood up. With all that was going on, the sporadic rain didn't really seem to matter.

* * *

Evie tore small pieces of pancake and fed them to Shiloh, who watched her carefully. Shiloh would do that—get a look on her face like she was waiting for the next thing to go wrong, not making any sudden moves. It unnerved Evie—that look from such a tiny thing.

"There's nothing to be scared of," Evie told her. "It's okay here. Jilly's nice."

The baby gestured for more pancake. Evie let her have it. She picked at the edge of her own. "We did it, Shiloh," she whispered. "You won't ever have to be scared of anything ever again." Her breath hitched, and she pressed her shaking fingers onto the table.

She'd left Seattle in the pouring rain in the middle of the night. She'd hurried six blocks, holding an old blanket over them both, taking the route she knew was safest, avoiding the dealers she knew would recognize her, stumbling twice. Her heart had raced so fast it hurt.

The bus had pulled up with the familiar whine of brakes and the release of air as the door opened in front of her. She hadn't moved, and the bus driver had leaned his head toward the door so he could see her. "You gettin' on?"

She'd felt the blood drain from her face as she stood. Then, as if pushed, her feet had carried her to the bus, up the stairs, into a seat.

She could've stayed on the bus. Ridden until it took her back to the stop. She could've sneaked back in, and Neil would have never known.

Neil. Evie remembered finding Neil and the girl. Her long silky hair, their legs tangled as they lay stoned on the floor of the bedroom.

She'd shaken him until he'd roused. He'd laughed at her anger. At her tears.

"What about me? What about Shiloh?" She'd felt little. Replaceable. She'd looked at the girl's long, smooth legs.

But they had Shiloh.

Neil had narrowed his eyes. "This deal I'm part of is so big . . . it's gonna *make* me." He reached over the girl and lifted a half-empty bottle of beer off the floor. He took a long swallow and, with a mild smirk, rested his head on the girl's bare shoulder. "What makes you think you even matter?"

"Dee dee." Shiloh reached out for more pancake.

Evie came out of her daze and wiped her eyes. She finished feeding the baby, holding her close.

Maybe she didn't matter. But some things did.

She kissed the top of Shiloh's head. "You're never gonna be scared again."

* * *

Jill held Hobbes as she pushed the cart. Baby shampoo, wipes, diapers . . . eight months . . . eight months . . . She grabbed the right package. A bottle, formula . . . She stopped in front of some jars of baby food. It wasn't on the list. She picked up a jar of bananas. Six months and up. She dropped it in the basket, along with some pasta and vanilla pudding, a bib, a package of pink and floral baby onesies, and a package of socks. That was the best she was going to do in the corner store. She turned her cart to the checkout and spied some red and white Blazers sweatshirts. She grabbed a tiny set with pants she thought would fit Shiloh and threw them in with the other things. Feeling like she'd already been away too long, she made her purchases, slipped her arms through the numerous bag handles, and led Hobbes toward the exit.

As she passed through the glass doors, one of the bags caught on a cart someone had left in the small causeway, drawing her attention, and she bumped into a passerby. "Oh, excuse—"

Scott Gentry blinked back at her, steadying one of her bags. Of course it was him. After all, there were only a dozen or more Walgreens in the city of Portland. Why *wouldn't* he choose this one? Tonight? She noted the umbrella hooked over his arm. Of course he'd walked. Of course he lived nearby.

"Jillian, I didn't see you. I'm sorry."

"No, that's all right." She turned quickly, her face flushed. Deciding to shop at a different Walgreens from now on, she continued through the doors.

"Wait, let me help you . . ."

She whirled. "Don't you think you've helped enough today?"

He froze, eyes open like he'd been caught—stealing. Scott carefully opened his mouth. "I just meant . . . you dropped some things here when the bag caught." He reached down and picked up the wipes, diaper rash ointment, and package of undershirts. She opened the torn bag. The gaping hole mocked her. She gritted her teeth and lifted her loaded arm to run her hand over her forehead. He brought the items over and found a place for each one in the other bags.

"Are you having a baby?"

She jerked her eyes up to his, and his mouth dropped open.

"Visit. I mean . . . having a baby visit. I'm sure you're not . . ." He blew out a breath and shook his head as her brow lifted. "I mean, not that you couldn't be—" Her mouth dropped open as well. "No—that's not what I—" He looked around like a trapped animal. "I just . . . when my sister comes, I usually stock up on this stuff." He took a deep breath and squared his shoulders.

She finally nodded, wanting to be gone, glancing at him in the store lights, feeling the heat in her cheeks. "My sister . . . It was unexpected . . ." Speech . . . not . . . working. Hobbes decided to make himself known with a loud bark.

"Is this your dog?" He was attempting to fix things.

She looked down at Hobbes, gathered her wits, and shook her head. "Mm, no. I stole him from a guy I wanted to impress." Speech working again.

Scott glanced sideways at her but said nothing. He bent down as her dog ferociously licked his hands. She needed a Rottweiler or a Doberman.

"What's your name?" When Hobbes didn't answer him, Scott looked up at her, waiting. What was it about guys looking up, all innocent and charming? Hobbes looked up too and cocked his head to the side.

Jill blinked and shook her head. "Hobbes. His name is Hobbes."

"As in Calvin and . . . ?"

She nodded and looked down the street, feeling a pull to get home. She had already been gone too long.

"Well, you're named after one of the greatest literary characters of all time, did you know that?"

"Of course he knows it."

He glanced back up at her, and she tried to breathe. He appeared apologetic but amused. "Well, enjoy your company."

She swallowed. He had no idea how complicated that would be. She turned away.

"Jillian."

She closed her eyes for a brief moment then turned back. "Yes, Scott?"

He ran his hand over his hair. "I wish there were some way I could make today right."

Today?

"I . . . can we start over?" He held his hand out, and she stared at it.

Long seconds sounded like gongs in her ears. She searched his eyes as long as she could allow then swallowed and felt the sting of saltwater settling into her lower lids. "I'm sorry, but . . ." She shook her head. "I just don't have that kind of time." She turned and took long, quick steps away from him and the bewildered look on his face.

Good. *Good.* But she didn't feel better. She felt miserable, and the rain suddenly mattered.

She opened the apartment door to the smell of something burning. She gasped. *The chicken.* She threw down the bags and let Hobbes scamper off, dragging his leash. The clamor roused her sister from sleep on the couch.

"Hmmm?"

"Evie, the chicken." Jill grabbed a hot pad and pulled out the dish, pulling off the foil with a groan. The rice was burnt around the edges, and the chicken was dry.

"I'm sorry," Evie said. "I fell asleep."

Jill bit back tears as she turned off the stove and opened the kitchen window. She inhaled the fresh air. After a few moments, she looked around, sensing something was missing. "Evie, where's the baby?"

Evie sat up straight. "She was right here. Shiloh?"

Jill beat her sister to the hallway. "Shiloh?"

"She can't open doors yet."

Jill opened the bathroom door anyway. Dark and empty. She heard a squeal, and they hurried to the bedroom. She flipped on the light and exhaled with relief. The baby sat on the floor, surrounded by squares of Kleenex and wincing away from Hobbes, who was licking her face and hands and feet.

"How about we give her a real bath?" She looked at Evie, who nodded, watching her child with utter adoration.

Shiloh's bath transformed her into a sweetly scented, shy, smiling girl. Evie showed Jill how to put on the diaper and snap up the onesie.

When Shiloh was settled on the floor with a clean, dry washcloth in her grasp, Jill said, "I think I can handle the bottle. It's your turn for a bath. Use anything you want. I'll find you something to sleep in." She moved to the dresser and pulled out a T-shirt and a pair of pajama pants. She held them out to Evie.

Evie looked at her as if she wanted to say something. She wrung her hands then wrapped her arms around Jill. Then just as quickly, Evie released her, took the pajamas, and moved past Jill and down the hall. Jill heard the bathroom door shut and the faucet turn on.

As needy as Evie seemed right now, it had been a long time since Jill had been hugged. By anyone. She rubbed her arms, holding on to the feeling.

With Shiloh on her hip, Jill frowned at the instructions on the canister of formula. She studied the measured markings on the bottle and went to work. She finished shaking the mixture and removed her finger from the tip of the nipple. White foam sprayed all over her face and the baby. Shiloh puckered and blew bubbles out her lips, waving the washcloth still in her grip.

Grabbing a dish towel, Jill shook her head and chuckled. "If you weren't so darn cute, I'd be crying right now."

Soon, however, the bottle was gone, and Shiloh was asleep in her arms. Looking at her niece's face, she guessed that her little life hadn't been this peaceful. Jill's chest tightened, and warm tears rolled down her cheeks. She laid her head back on the cushion.

"Please, God, help me help them. Help me know what to do." She drew in a choppy breath. "And please let this horrible day be over. I don't want it anymore." She wiped away the tears. She counted the blessings she could remember, asked a blessing on those she loved, and closed her prayer. She heard the bathroom door open, and her sister padded out in the pajamas, looking like a little kid. She still wore her sweatshirt over the T-shirt. To hide the user marks, Jill was certain. She wiped her eyes once more.

"Here, you take her, and I'll pull the bed out." Jill had bought the convertible sofa for the one-bedroom apartment in case she ever had company. This was the first time she'd had a chance to use it. She passed off the sleeping baby, tucked in the sheets and a quilt, and brought out the spare pillows.

"This is so nice. Everything is so nice," Evie said as she laid Shiloh down.

Jill glanced around. It was simple, but, yes, nicer than anything they'd had growing up. She turned back to her sister. "Evie, who is Shiloh's father?"

Evie's eyes darted up then around the room as she chewed her lip. Her arms folded across her stomach. Finally, she whispered, "Neil." She squeezed herself tighter. "There's only been Neil." Her eyes turned glassy. "But you have to promise me you won't try to find him." Her expression turned to one of panic. "You have to promise me."

The quiet intensity in Evie's voice sent a chill through Jill's bones. She nodded.

She placed a hand on Evie's arm, trying to appear calm. "You're safe here. You know that, right?"

Evie looked away. "Shiloh's safe here."

Jill reached and tucked a lock of damp hair behind Evie's ear. "You both are."

Evie sat on the bed and pulled her knees up to her chest, watching Shiloh sleep.

"I hope you're comfortable. Will she be all right?" Jill asked.

Evie nodded. "Oh, yeah, we sleep together all the time."

As Jill left the room, she reached to turn the light off. She paused. "Evie?"

Her sister drew in a ragged breath, as though she were fighting tears. "Hm?"

"Do you think we could call Dad tomorrow?"

Silence.

"Well, think about it, okay?"

"'Kay."

She flipped the switch. A smile crept onto her face. "Good night, Everlisse."

There was a pause. "Good night, Jilly-pill."

Jill walked down the hall and turned on the little lamp next to her bed. Hobbes hopped up and curled into a ball at the end. Exhaustion weighed her down, her thoughts whirling in a muddy mess too heavy to lift and scatter away. She pulled back the covers, and her stomach growled. She flopped down onto the mattress. "I forgot to eat," she moaned.

She leaned over and rummaged in the drawer of her nightstand, glancing past the now-overstuffed box of tissues hastily put back together. *Bingo.* A near-empty bag of chocolate-covered cinnamon bears. She bit one in half, sinking her teeth into the soft, spicy inside. Mmm. She fluffed her pillows up and leaned back, closing her eyes. She finished the one and reached for another. She would brush her teeth again later. This one she popped in her mouth whole. She pulled the covers up under her chin and chewed, letting the chocolate melt and slide over her tongue. One more. She held the little bear up and looked at him with one eye.

Scott Gentry.

She bit the bear's head off. Sighing, she finished it and rolled up the bag. She set it on her nightstand and leaned back, watching the fan spin around on the ceiling. She remembered other fans, woven wicker hanging on long stems from white stucco ceilings, moving the soft air around so you could feel it was there . . .

The air in Costa Rica was not room temperature. It was body temperature and so humid you never needed lotion or lip balm. So wet that makeup became a nuisance and a waste of time. So full of moisture that naturally curly hair tightened up into a floaty, frizzy mass you fought and pulled at until surrendering to the tightest, flattest French braids your friends could manage.

She was too exhausted to stop the images and longed too much for an escape to push them away. The memory opened like a file on her laptop: costaricajunioryear.doc. Keyword: *Scott Gentry*.

CHAPTER 3

June—school was out, and she was on a bus with a group of her third-year Spanish classmates—most of them graduated seniors—heading for the Portland International Airport, where they would catch a flight to Dallas then Costa Rica.

She was doing it . . . getting away. She'd put in as many hours as she could bagging groceries at Safeway, earning the money that would give her freedom and adventure as she had never had it. Ten whole days. She soaked it all in and wrote furiously in her journal, trying to capture every event, large or small. As the airplane began its descent over the sprawling city of San Jose, Jill's anticipation heightened, along with the butterflies in her stomach. She wasn't used to flying. The city was nothing but a blanket of lights. She would have to wait until morning to see it in detail.

At the hotel, they were given a meal of rice and black beans, and grilled carrots and chicken. Everyone ate gratefully after twelve and a half hours of travel.

In the morning, they met the other high school students they would be touring with throughout their stay, a large group from California. Jill scanned the strangers and found one of the boys staring at her. She looked down and folded her arms over her middle, but when she raised her eyes, he had looked away. She bit her lip and joined the other girls, lining up for the tour bus they would claim as their own for the next week and a half. She glanced behind her, seeing the boy again a few seats back, and this time he smiled. She quickly turned and found a seat next to the window. As the tour guide droned in Spanish, then English, the noisy traffic and crowds of the city gave way to sprawling green coffee plantations and lush, towering mango trees, branches full of fruit dipping right over the pot-holed road. The countryside flourished in the tropical climate.

But even on the air-conditioned bus, humidity raged a war with Jill's hair. She ran her hand over her unruly curls.

"Here." Michele, a senior sitting behind her, undid Jill's clip and divided her frazzled brown hair down the middle in the back. She expertly wrapped a side section into a knot behind Jill's ear and fastened it in place. She did the same with the other side. "Look at me." Jill obeyed, as Michele twisted her hair in front to the side and slid in a bobby pin. She pulled out a small mirror from her pack. "There."

Jill turned her head in the mirror. She smiled, feeling the cool air on the back of her neck. "Thanks."

"*No problema, chica.*"

The bus stopped at a wildlife refuge. Their large group hiked through tall, ancient trees, the broad spreading roots sheathed in leathery bark. Sweat dripped from the students' brows as they sipped from their water bottles. The air filled with staccato hoots.

"Howler monkeys," the guide commented.

Mango pits littered the ground beneath their feet. A boy, the one who had smiled at Jill, cupped his hands to his mouth and hooted back. The monkeys answered, but the boy had to duck as a pit came hurling in his direction. Nervous laughter erupted, and he turned his astounded expression to Jill, who pressed her lips together to smother her own amusement. He looked down and toed the pit.

"*Cuidado*, Scott," the guide warned.

"*Sí.*" Scott called up to the trees, "*Lo siento, monos de mangos.*"

Jill giggled at the translation: *Sorry, mango monkeys.*

The jungle surprised her. She had seen paintings, vivid murals, and illustrations in children's books of the intensity of color and movement but always thought it was an exaggeration, a caricature of reality, an attempt to combine all the elements that can be found in a jungle into one square area of artwork. But it was no exaggeration. Red bromeliads, orange and purple birds of paradise, vines of jasmine with pure white trumpet flowers, golden orchids, banana trees, all on a background of deep emerald green leaves bigger than anything that grew back home. She looked and looked and then attacked her journal before she lost it all to time.

On another outing they hiked up a mountain and zip-lined through trees, higher and higher, skimming branches then leaves then mist, unable to see the landing platform through the clouded forest.

"Shout it." The voice in her ear gave her shivers on top of the butterflies in her stomach.

She gripped the handles of the pulley, hesitating, looking down at nothing but dense white air, knowing there was a rainforest below somewhere.

"Shout it," she heard again.

She turned to the face near her shoulder. Scott grinned and nodded. She couldn't help but smile.

She looked ahead, taking a deep breath. "*Pura vida!*" she yelled as she jumped off the platform and zipped into the swirling soft void.

The students enjoyed a shopping excursion, buying chair hammocks, straw bags, and machetes. She allowed herself one purchase: a small puzzle box in the shape of a hummingbird, inlaid with all the scented hardwoods from the region. The clerk wrapped it for her and smiled broadly.

"*Gracias,*" Jill quietly said.

"*Con mucho gusto.*"

They spent a couple nights at a resort known for its natural hot springs and mineral pools. Jill stood in front of the mirror, wearing her swimsuit. She had dreaded this part . . . the swimming . . . which required swimwear. But as she looked in the mirror, she didn't grimace. She was tan now. All the girls had stopped wearing the futile makeup, and everyone had their hair pinned up and away. With all the hiking and sweating and good food . . . *comida tipical*—rice and beans and piles of fresh fruit the *Ticos* were very proud of—was it just her, or had some of her curves settled down to where they should be?

"Here, gorgeous, tie me up."

Jill blinked at the term and watched for sarcasm from Michele. But there was only patience as Michele held her swimsuit straps behind her neck. Jill tied her and took another look in the mirror. Could she pull that off? Maybe not that word exactly, but . . . cute? In a swimsuit? She tilted her head.

Michele's bright face appeared next to hers in the mirror, full of confidence and all-American blondeness. "You have pretty eyes. And a great mouth. Smile."

Jill smiled skeptically.

"Yup. You should do that more often. A real one." She turned and threw a towel at her. "You look hot. Let's go."

Jill reached for her T-shirt and grappled it over her head, shimmied into her flip-flops, and left for the pools.

And there he was, eyeing her shirt again. What was with this guy? She folded her arms and shifted her weight as he walked over to stand behind her in line at the hut selling drinks and snacks.

"Hi, I'm Scott."

She answered. "Jill."

He pointed to her shirt. "You LDS?"

Ooh. She looked down at the blue cougar on the front, leaping across the gold letters *BYU*. She breathed out, a little relieved. "Yes."

"Me too. I'm going to the Y next year before my mission."

She smiled. Why was it so much easier after that? They talked and hung out with the others, laughing and teasing like it was natural all of a sudden. They had something in common. Her faith was a really big part of her life, and he understood it. His group joined hers at dinner, and the seating on the bus mixed up more frequently now that everyone was finally getting to know each other. He called her Cougar. She liked it. The nickname made her feel like she was someone else—a new Jill.

All too soon, they were at their last stop of the trip. Punta Leona, a beach resort on the edge of the tropical jungles, with white sand and bowing palm trees. After a lunch of *pinto gallo*, the traditional rice and black beans, with cabbage and pineapple salad, they walked on the white path to find their rooms. If the earlier part of their trip had been a dream, then surely this was paradise. They walked around two large pools, a high, thatch-covered *discoteca*, a little store, and a church, glimpsing the beach along the way, and found their white stucco bungalows hidden here and there in the trees and giant ferns. After opening the carved wood doors and feeling the red clay tiles beneath her feet, Jill was not at all surprised by the iguana sitting on the wall above her bed.

"Ohh, *que tranquilo*."

Jill agreed with Michele. And then Michele turned the air conditioner up to high.

They changed into their swimsuits and met the others at the beach, swimming and bodysurfing until dinner. The sun set as they ate, and lights came on all over the resort.

"Are we dancing tonight?" one of the kids asked their guide, who nodded.

"*Si*. You get to dance the night away. *Toda la noche*."

Everyone hurried to freshen up and put on something as light and dry as possible, something that hadn't been rained on or sweat through during the hikes. These were their last few nights, and each one was to be a party.

Only, it was not the kind of party Jill had in mind. After a few hours of dancing, laughing, and having fun, the chaperones went to bed, exhausted, and gave instructions to the kids.

"Don't stay up too late, and don't get in trouble."

That's when the drinking started. The chaperones had asked the bartenders not to sell to the kids, but it was soon obvious that money was more important than morals when the teenagers were willing to pay and no legal limits were set. Jill watched her friends go from happy, cute, and flirty to loud, brash, and dangerously drunk.

"C'mere, Curly Sue."

Jill turned to Michele. "Me?"

"M'hm. C'mere. Look. Look at this girl's hair." Michele reached over and began to paw at Jill's hair while a few others looked on, laughing at nothing.

"Michele, don't." Jill turned her face away, the smell of Michele's breath all too familiar.

"No, really." Michele pulled out the clips holding the two knots in place. "Have you ever seen hair like this? I mean," Michele stretched out the curls, pulling Jill's head, "it's crazy. Like a clown." Michele leaned heavily against Jill.

No, not this. Not here. Jill pushed her away to lean on someone else, trying to calm her fear. Trying not to show how quickly she could lose her grip on her newfound peace of mind.

"Stop." Jill didn't want to see Michele like this.

"Oh . . . oh, Jill, don't cry. I like the curly hair. I like it all boingy. Boingy boingy." Michele suddenly looked bored then took a few staggered steps off to the edge of the dance platform and threw up into the giant azalea bushes. Laughter followed her.

But Jill turned, leaving the *discoteca*, rushing away from the noise and lights, fighting nausea herself. She followed the white paths to the pools connected by a low bridge. She attempted to breathe it away, taking in deep gulps of air, but sobs overcame her, and she had to stop. She sat on the bridge and dropped her feet in the water.

"Hey, Cougar."

Jill wiped her tears and sniffled. She grabbed her hair in her fist and turned away. Still, he closed the gap and sat next to her. She wished her thighs were slender.

"Are you all right?"

She nodded and shrugged. She peeked over her shoulder, past him, toward the sound of the music. "I don't like it when they drink."

He looked back too. "Pretty lame. But not all of them are drinking."

She was silent.

"But your friends are," he added.

She nodded.

"Why do you let it bother you so much? You know they don't know what they're saying. She won't remember that in the morning."

"I will."

Scott didn't respond. She watched his leg kick slowly through the water.

Jill shook her head. She wanted to tell him. Why not? She'd never see him again. And she needed someone . . . to understand. She wiped her tears and took a deep breath. "My mom drinks." She watched him, seeing his discomfort.

"Oh." He ran a hand over his head. "A lot?"

She nodded. "This was supposed to be an escape from all of it . . . for the first time . . . a break from that endless nightmare. But if they keep doing this the next couple nights, I'll be the one who has to take care of them in the morning when they're hung over and regretting it and not wanting the chaperones to know . . . Then it will be time to go home. This . . . this was heaven." She gazed out at the beach beyond the pools. "But now, it smells like alcohol."

She felt his arm around her shoulders, and he pulled her next to him. "I'm sorry. You don't have to take care of them, you know. They're doing this to themselves."

She looked at him doubtfully.

"Just . . . just get up and come find me in the morning."

She raised her eyebrows, and he nodded at her.

They sat together, and she calmed, though she felt nervous in another way. She wasn't used to being hugged, being so near someone. Especially someone like Scott, with hairy legs and muscular arms and blue eyes that changed color with the sky.

He tried to look stern. "Maybe . . . maybe we could march over there and give them a good sermon on choice and consequences. Or the Word of Wisdom."

She looked at him, and he grinned. She shook her head.

"No? Well, maybe we could do something to take your mind off it?"

"What?" She circled her feet in the warm water. Everything here was warm.

"Well . . ." He slowly reached down next to him then flipped a handful of water in her face.

She gasped, stunned, but his grin was still there, hopeful. She scooped up a wave of water, drenching his neck and shirt.

"Oh no you didn't." He laughed.

She squealed as he pulled up an armful and doused her. She was pulled off the edge and into the pool, laughing, splashing, gripping his arm and pushing water toward him, giving as much as she got, putting everything she had into the effort.

"Okay, okay, Cougar." He shook his blond hair, and she shielded herself from the spray. Her hair hung in her face in stretched, wet, curly tendrils, and she went under, tipping her head back as she came up.

"Whoa, your hair is longer when it's wet."

She nodded, and a stray giggle bubbled up. She felt his fingers weave through hers, and her heart jumped in . . . fear? No. But then he pulled the hand he'd entwined in his, and she allowed herself to follow the movement. He studied her face, making her heart flop like a fish on land. She needed to look away but couldn't.

"Is this better?" he asked.

She nodded. So much better.

"Good." His dripping hand came up, and he gently played with a curl. He leaned, studying her mouth.

She watched his wet lashes lower and his lips part. Was this happening? She closed her eyes. The kiss was so unexpected, so much more than she'd been wishing for a few minutes ago.

She let him kiss her then followed his lead and learned. She was barely aware of her hand still gripping his, but as his other hand drew around her, she felt a brief twinge of self-consciousness that quickly faded as her focus turned back to his mouth.

So much better.

The days were the same after that. Fun, adventure, friends. She would find him in the mornings, and they would eat and walk and swim. But those last nights, after the chaperones went to bed and the party started, she would watch, and he'd catch her eye and say good night as he walked away from the crowd. Then Jill would fade away and find him waiting. She'd never understood the allure of kissing. By the lights of the pool, the torches on the beach, the lamp behind the bench in the colonnade of palms, they kissed. She was getting a better grasp of the concept.

Then the day came to say good-bye. Everyone hugged everyone else, and every few good-byes she would slip her hand in her pocket to make sure the paper with her e-mail address and phone number was still there. She sped through the good-byes until it was his turn. He stepped to her, and the hug was good, warm, strong.

"I had a great time."

She smiled. "Me too."

He whispered in her ear, "Try not to let it bother you." He pulled back and gave her a meaningful look.

She understood. He hadn't pushed any more conversation about her mother, but once or twice, when she'd turned quiet, thinking of going home and facing things again, he'd squeezed her hand and given her that too-simple piece of advice. "Thanks. I'll try."

He let go and stepped away with an encouraging smile. He pressed a small, perfect spiral seashell into her hand. Then his friends were pulling him to the bus, a little too soon for Jill.

"Wait . . . Scott, here." She rushed forward, reaching in her pocket, and put the paper in his outstretched hand. His fingers pulled along hers.

"Thanks, Cougar, for everything." Then he was on the bus, and the doors closed. She watched his silhouette through the tinted windows and then followed her group to their own bus.

It wasn't until weeks later that it occurred to her that maybe his last piece of advice referred to the fact that he knew he wouldn't call her—that he wouldn't write.

Try not to let it bother you.

She tried.

CHAPTER 4

The basketball bounced off the pavement into Scott's hands in the early misty hours of a Portland Saturday morning. He hadn't slept well, finally giving up and coming to the nearby elementary school playground to pound away some of his frustration. The familiar hollow echo of the ball sounded a few more times as he dribbled. He lifted and shot but missed. The baskets were lower to accommodate the smaller players out on recess. He jogged after the ball as it rolled under the net then gripped it and pushed himself forward for a lay-up. The ball rolled around the inside edge of the rim and spun itself back out. Scott stood with his hands on his hips, watching the ball bounce lazily away.

No loss.

What did it mean, she didn't have that kind of time? What he had done at the office was stupid, yes. Thoughtless. Self-serving and brash. And it had nearly cost her a chance to put her book directly into hands that could move it to the public eye. He knew what that meant. Two manuscripts in a hundred make it past submissions, let alone to the managing editor.

But he had tried. He had done what he could to help after scattering her manuscript all over the floor. And when he'd run into her, literally, again at the store . . . he'd only asked for a chance to make it good. Just to start fresh. And for a minute, he'd seen something in her eyes, some sort of . . . *connection*. Her eyes had softened . . . had asked a question he wanted to understand . . .

And then she'd slammed him.

He walked over to retrieve the ball and squeezed it between his hands before throwing it hard at the backboard, where it ricocheted through the hoop.

What was it about Jillian Parish that drew him? It had to be more than her glossy dark hair that fell just past her shoulders, her eyes . . .

the definite curves on her petite frame. He shook his head. He'd thrown himself into traffic, and she'd run over him with her armored truck. And he still couldn't shake her.

He'd seen her at the singles ward and asked casually about her, always a risk when talking to Trey or anyone else in his family. He mentioned a girl and they either scrambled to set him up or demanded details, the level of commitment, and why there wasn't any. But Jillian had caught his eye at the beginning of the meeting and, for a moment, met his gaze. And just for that moment, it was as if time had stopped, distance across the pews had disappeared, and he'd almost smiled, a real smile from somewhere deep inside him. It was a risk, but Scott had come to Portland to make a fresh start, so he'd asked Trey about her.

Dude, don't even try. He was surprised by Trey's discouragement. She didn't date. Period. There wasn't a guy who hadn't tried.

When Scott had turned back to the girl, she'd looked away and avoided him the rest of the meeting.

But when Trey caught Scott watching her again in Sunday School, the wheels started turning in Trey's head, and Scott became a willing player in his brother's ill-fated scheme.

And now Scott was crushed. Pathetic fool.

No loss. Let it go. Other fish in the ocean. Or is it sea? He turned his gaze to the west. He hadn't been home since he'd moved in with Trey. Maybe he'd pay his mom a visit. Trey had his *date* tonight . . . and then Scott wouldn't have to face *her* at church tomorrow.

Yeah, a trip home would be good. It was Labor Day weekend. He had Monday off. Why not?

He packed, and a couple hours later, cool, piney air filled the car, and shadows from the overhead trees rippled over the windshield and sunroof. Scott maneuvered the blind turns and gentle rises and falls of the woods with ease. He enjoyed this drive and allowed its calming effect to wash over him. Maybe if he could just get her out for a drive—*Idiot. Stop thinking about her.* He took a deep breath and focused on catching that first glimpse of the ocean just coming up after the next few curves. *Curves.*

Geesh, get her out of your head. That shouldn't even be—

He slowed and pulled off at the viewpoint.

He stood at the railing, tucking his hands in his jacket pockets. The pale beach stretched in front of him, the gray-blue water crossed by white strips of breaking waves rushing at the shore, relentless, reliable. He closed his eyes and listened. The wind pulled at his hair.

His cell phone rang, the guitar starting and drums joining in—an even, steady rhythm he knew would give way to lyrics he could recite backwards if he felt like it.

"This is Scott."

* * *

Jill woke up to the little snores of a curly brown mutt nestled into her side. Saturday. She ran her fingers through Hobbes's hair and then rolled and stretched. She blinked up at the ceiling fan and smacked her tongue from the roof of her mouth.

Eww. She hadn't brushed her teeth after biting Scott's head off. She watched the fan blades spin around. She hadn't meant to let the memory slip that far. She'd only wanted the escape of the tropical scenery, the adventure. She ran a hand through her hair.

Even though she was frugal with her money, Jill had made one decision after that trip that would bite into her bank account monthly. She had started going to a salon to have her hair professionally straightened. The results of her transformation were immediate. All of a sudden, she had eyes, and people looked at her and listened to what she said, gave her compliments on her clothes and noticed when she lost weight because she had insisted her dad start cooking like the Costa Ricans, which was great with him because it was easy and cheap.

Her dad started worrying about boys, but she only worried about one boy—and then stopped worrying, and after a year at home, working and attending the community college, chose the University of Oregon over BYU, took the scholarship, and seldom looked back. When the budget was tight, she'd grown out her curls again, which wasn't so bad. They weren't as tight as before—she knew more about styling products—and she'd gained enough confidence to wear them without the suspicion that everyone was laughing at her.

But when she began applying for jobs, she splurged again, and she'd kept her hair straight ever since. Comfort, ease, one less thing. Like a wall painted a color you hate . . . always there, keeping to itself, but somewhere in the back of your mind, it's itching, crawling at you, bugging you. Then the wall gets a new color, and you like it, and pretty soon you're not thinking about it anymore. Just an occasional thought of gratitude for one less thing pulling at your insides. More space for good things. Happier thoughts. Outside yourself.

She thought of her book in Rowena Martin's hands and decided she would definitely make hot cocoa with breakfast.

The thought was immediately punctured by the sound of a baby's cry, and she snapped upright. Pushing off the covers, she slipped out of bed and walked a little groggily down the hall.

Jill should have expected it. She should have seen it coming as soon as she'd opened the door last night.

Evie was gone.

Shiloh leaned against the back of the sofa, her socked feet buried in the mess of covers on the mattress. The pout on her face turned to Jill, but the wail stilled for only a moment. The baby must have seen the shock, the fear, the dread in her aunt's eyes because her face crumpled and she pushed out another cry.

Jill hurried back to check the bathroom, Hobbes at her heels. Nothing, dark.

"Evie!" she called.

She yanked open the front door, running down the steps, stretching up on her bare toes to see as far as she could in either direction. "Evie!"

The baby wailed. She rushed back to the front room, wrenching the door closed behind her and pulled Shiloh to her, desperate anger welling up inside her chest. "Okay . . . okay . . . okay . . ." She bounced her niece as she paced, not really seeing, searching her thoughts for some direction, some sign that all would be well. Shiloh's crying intensified, and Jill spun in a circle, frantic for someone to tell her the next step.

"Ma ma . . ."

"I know, I know . . ." She paced to the back door where Hobbes slipped out as she opened it. "Evie, are you out here?"

She wasn't.

"Ma ma . . ."

"Shh . . ." She hurried to the cupboard and prepared the bottle. Shiloh's crying slowed as she watched the powder being scooped into the bottle. "Maybe she just went to the store," she said aloud, more for herself than the baby. "She'll back any minute." But the gnawing ache in her chest wouldn't ease. She filled the bottle with water from the faucet and screwed on the top.

"Dee dee?"

"Mm-hm." Jill didn't know what *dee dee* was. Probably not hot cocoa. She shook the bottle hard and moved her finger off the tip of the nipple.

"Aaahhh." The spray was not as amusing this time, but Shiloh took the bottle out of Jill's hand and crammed it in her mouth. Jill wiped her face and listened to Shiloh breathe between gulps, interrupted here and there by a shudder. She wiped the baby's tears and carried her to the sofa. She sat on the mattress, looking at the space where her sister had slept. Her eyes swept the room.

"No note?" She spied the blank notepad and pen and closed her eyes against the tears. Had Evie just stepped out for a minute? Gone to Walgreens? Her mind drifted to other possibilities, and she hated the idea that those possibilities could be connected to her sister. She moved Shiloh to a cradled position and ran her finger over the baby's cheeks. Shiloh watched her, wary. "How could she just leave you?" The words tore at her. "How could she leave when she knows how it feels?" Tears slipped down, and she took a deep breath. The minutes ticked slowly by on the clock, and with every tick, Jill's suspicions gained strength. Her sister might not return.

"What am I supposed to do?" The sound of sucking an empty bottle and the pop as Shiloh removed it from her mouth made Jill look down and sniffle.

"Do you want something to eat now?"

"Dee dee."

"Okay." She wiped her nose and walked to the kitchen, Shiloh stuck to her hip.

By the time she got a little oatmeal in Shiloh's belly and on the table, the floor, Jill's pajamas, and face, Jill had decided to call the only person she knew with kids—the singles ward bishop.

Jill tried to keep her voice steady while she quickly explained what had happened.

"Have you thought about calling the police?" Bishop Thornton asked over the phone.

"Yes, but I don't know what that would do. All I could give them is a description, and if they found her, what would they *do*?" The panic she was keeping submerged struggled to be free, and she swallowed. "She's young. She's probably scared to death." Jill remembered the looks of devotion Evie had given Shiloh and the fearful, nervous way she'd held herself.

"But she may be headed back into danger. You don't have any ideas about where she would have gone?"

"She wouldn't tell me where she'd been. She was in Seattle for a while, but that was two years ago." She pushed her hair out of her face. "Maybe I'm overreacting. Maybe she'll be back tonight. Maybe she just—" *had to find a fix*, she finished inside her head.

"Did she say anything last night about going anywhere?"

"No. I mentioned calling my dad . . . She didn't seem to like that idea."

"Have you talked to your father, then?"

"No."

"Jill, I think you should call the police then talk to your dad."

"But—"

"What if you don't?"

She thought of the possibilities. "All right."

"Would you like some company?"

"Yes."

"Laura and I are on our way. What about the baby? Do you have some things for her?"

"Only a few things. I was going to take them shopping today. They had nothing, not even a change of clothes."

"Oh boy." He sighed. "I'll ask Laura if we have anything extra, an extra car seat lying around somewhere, stuff like that."

A car seat? She hadn't even thought of that.

"Hang in there, Jill. We'll be over in a few."

Jill gave up trying to get the oatmeal out of Shiloh's hair. "C'mon, let's bathe you."

Twenty minutes later, the doorbell rang just as Jill pulled Shiloh's Trail-blazer sweatshirt over her head. Jill hurried to the door, and she opened it to startled expressions.

"I know . . . I'm sorry . . ." Jill wiped her eyes, knowing she looked horrific. Not put together. Not calm. "I couldn't figure out how to shower . . . She crawls all over, and she keeps crying for her mom—"

"Shh . . . It's all right." Laura Thornton came in and confidently lifted Shiloh out of Jill's arms.

"Have you called the police yet?" Bishop Thornton followed his wife into the apartment.

Jill pulled at her sleeves and wiped them again across her face. "No. I couldn't bring myself to . . ."

He put his hand on her shoulder. "I'll do it. All right?"

She nodded.

Laura reached out. "You go take a quick shower. You'll feel better. We'll bring stuff in."

Jill peeked around to the porch. An unidentifiable piece of equipment leaned against a highchair and baby car seat. Bishop Thornton held a duffle bag stuffed tight. She raised her eyebrows.

"Is that all for the baby?"

Laura gave a soft chuckle. "You'd be surprised. They come with their own world."

Jill gulped and let Laura turn her around toward the bathroom. "Go . . . be quick. Grant will get on the phone."

Jill had never showered so fast. She wiggled into jeans and threw on a shirt she didn't even look at. Still, when she emerged from the hallway, hair wet but brushed and no make-up, a pair of police officers stood in her front room. The sofa had been made up, and the bedding was folded in a neat pile. Shiloh sat in a highchair, banging a rubber toy on the tray. Beads bounced and clacked on a brightly colored curly wire suctioned there. Laura looked up from the sofa and gave her an encouraging smile.

One officer stepped forward, his hand outstretched. "You must be Miss Parish." She shook his hand. "Officer McKay. This is Officer Kent. Mr. Thornton has given us the basics, but can I ask you a few questions?"

Jill nodded, and he held his hand open to the dining table where Bishop Thornton sat.

"Your sister's age?"

"Twenty. She turned twenty this July. July seventh." She took a seat and rested her hands on the table, fighting to keep them still.

"Full name?"

"Everlisse Claire Parish, but she goes by Evie."

"Spell that please."

She did.

"Single?"

"Yes, but she's been living with a guy . . . Neil Bradshaw." Something occurred to her. "She never said anything about getting married, but I guess it's possible. I haven't heard from her for a while."

"Do you know how recently they were together?"

"I'm not sure. They'd been together since high school. They left for Seattle as soon as Evie turned eighteen. She contacted me once, said they moved around a lot, that I couldn't call because the phones were always changing, and that was the last time I heard from her . . . until last night." She looked at Shiloh and did the math. "They were definitely together seventeen months ago.

"Are you sure?"

Jill nodded. "Evie told me Neil is Shiloh's father. I believe her."

She waited for a judgment, some sort of eye roll because she believed a person who would disappear and then turn up, only to disappear again, leaving something as important as a baby, but Officer McKay just glanced over his notes and went to the next question.

"Do you have any photos of your sister?"

Jill nodded. "They're old. My high school graduation."

"We'll need one. Is anything missing?"

"Missing?"

"Stolen?"

She understood why he asked, but a knot of anger tightened in her stomach. "I haven't had a chance to look for anything like that."

He nodded then frowned. "Miss Parish, was your sister involved in any drug-related activities?"

Jill stared then swallowed. "I don't know." She lowered her eyes. "It's possible."

She considered her sister's habit. She thought about how she'd gotten involved in something so destructive so young. Jill's father had converted to the Church as a young man. He'd attended off and on then met Jill's mother, a recovering alcoholic with a beautiful smile, a girl in desperate need of kindness. If Jill's father was anything, he was kind. They married, and he told Jill that when she was born, he made more of a commitment to the Church. He wanted that for his family. His wife would have nothing to do with it. She'd started drinking again, quietly at first. And then it wasn't quiet. It was angry, hurtful. Confusing. And then Evie was prematurely born, with tubes and incubators. And the drinking became a monster. Jill's father protected them as well as he was able, took care of his wife with every hope for her recovery, but kindness isn't always enough. Love isn't always enough.

Whereas Jill had thrown herself into school and books and had clung to Primary, Young Women, seminary, and the safety there, Evie had not been a great student, had not been absorbed by her own findings in the gospel, and had found safety in the rougher crowd . . . the crowd who welcomed anyone they could hook, no matter what their background.

The more Jill had pulled, coaxed, fought to save her sister, the more Evie had withdrawn and the more their mother shouted to leave the girl alone, let her do what she wanted . . . *Not everyone can be holier than thou, Miss Perfect . . . Miss High and Mighty Jill, wearing those new clothes, thinking you're better than us. Traipsing around with your fancy friends who will drop you the minute they know who you really are, a nothing . . . just like your father. Nothing from nothing, that's what you are, and Evie's no better, but at least she knows it. Don't you, Evie? Don't you know you'll never amount to anything? Evie, are you listening to me, you pointless little . . .*

"Miss Parish?"

"Mm, I'm sorry. What?"

"Did your sister mention anywhere she might be headed?"

Jill shook her head. She ran through what little conversation had taken place. "I didn't think she would leave . . . She seemed so relieved to be here. I don't even know how she got here. She didn't have a car."

"Bus?"

"Maybe."

"We'll check out the stations, ticket records. Do you have any other family she would seek out?"

"My father lives down in Lebanon, but I don't think she'd go there. I was going to call him. They . . . they aren't close."

"Your father's name?"

"Jeremy Parish."

"Your mother?"

"Dead." The word came without emotion.

"When?"

"Four years ago. I even came home from college, took a semester off. Evie was sixteen. We tried counseling. She dropped out of high school the following year. There was nothing I could do." A look did come then. But it was one of sympathy.

"Any other relatives?"

"None that she would think of."

Officer McKay straightened up. "Do you think you could find that picture?"

She pulled herself from the chair, feeling heavy, and made her way to her bedroom closet. She pulled an album down. It wasn't thick. She had very few pictures, and the few she had were tainted with sadness, regret, and anger. Her eyes blurred with tears, but she continued to thumb through the pages until she found it. She stopped and blinked. Jill with her arm around Evie, Evie looking wide-eyed, a little scared, a little proud, hunching in her shoulders. She actually hadn't changed all that much. A scared little girl, wanting to be somebody but knowing she couldn't. Believing she couldn't.

Until she had a baby. Jill had seen it. The purpose . . . the pride. It was *real*. Evie was a mama. Jill shook her head. How difficult had it been to leave her sleeping baby? Why would she?

"Why?"

She pulled the picture out of its sleeve and closed the album. She wondered if Evie had an album somewhere and guessed not.

Jill paused at the bathroom on her way back. Her jaw clenched as she eyed the medicine cabinet. Unwillingly, she stepped forward and opened the mirror door. She scanned the shelves and moved a few things, looking behind a bottle and some tubes of ointment. She sighed.

"Here's the picture." Jill returned to the front room, where the officers waited by the front door.

Officer McKay took it. "Thank you. We'll get it back to you after we make a copy. Here's my number if you should remember anything."

"I just looked on my way back in here, and an old prescription of hydrocodone is missing from the medicine cabinet in the bathroom." The words tasted of betrayal. "There were only two or three pills left though."

The officers glanced at each other, and Officer McKay nodded. "I'll make a note of it."

"What happens now?"

"I file the report, run the names through the computer . . . check out the depot, train station, parks," he lowered his eyes, "any drug-trafficking areas, the hospital . . ."

Jill pulled her arms around her middle. "What happens if you find her?"

"She'll be brought in. She could be charged with abandonment . . . It depends on how we find her."

"Please . . . try not to scare her."

He nodded. "We'll do our best, Miss Parish. I do hope we find her."

"What should I be doing?"

"Try to sit tight. She may come back." He glanced at the baby, who was accepting a raisin from Laura. "Call your father . . . anyone else you can think of with a connection."

Jill opened the door, and he stepped out after his partner, placing his hat on his head.

"What about Shiloh . . . If you don't find Evie . . ." Jill bit back the words. "I don't want Shiloh to be taken away to strangers."

"Some of that will be up to you. Some to the state. In cases like this, where a relative is willing to take custody of the child, we contact DCFS, and they conduct an evaluation. It's a holiday weekend, so we'll keep her in your custody for now, if that's what you'd like."

"Thank you."

He nodded, his lips pressed in a line. He gestured to the card in her hand. "Stay in touch."

She closed the door and turned. Laura had begun sorting through a stack of clothes from the duffle bag, her long legs stretched out and crossed in front of her.

Was this happening? She watched Laura work, and guilt overwhelmed her. "I'm so sorry. I had no idea . . . I . . ."

Laura stopped folding and pushed a lock of dark hair off her rosy face. "Oh, Jill, it's not your fault. We're glad you called us." She shook her head. "I hate to think of you handling this on your own. I don't know how I would."

Bishop Thornton paced around the kitchen, the phone pressed to his ear as he absently touched things. Looking at the couple, Jill found it hard to believe they had two grown children in addition to the three still at home. Bishop Thornton was tall and thin, and his round head was topped with plenty of straight brown hair, parted on the side. He was forever adjusting the frameless glasses sitting on his nose and was known for his sense of humor with the young adults in the ward. He was serious now though.

Jill slowly walked over to the highchair and took Shiloh's hand, needing the physical reassurance this connection with Evie provided. She looked over the tray and felt around the sides.

"I don't even know how to work a dumb highchair." She felt the heat of frustration rise in her cheeks.

Laura reached over and pushed a lever at the front of the tray. It slid loose. Jill shook her head and lifted Shiloh, only to find her stuck.

"What am I doing wrong here?" Aside from everything.

"I belted her in. Here." Laura unbuckled the strap, and Jill felt the frustration turn into embarrassment.

"I don't know anything . . ." She gestured at the paraphernalia in front of the sofa. "Any of this. What am I going to do? How am I supposed to work? Find somebody to watch her? I can't leave her, can I? She's already been left—" Jill swallowed past the tightening in her throat, blinking under Laura's patient gaze. She worked to quiet her voice. "I don't know how to do any of this. Evie only showed me how to change her diaper and—"

Laura furrowed her brow as Jill paused.

Jill's stomach knotted. "Do you think she knew? Do you think this was the plan?"

Laura considered. "It's possible. But maybe after getting here, she just got scared."

"Of what though?"

Laura shrugged. "Of not being good enough."

Jill looked down at Shiloh in her arms.

"Shiloh's safe here," she murmured.

"What?"

She lifted her gaze to Laura. "Last night Evie said, 'Shiloh's safe here.'"

Laura's brow lifted a fraction, but she said nothing. Jill held the baby tightly to her and smelled her hair. *Safe from what?* She kissed her forehead. "I need to call my dad." She found her phone and sat down at her desk. Shiloh reached for a Harry & David catalog, and Jill let her have it.

"Hi, Dad."

"Jillian?"

She winced at the surprise in his voice. He sounded tired. "Yeah, it's me. Hi."

"Well . . . how are you? Is everything all right?"

They had never been a family for small talk. "Umm, no, actually. It's not. Evie was here."

The silence on the other end confirmed her suspicion. Evie had not been in contact with her dad. Not ever.

"She . . . is she all right?" She heard the emotion in his voice. She took a deep breath and explained everything to her father. He listened quietly while Shiloh tore pages and let the pieces fall.

"Dad, are you still there?"

She heard him take a breath. When he spoke, he sounded old.

"Yeah. I . . . I'm sorry, Jillian. I wish I'd done better . . ."

"Dad, you did your best. Both of us know that."

"The baby . . . is she . . . is she okay?"

Jill told him everything good she could about Shiloh, beginning with her hair. His hair. "Maybe after we get this worked out, we can come see you."

"I'd like that. I would."

"Dad, you have to let me know if you hear anything, all right? Anything at all."

"All right."

"Good-bye, Dad."

"Bye."

Click.

There was a yip at Jill's feet. "Oh, Hobbes, I'm sorry." She pushed her chair out and hurried to get Hobbes some breakfast while Shiloh leaned as far as she could, trying to touch the doggie.

"It's all right to set her down, Jill."

Jill looked up. "Oh. I know . . . I just . . ." Her grip tightened around the baby, then she set her down to play with Hobbes. "I feel like I can't let her go."

Laura nodded understandingly and stood. "After you finish with that, *we* are going to have some lessons."

"What kind of lessons?"

"Baby lessons."

* * *

Evie had easily found a motel on the other side of the city where she'd blend in. Checking in at three in the morning had annoyed the guy at the desk, but she hardly cared. She'd shut herself in her room and cried for hours. The pills she found at Jill's helped.

As soon as the buzz wore off, she made her way to the closest store she could find. She looked through a rack of clothes at the thrift shop, biting her nail. Her eyes darted around the store every few seconds until they landed on a guy who was watching her.

She knew a dealer when she saw one. The same way he knew a user. She turned and sorted through a different rack. She pulled out a jacket and moved over to the jeans. The store's bell jingled, and she peered behind her at the door. The dealer was leaving but caught her look. He continued outside.

She found a few more things and went to try them on. The changing room smelled like a toilet. She pulled the curtain closed and turned to her reflection in the mirror.

She was empty. She'd always been empty.

No. That wasn't true. Jilly had taken care of her. She was safe with Jilly—most of the time. But then Jilly left. She'd had to leave. And Evie wouldn't have gone with her.

And Shiloh. She hadn't been empty with Shiloh. Evie held the clothes against her. Against the hurt.

Shiloh was good. Shiloh still thought her mama was good. Even when—

Evie brushed the tears away and pulled on the jacket. And Neil. She hadn't felt empty after she'd met Neil. She fumbled with the zipper as her eyes blurred with fresh tears.

She'd met Neil at a party, and he'd noticed her, smiled at her, even teased her, calling her over in front of everyone. No boys had noticed her, not like that. He was older, a senior, and she was just a freshman. Kids grouped around him like he was some kind of rock star. He'd kept her close by, just with his glances, the whole night, and then a few days later, he'd called her; he came to pick her up at her house.

Evie remembered her mom's drunken, mocking words, calling Neil her white knight, telling Evie the extra make-up made her look like a tramp and who was she trying to impress . . . When her father had stepped in, her mother had said, "Let her go, Jer. Let her find out what being a big girl is all about." Then she'd laughed and stumbled, and her father had caught her.

He was always catching her. Always making excuses. Always quiet. Without saying a word, he'd carried her back to the bedroom, while her mother wondered aloud why Evie had even lived past all the tubes and complications and crying. Ungrateful—

Evie had watched her father go. He'd always been the buffer between her and her mother. But she was growing up. He wasn't the hero she'd thought he was. He was nothing. Just like her.

Neil had reached out his hand, and she'd taken it, and she hadn't let go all night. Had never really let go—until now.

Evie pulled off the jacket and her shirt, not looking at the marks up her arms. She pulled on a sweater.

Neil had made things easier. Better.

But she'd become Neil's mistake. She wouldn't become Shiloh's.

She pressed shaking fingers to her mouth. She was empty again. And the pain was unbearable.

She left the thrift store, where the dealer was leaning against the side of the building, waiting for her.

* * *

Jill ran through a mental to-do list as she drove home from church. Laura had offered to take Shiloh on the days she didn't work at the library, but Jill still had to find someone to watch Shiloh for the remaining days. Combining sick days, which she never took, and personal days, which had pitifully accumulated, and adding those to the three-day weekend, she hoped she had the time she needed to find daycare for Shiloh. Having an income had never felt so crucial. She had no idea if it would be enough. She had no idea if she would be enough. And she still had to hope Evie would come back, that they could do this, do *something*, together.

Jill glanced at Shiloh in the rearview mirror. She slept in her car seat, finally succumbing after the long three-hour block of meetings. They had almost made it. Shiloh had been fairly good through sacrament meeting, thanks to the diaper bag Laura had packed with snacks, toys, and hard little books. When asked, Jill only said she was watching her niece for a week. Nobody knew Jill well enough to question her further. They'd spent most of Sunday School out in the halls, where Shiloh had crawled endlessly, but in Relief Society, the baby'd had enough of church and snacks and bottles, and though Jill had received plenty of offers of help from girls who had barely spoken to her before, Shiloh would have nothing to do with them. With half an hour of lesson left, Jill left the building with Shiloh, buckled her in her car seat, struggled to keep her own tears at bay, and drove the long way home. At least Scott hadn't been there.

She turned the corner onto her street, pausing at the gathering of people at the end of her block who watched with fearful, curious expressions. Then she brought the car to a stop as her heartbeat sped up. A group of police cars with lights flashing blocked the front curb of her brownstone apartment, and one officer spoke into a radio. Jill pulled over and parked, holding her breath as more officers with weapons already drawn approached her steps and porch. After some shouts, they kicked open her door. Jill jumped at the impact, her hands covering her mouth.

That's my home. I'm right here.

Shiloh woke up with a wail. Jill's attention turned. As Jill vacillated between trying to pacify Shiloh and keeping her eye on the officers now swarming in and out of her apartment, a sharp tap on her driver's side window nearly sent Jill flying through the roof of her Honda Accord.

She tried to compose herself and carefully opened the door to Officer McKay.

He blinked his eyes in a look of relief. "Miss Parish. Are you all right?"

She nodded. "We just pulled up, and the lights and the guns . . ." Her voice rose in fear. "What's happening?"

"Your place was broken into. The perpetrators are gone now, but I'm afraid they left a mess. When we couldn't find you or the baby, we suspected—"

"I was at church." She looked again toward her apartment, her heart stuttering in her throat.

He nodded. "It's a good thing you were." He pulled out a radio and reported her presence. After receiving a response, he put the radio away and turned to her again. "You'll need to take a look."

Her head swam. Officer McKay held out his hand to her. "It's safe now."

Safe? *Safe?*

"Wh—who was it?"

He shook his head then nodded up the street. "Your neighbors called it in. Whoever did this kept things real quiet until the end. They did a thorough job."

Realization struck her, and she moved to get out of the car. "Hobbes." After getting Shiloh out of her car seat with some difficulty, she followed Officer McKay up the walk and into her home. Shiloh had quieted; though whether it was from sensing Jill's concern or being taken by the lights and movement, Jill couldn't tell.

The deadbolt was still attached to the open door, the space where it had been locked in the jamb splintered away. So much for *that* little peace of mind.

She gasped as her gaze drifted around the apartment. It was like . . . confetti had exploded from every possible corner. The bag of baby clothes was ripped to pieces, the contents scattered everywhere. The highchair was tipped over, legs broken and bent. Someone had broken a small hole in the back door window. Her TV was smashed in, and her CDs scattered, some crushed. She tried to swallow. The drawers of her desk were pulled out and overturned, her files thrown on the floor, her lamp broken. She took a step and felt an awkward lump under her foot. She pulled back and bent down, pushing some torn pages aside.

The hummingbird puzzle box. It had been years since she'd opened it. Her eyebrows drew together as she pulled the key piece in the bird's tail, slid the top forward, and removed the inner lid. A tiny, spiral shell remained in one piece. Jill swallowed her emotions and slid the pieces of the box back together. She lifted her head then searched the room again, fear taking hold.

"Hobbes?" she called, sounding like a stranger to her own ears. "Hobbes?" The name caught in her throat. Understanding came to Officer McKay's face, and he strode to the back door, pushing it open.

"Hobbes!" he called outside then whistled.

A whimper sounded from the corner of the room, where the bookshelves leaned askew.

Jill bolted, nearly dropping Shiloh as her heart leapt to her throat. "He's in here!"

Officer McKay returned. Jill was already kneeling, moving books out of the way and clutching Shiloh with one arm as the sounds coming from her dog grew louder. Officer McKay steadied the shelves above and called for more officers to help. "Get medics in here."

Medics? She removed a copy of Marjorie Kinnan Rawling's *The Yearling* and several copies of *Writer's Digest* and finally felt a wet tongue and furry muzzle.

"Oh, Hobbes. I'm so sorry."

A medic looked Hobbes over and carefully wrapped his front right leg. A space had been cleared on the sofa, and Hobbes now lay against a pillow the medic had brought in from the ambulance. She stood, gathering her things. "He should be all right. I don't think the leg's broken, but he's favoring it pretty well. You'll need to get it examined by a vet, today if possible. Might be difficult being the long weekend. But it's wrapped up, and I don't think you'll have to worry about him trying to walk on it too much for a while anyway."

"Thank you."

The medic nodded and turned to the little dog. "Take it easy, Hobbes. You're one brave pup."

Hobbes lay his head down on the pillow.

"Miss Parish?"

Jill turned to Officer McKay in a daze as the medic excused herself. "Yes?"

He stood next to an official-looking man she hadn't seen yet. "Miss Parish, this is Detective Okada."

Jill took the offered hand, barely aware of the firm handshake and large notepad the detective held in his other hand. Hobbes had been found and would be all right, but the apartment was still in shambles around her, and people kept coming and going as if . . . her eyes fell on her desk. "Oh no." She pulled her hand out of the detective's grip and stepped over debris to get to her desk. She shifted Shiloh to her other hip and ran her hand around the spaces on the desktop, peering around the base of the desk. "My laptop." She looked up, over at the men. "My laptop is gone."

The detective nodded. "You're sure?"

She searched the floor, scanned the overturned drawers. "I don't see it. It should be here. It's always here." Panic gripped her, but she remembered the flash drive. All her novels were on the flash drive. The work stuff could be retrieved at the office. She steadied her breathing and focused on the serious man before her. The detective surveyed the room.

"You'll need to make a list of any missing items." He turned, now searching her face. "Miss Parish, I'll be handling this case from here on out."

"Case?" Books lay at awkward angles at the base of her leaning book-shelves, pages torn out of them. Even the pictures on her walls had been knocked out of their frames. This wasn't a burglary. Someone was angry. She turned to the kitchen. A sound escaped her throat. All her dishes, all her glasses, all the contents of her cupboards were in fragments on the floor. Her refrigerator door stood ajar, contents tipped over and spilled. She could make out strawberry jam and pickle juice, smeared like finger paint. Someone was collecting fingerprints from it, and Detective Okada was saying something about the back door and the secluded alley—no witnesses. She turned and walked to the hall, fighting tears.

"Miss Parish, be careful."

The bathroom light was on, the medicine cabinet empty except for some dental floss and a squashed tube of toothpaste on the counter, but what sent a shudder through her entire body was the mirror. It was smeared with toothpaste. But it wasn't just streaked. The letters were defined.

EVIE.

"Miss Parish?"

"Jill." She turned, trying to keep her hands from visibly shaking. "Call me Jill."

Detective Okada nodded. He held her arm and directed her to the bedroom. Toilet paper ran from the bathroom down the hall.

Her fingers came to her mouth. Her top mattress was pushed over the base of the bed, all of it heaved up at one corner and shoved into the plaster wall. Pictures were smashed and clothes scattered. A man with a camera snapped away and another lifted prints off a lamp base. She turned to Detective Okada, who held her photo album with latex gloves. She wrinkled her brow.

"Are any of these missing?" he asked.

She stood, shifting Shiloh to her other hip. She reached but he pulled it away, shaking his head. One by one, he turned the pages from the beginning. Pictures of Dad next to a rebuilt Chevy Bel Air. Mom looking up at the camera, holding Jill, when drinking wasn't the only thing Mom cared about. Dad in his swimsuit in front of the ocean, lifting Mom, her toe pointed. Jill, riding a tricycle. Jill, a space where her permanent front teeth would grow in. Mom, holding baby Evie with tubes in her nose. Mom looked away instead of down at her tiny daughter. Jill, with her arms wrapped around her little sister, both looking too serious for their ages. Jill, looking overwhelmed in front of the rebuilt Beetle her dad had given her for her sixteenth birthday. Her life in a few pictures, glossed over. The pages kept turning, each one a step closer to the disarray surrounding her.

"Stop." Two pages had blank spots. She pointed. "This was a picture of my dad."

"When was it taken?"

"A year ago. At Thanksgiving. And this was a picture of . . ." her eyes met the detective's, "his house." Her dad had moved across town after her mother had finally pushed herself over the edge. His own way of leaving the past behind him. Dread came over Jill, and she felt light, like her insides were just space, enlarging, expanding. "Dad," she mumbled as she looked for a place to sit down and as Shiloh began to slip out of her grasp.

"Guys." She heard the detective's voice and felt hands at her elbows. Somebody took the baby as the room spun to black.

* * *

Cold pressed against her forehead, and someone placed something over her mouth. She breathed the saccharine air and promptly removed the oxygen. "I have to call my dad."

Detective Okada nodded. "I would agree."

Later, as Jill sat on the sofa with Laura, Bishop Thornton spoke quietly on the phone with Jill's father. Mrs. Holbrook, the landlady, was talking to the police officers. Hobbes lay on his pillow at Jill's feet, occasionally reaching up to nuzzle Jill's leg. Shiloh slept on Jill's lap.

"Let me put her down," Laura said.

"Where?" The portable crib Jill had just learned to set up was broken and out of joint. "I'm fine. She's fine. It feels good to hold her."

Detective Okada walked in through the front door, where a tarp had been hung to keep out the brisk air. "Jill, do you have a place to stay?"

Jill knew she couldn't stay here. She wouldn't. The questioning had sharpened her sense of reality. The police officers had just left with bags of possible fingerprints and clues.

"She'll stay with us."

Jill shook her head at Laura. "But I couldn't . . . what if they find out?" Of course, their main suspect was Neil—and anyone connected to him. Even Evie.

Detective Okada looked up from his notepad. "Actually, I don't see how a connection would be made between you and the Thorntons."

"Jill."

Jill turned to Laura.

"We had planned a trip to the ocean for the long weekend, you know, last of the season. But when we got your call yesterday—"

"Oh no—" She'd disrupted their plans.

Laura put her hand up. "No, we are so glad you called us. But we do have the cottage for the week. I was thinking you might like to come with us, you and Shiloh . . . maybe stay there for a few days to get away from this?"

The thought of reprieve steadied Jill. Yes . . . the ocean . . . escape. Then she jolted. "But what if Evie comes back? What if she changes her mind? Realizes she can't—"

Detective Okada spoke up. "We'll be watching the place. We *are* looking for her, Jill."

His nearly black eyes were steady. She had to trust him. "What will happen here?"

He gave her a shrug. "It will take the insurance company awhile to process this. You need to gather anything of value, remove it, make sure everything is listed. Then we'll board up the doors, and the insurance people will contact you."

"What about cleaning?"

Laura spoke up. "We'll pick up some of the food, your valuables . . . the toothpaste." She shuddered. "We can have the ward in here to help—"

Jill's startled expression must have given away her thoughts about that idea. Jill wasn't ready to be exposed to the ward in such a way.

Laura switched gears. "We'll talk to the landlady and see what she wants to do."

The detective nodded. "The insurance should cover the cost of any damage. I won't lie to you. It takes a long time. Weeks. Sometimes more."

Jill sighed and looked around. "I can't believe this is happening."

Laura shook her head. "I can't believe you're holding together so well."

Jill dropped her eyes and rubbed her thumb over Shiloh's fingers. "Years of practice."

Bishop Thornton walked to the sofa. "Jill, your dad wants to speak to you."

She took the phone. "Dad? Are you leaving?"

"I guess. Ol' Pulsifer will let me stay at his place. Are you all right?"

"Yes. I think I'm going to the coast for a few days with the Thorntons."

"That fellow, Grant, said that might happen. That's good, Jilly. Take it."

He'd said that when she had been offered her scholarship and again when she'd been offered the job at Brasher. Friday at the office seemed like forever ago.

She wasn't sure what else to say. She and her father, though close in some ways, had never been very expressive of their feelings. Feelings were something to protect. Something fragile. Jill's gaze followed Laura as she got up and walked to the kitchen.

"Grant says I could come out to the beach with you all . . . see that little granddaughter of mine."

Granddaughter. "Will you?"

"Well, I've got a little '56 Fairlane I'm fixing up for Tom Dickerson. Some good money in that. But if I get a day, maybe I'll make the trip."

"That's great, Dad." There was another pause.

"Jillian . . . I'm really glad you weren't in the house." His voice wavered. "So glad." He drew in a quick breath and blew it out.

"Me too." She gazed around at the hateful destruction. She didn't remind him that these were probably the people Evie had been *living* with. "I'll let you know if anything happens."

"Thanks, Jilly. Take care of yourself . . . and that baby."

After she hung up the phone, Jill lifted Shiloh from her lap to sleep on the sofa and went to help in the kitchen, where Laura and Bishop Thornton were salvaging anything unbroken.

"Thank you, Bishop Thornton. You've done so much. Are you sure about bringing me to the beach? I could get a hotel room."

Bishop Thornton held up his hands. "Enough of that. If it makes you feel better, I do require one thing if you come with us to the beach house."

"Anything."

"Promise me that while we're there, you'll just call me Grant."

Jill felt the corner of her mouth come up. "All right. Grant."

He raised his brows. "Not until we see the ocean."

She laughed. It felt good.

"Oh, look." Laura pulled out a small plastic bag from the mess. She waved it a bit triumphantly.

Jill sighed. "Yes." Her emergency stash of European chocolate.

Laura opened the bag and withdrew the partially frozen bars. She handed one to Jill, who took it gladly.

"The losers missed out in their haste. Do you mind?" Laura held up the other bar.

Jill had already bit into hers, breaking it off with a snap. "Not at all."

CHAPTER 5

Jill had never slept so soundly in a car. The *ding ding* of the open car door forced her out of the deep sleep.

A porch light blinked on not far from the car, revealing Bishop Thornton, or Grant, and the kids, who were already unloading the Thorntons' minivan.

"Are we here?"

Laura removed the keys from the ignition of Jill's Accord. "Yup, listen."

Jill closed her eyes and breathed, hearing the waves rolling, pushing against sand she could almost feel beneath her feet. She opened her eyes, and Laura held out her keys. Jill took them. "Thanks for insisting on driving. I really didn't think I could sleep. I guess I was wrong." She looked behind her. "Are you asleep, baby?"

"Dee dee."

Not asleep. "I think that means she wants to eat."

Laura nodded. "I wouldn't be surprised. I'm hungry myself."

None of them had felt like eating much more than the chocolate earlier, but after the long drive, food didn't sound so bad. Jill's landlady was hiring professionals to clean up the mess, but it had taken a couple of hours to find and pack up any valuables and then pack a bag for Jill and Shiloh. It had been hard to leave the kitchen the way it was, with all the shattered glass and dishes embedded in sticky food. Laura had made Jill put the broom away twice.

Then Jill had been able to get Hobbes an emergency appointment with the vet. His leg was rewrapped, and she was given a cone she hoped she wouldn't have to use on the poor dog. She wasn't looking forward to the bill, but it was one less thing to worry about.

Today had been one of the longest days of Jill's life. The clock on her cell phone read 10:08 p.m.

Jill peered out the window. "This is your family's?"

"Grant's. We have a rotating schedule among all the siblings and Grant's parents. Sometimes we share; sometimes we get it to ourselves."

"Will there be enough room?" She looked over the one-level cottage. Hollyhocks stood against the front of the house, and sea grass lined the broken walk to the shallow front porch. Blinds were drawn over the windows.

"Oh, sure. We've squeezed twenty of us in here before."

Jill raised her eyebrows.

"There are only two bedrooms and a sleeper sofa in the front room, but we throw all the kids in the big rec room in the back. They love it."

They got out of the car, and the rest of the family returned to help bring everything in.

Hobbes gingerly found the edge of the yard to do his business and then returned to the front screen door.

"Come in, pup." Laura let him in, and he carefully explored the new space, limping with his little cast. "Jill, you and Shiloh will be in the second bedroom. Grant and I have this one here. Bathroom is down the hall . . . only a shower, but the kitchen sink is big enough for the babies. You saw the kitchen on the way in, and that hallway leads to the rec room."

Territorial shouts rose from the back of the house where the kids were already making themselves at home.

"There are books here and some in your room, towels in the hall closet, extra blankets . . . Hmm, I think Grant has your things in here already. Yup."

They stepped into Jill's room as Grant popped up another portable crib. He answered Jill's questioning look.

"We keep a couple here . . . Lots of babies in the family." He spread a sheet over the little mattress and stood up, stretching his back. He took in the small space. "It'll be snug."

"I don't mind." She looked back and forth between the two people she had come to rely on so heavily in such a short time. "Thank you so much." She couldn't say anything else.

"Dee dee." Shiloh rubbed her eyes and whimpered.

"Come on," Laura said. "Let's get her some dee dee."

After they had eaten a late dinner of sandwiches, Jill tucked Shiloh in, and Hobbes settled onto his pillow. Jill wandered out to the front room and stood at the screen door. The breeze felt cleansing, milder than the colder air in the city.

"How close are we to the beach?"

"It's just a walk across the road. There's a path between a couple homes leading over a dune, and there's the beach." Laura looked up from the box of food she was unpacking. "Would you like to walk over?"

"Now?"

"Sure. We have a couple flashlights here. Grant and I sneak out after the kids quiet down. The beach is pretty at night, especially with the moon."

She brushed her hands on her pants and tossed the empty box in a corner. "I'll take you, and then you'll know the way." She turned and called quietly to the bedroom. "Honey, Jill and I are going for a walk. Want to come?"

The reply was a muffled grunt.

"I think he's asleep back there."

Footsteps sounded from the back room. "Can we come?" Three sets of big smiles and bright eyes waited expectantly. The remaining Thornton kids were ages twelve, thirteen, and fifteen, all boys, and each a perfect blend of their mother and father.

Laura chuckled. "Sure . . . Grab a flashlight and jackets. And turn the lights off back there." She shook her head at Jill as the rumble faded away, and then she handed Jill a flashlight. "Next time I won't announce our sneaking away."

Jill smiled and followed her out.

"See those two houses? The path is there. This beach is private access for this neighborhood, but you can pretty much go as far as you want either way. Public access is up that way." She pointed north. "The cape ends in tide pools and a big sand dune. It's a fun little climb—about once every couple years." Jill laughed and Laura smiled. "The tide pools are fun though. You have to get up pretty early." She motioned north again to a small cluster of lights. "Have you ever been to Pacific City?"

Jill shook her head. "We would go to Newport, mostly. Once, though, we went to Lincoln City."

"Well, that makes sense, being from Lebanon. And everyone goes to Lincoln City. Did you like it?"

"Mm-hm. I remember the kites. And the wind." The breeze brushed her hair as they passed the dark houses and rose over the dune. The beach grass swiped against her jeans. She paused, bending down to pull off her shoes and socks. Laura joined her, and they rolled the hems of their pants while the kids caught up.

Her bare feet sank into the cool of the dune then flipped little puffs of it up as she walked. The sound of the waves grew louder, and her feet hastened to get her to the top.

The night stretched out, black sky meeting black water in motion, the moonlight bouncing off the gentle crests of each low wave running to the shore. Jill took a deep breath as she stood, absorbing it.

Laura sighed. "I never get over it."

Neither did Jill. The beach was the one place—the *one* place—with only happy, peaceful memories. Her mother must have loved it enough. They hadn't gone often as a family. Maybe that was a factor. "It almost makes it all go away," she whispered, unsure if she meant the last weekend or her troubling past.

She heard a bang, and the sky to the south momentarily lit up, light streaking into the sky, then fading.

"Cool, somebody's doing fireworks!" The kids ran past them onto the beach.

"Brady, stay out of the water," Laura called. "Watch out for your brothers." The tide was in this time of night. Jill imagined the beach would stretch a lot wider in the morning.

"Tell me about your book. What's it called?"

Jill felt the nervous flutter in her stomach that always came when someone asked her about her book. As much as she loved writing, she found sharing it with others a daunting task. But if she were to be published someday, she'd have to get over it.

"It's called *Saved by Grace and Chocolate*."

"I like it already."

Jill smiled. Most people had that reaction.

"Explain the title."

"Well," Jill flipped a bit of sand out in front of her with her foot, "*grace* has a couple of meanings, right? There is physical grace, movement and flow of the human body, or words, *She walks in beauty like the night*—that sort of thing. Objects or people or nature. We tend to judge whether things are graceful or not, usually valuing and praising what is and pitying or dismissing what isn't."

"Hm. There's truth to that."

"Yes. And then there's God's grace. Those things that happen and, for all the laws and powers of reason, they shouldn't happen, but they do, and someone is given a chance . . ."

"Mercy."

Jill turned to Laura. "Yes. Mercy." She swallowed. "The book is about a girl who is given mercy and then learns that mercy, that *grace* . . . is not always painless." She lifted her brow. "It's not always . . . graceful."

Jill paused. She'd found her two-sentence hook.

"And the chocolate?" Laura asked.

Jill grinned, feeling a small triumph. "Well, it's *chocolate*."

Both women laughed.

They continued to talk about the book as they walked toward the fireworks. It was nice to share this with a woman who seemed content to just listen and prod Jill only enough to keep her talking. Jill slowed before they got too close to the launching site. As nice as it was to talk with Laura, Jill wasn't in the mood to be social. "Can we sit here?"

"Sure." They dropped down on a bleached log and watched the fireworks, the surf, and the moon until the fireworks ended. Then they called the kids, and Jill felt like maybe she could sleep soundly.

She was wrong.

She'd been dreaming of her house back in Lebanon—the mess it always was—and then someone broke the window, and they were trying to get her and her dad, and then a few people got inside, and one of them was Evie, who laughed at their fear as if they shouldn't be afraid, and her dad was old . . .

And then Shiloh woke up, crying hard. Jill had come to with that disoriented feeling of not knowing where she was. She'd held tight to the covers, then as Shiloh's cry escalated, it drew Jill out of the dream and back into reality.

"Ma ma . . . ma ma . . ."

"I know. I know. Shh." Jill paced the floor, bouncing Shiloh. It was futile. She sank down onto the edge of the bed.

"Do you want a bottle?"

Shiloh pulled in her breath and stuck her fingers in her mouth. "Dee dee." Jill moved.

She rummaged through the diaper bag until she found what she needed, picked up the baby, and stumbled to the kitchen to make the bottle. Her head nodded and bounced a few times as she sat in the chair, feeding Shiloh. When the bottle was empty, Shiloh whimpered and cried less heatedly but did not want sleep.

"Are you having bad dreams too?"

Shiloh reached for the napkin holder on the dining table. Jill removed the napkins and gave the holder to her niece. While the baby was occupied, Jill took in her surroundings.

Even in the low light of the stove lamp she had turned on, it was a cheerful place, *nostalgic*. Each cupboard door was a different color: sunset orange, green, like the sea grass, faded buoy red, and soft yellow, the sun behind thin clouds. The counters and the floors were the same sandy pattern and color, probably a good choice. She pressed her fingers along the deep, dark wood of the table. The piece was heavily varnished and deeply carved on the legs and chairs. She imagined someone had chosen the weighty set for longevity. None of the silverware or glasses matched, but the dishes in the happy colors of the cupboards brought it all together . . . creating comfort she hadn't known she'd needed until three in the morning when the baby was crying and the world was turned upside down. Jill shook her head and allowed a slight smile. A colorful kitchen. Of course that was the answer to all her troubles. She looked down to see Shiloh's eyelids drooping. Carefully, she took the napkin holder from her little hands and rose from the chair.

Shiloh's eyes flickered open, and she whimpered. Jill sat back down and gave her back the napkin holder, which she clung to with desperation.

"You're a little out of it too."

She leaned on her hand and sighed, her lids heavy.

Jill's head jerked in her hand, and she blinked awake. The sky behind the blinds had begun to lighten, and the house was still quiet. She looked at the sleeping baby in her arms and pulled herself up so she could walk down the hall. Hobbes greeted her in the bedroom, tail wagging expectantly. Jill lay the baby down in the crib and considered going back to bed. She stretched and yawned and, after some thought, gathered her clothes and toiletry bag and headed for a shower. "Give me a sec, Hobbes."

When she returned to her bedroom, Shiloh stood peeking over the edge of her crib. Jill looked from her to Hobbes. "Okay, let's go."

She left a note on the big table, and they stepped outside into the ocean air.

Jill felt a tug at her hair as they walked along the sand where foamy water ebbed and then was pulled back into gray-blue ocean. She had decided to try the baby backpack Laura had shown her and was pleased she'd figured it out. Shiloh seemed to be pleased too. She held tight to a lock of Jill's hair and babbled and squealed at a bird overhead or a wave that came in particularly close. They had the beach pretty much to themselves at six o'clock in the morning. A jogger ran past, and Jill spotted another figure up ahead, but that was all.

The day would be bright. The pale sky was clear, and there were no clouds on the horizon. A large rock the shape of a haystack loomed off the coast to the north. She couldn't judge the distance, but the harder she studied, the more she could see the outlines of plants—or were those trees?—clinging to the exterior. She assumed the tiny fluttering white flecks were seabirds fishing around the island. But the rock fascinated her. It stood alone, beaten by the waves surrounding it.

She felt the past, the parts she wound tight and kept hidden from her organized world, begin to unravel again as she watched the relentless waves. The last three days had brought wave after wave of disruption, change, hurt . . . everything she'd tried to escape had been hurled at her in battering waves.

Make it stop.

She clenched her fists at her side, fighting for the control she needed. She straightened and turned away from the rock, looking back the way they were heading, south. Hobbes barked at seagulls. Jill took a deep breath and watched him, finding the calm she needed in his familiar form and sound, even if he was gimping a little on his injured leg. He walked out in front, unleashed and free to explore without the fear of cars or buses.

"Hobbes, stay close." He'd wandered over to a pile of washed-up sea plants and driftwood. After sniffing around, he raised his head, looked down the beach, barked, then took off. "Hobbes." He headed for the launching site of the fireworks, where the lone figure she'd seen before was cleaning up.

She watched as Hobbes ran to the man in a hooded sweatshirt. He bent down to greet the dog as it neared. She didn't feel like speaking to anyone but followed after her entirely too-social dog. The figure abruptly stood, looking down at Hobbes then up to her.

She halted, gaping from where she stood in the sand. Blue eyes. Gold flecks.

* * *

Scott Gentry stood very still, his mind working as his brow furrowed. He flexed his fingers and blinked. He looked toward his parents' house then back at Jillian Parish. It was her. This was her dog . . . Hobbes. With a bandaged leg. And she had a baby on her back.

He pressed his lips together. He wouldn't say anything. She'd been very clear about how she felt about him. He watched her face, though, for any hint of what he should do.

He couldn't read it. Her brown eyes, those eyes that haunted his thoughts, were round and unblinking. She bit her lip, seemingly as surprised as he was. If he didn't know how much she despised him, he would think she wanted to say something to him. Maybe it was more of those words he deserved to hear.

Well, he wasn't going to stick around to hear them. He'd apologized, and he'd meant it. He nodded brusquely and turned to climb the grassy slope to the long boardwalk leading to his parents' house.

But the dog had other ideas. He yipped and jumped close to Scott's legs and tripped him up in the loose sand as he tried to avoid injuring the animal further. He half turned. "Would you mind calling your—?" He caught the devastated look on her face, the lift of her shoulders, and now, the tears slipping down her cheek.

She gasped and wiped the water away as she turned from him, but the quiet gasping continued, and soon her head dropped into her hands.

His compassion overrode his pride. Slowly, he walked back to her.

"Jillian . . . I . . ." He didn't know what to say, had no idea what she wanted to hear. The child in the backpack patted her head. "What can I do?"

Jillian shook her head. "Nothing . . ." She drew in a breath. "Nothing." She lowered a hand and held it away from her. "I'm sorry. It's just been a really hard weekend." Her shoulders began to bounce again, and he looked at the child's big brown eyes staring at him as she leaned her head toward Jillian's.

Carefully, he reached and brushed the little girl's curls with his fingers. Quietly, he asked, "Is this your niece?"

Jillian nodded her head jerkily and sniffled, still facing the morning waves.

"She looks like you."

A sort of choked laugh came from her throat. She mumbled something about how would he know what she looked like, and he didn't understand. But he could tell her tone was headed in the same direction it had the other night.

"Listen, I don't know—If I had known my actions would affect you this way, I never would have even attempted to get your attention. I only thought . . . maybe we had some things in common, and it's hard . . . being single and getting older and everyone thinks you're not trying. But the truth is—"

She laughed in an I-can't-believe-this sort of way.

He took half a step back as she turned to face him. Some of her hair blew across her face. Her eyes were red, and he couldn't read her expression. Not disgust or annoyance—

"What brought you here from California? The rain?"

"No, I . . . my parents moved here after . . ." Had she asked someone about him?

"Look at me, Scott."

The request startled him. He couldn't look anywhere else.

"I have curly hair . . . and a tan . . . and I have a little more weight in places I hate . . ."

He tried to follow her, sensing from her steady gaze that this was important.

"I'm crying, and you help me. You make it bearable."

He furrowed his brow, trying to make sense of what she was telling him. He was *helping* her now?

"And I wait and wait to hear from you, but you don't call . . . Nothing . . . You forget. Because I was just a distraction in Costa Rica . . . a distraction you called Cougar."

He drew in a slow breath as his face warmed. He swallowed, and his pulse began to race. "*Cougar.*"

She let him absorb the realization. He searched her face, hair, arms, and figure. Her eyes. Eyes that waited to be given a reason to smile. Eyes that challenged him. He took a step toward her, but she stepped away just as quickly.

He reached a hand out. "Jill?"

She nodded, her eyes hardening. "Parish."

"*Jill Parish*, from Oregon." Saying it out loud helped a little. Was it possible?

She folded her arms. "Is it coming back to you, Scott Gentry?"

He clenched his jaw and nodded. Deep brown eyes, lost, hurt, soulful, searching, full of wonder.

She dropped her gaze and toed the sand with her bare feet. He remembered those feet. Tan. Her voice was hushed. "I think if I would have been another kind of girl, from another kind of world, this would all be pretty funny. Almost entertaining." She raised her narrowed eyes to his. "I'm sorry—*really, very sorry*—I wasn't that other kind of girl."

Her words struck him because he knew she wasn't that other kind of girl. He knew why he had been drawn to her, why he had tried so hard to distract her, to make her smile. To find that look of wonder. "I . . . can't believe—"

"That it caught up to you?"

He nodded, his mouth open. He blinked. "No, I mean—"

"Save it, Scott. Life is way too complicated right now for me to even give you a thought, and it really irks me that I have. I just wanted you to know so you can leave me alone."

He swallowed. He didn't want to leave her alone, not like this. "Please, listen. I—"

"No. *No.*" Her eyes were filling with emotion again. "Trust me—"

"Dee dee."

Scott looked at the little girl holding Jill's hair. Jill sniffled and wiped her sleeve across her face. "You hungry, sweetie?"

"Dee dee."

"Let's get you something to eat." Jill turned without looking at him. "C'mon, pup." Hobbes quickly followed her.

He couldn't just let it go like that. "Jill."

She turned, tears on her cheeks again. And he could see her. He could see the girl. Without her make-up and with the wind messing up her hair, she was no longer the closed woman he couldn't shake. She was a girl sitting on the edge of a pool, wondering how to live in a cruel world. Shame filled him.

She took a deep breath. "Don't. It was a long time ago, right? Long, long ago, in a faraway land." She forced out a short laugh. "You actually made the right move, you know? This?" She gestured to herself, the baby, and the dog. "It's kind of a mess. You are so much better off in your world, Scott. I just wish—" She stopped herself.

He waited, breathing in and out, waiting to know what she wished. He stepped toward her again. "What?"

She steadied herself and pulled her hair behind her ear. "I wish I had forgotten you too." She turned and walked away, leaving footprints behind her, the baby sucking on her fingers and looking back at him. She pointed her tiny finger then turned around and pointed to the dog below her, and the breeze carried away her jabber sounds.

He stayed and watched until her distant figure turned and disappeared over a dune. He rocked back and sat down hard in the sand then dropped his head in his hands, remembering. A penance.

* * *

"So what was with you and the chubby girl?"

The smaller bus pulled onto the palm tree-lined road leading away from Punta Leona.

Scott pulled his eyes away from the window and the last few kids from Oregon boarding the other bus. "What are you talking about?"

"Oh, come on. Like we don't know."

Scott scowled, forcing a smile. "I don't know what you guys are talking about."

"Yeah right." Someone pulled the paper from his hands.

"Hey!"

"Oh c'mon, man. She lives in *Oregon*."

"Hey, knock it off."

"I think Gentry likes himself a little Oregonian *curvature*."

"I do not. She was fun. Now give it back."

"Yeah, I bet she was. *Geesh*, man, Erica is so much hotter than that."

Scott sat back in his seat, red and scowling. "Whatever." He stared out the window as the bus pulled away.

"Oh, *Scotty*."

He had to look over, and his stomach dropped along with the paper out the opened window. He lurched out of his seat toward the kid who had dropped it, smashing into his chest and hearing the grunt whoosh out of the kid's lungs as he hit the window.

"Hey! Gentry, Thompson! Cool it! Gentry, get back to your seat."

Scott gave one last shove as he backed out of the fight, straightened his shirt, and returned to his own seat. After everyone else slowly sat down, he put his head in his hands.

He didn't even know her last name. Jill . . . Jill something. Jill Cougar. From Oregon. He grimaced at himself and sunk lower in the seat.

"Geesh, Gentry. Get over it."

"Yeah, man. Don't let it bother you."

* * *

Laura turned as Jill came through the door. "Hey, there you are. I saw your note—" She stopped stirring the pancake batter, set down the bowl, and hurried to Jill. "What happened? Is something wrong?"

Jill shook her head and let Laura lift Shiloh off her back. "No . . . Well, yes. But—"

Laura gave her a concerned look as Grant walked out from the hallway. "Good morning, ladies. Hope you enjoyed your sleep. I myself slept *quite* well. Mm, is that pancake batter? Do we have blueberries?" He halted halfway to the freezer, seeing his wife's glare. He pushed his glasses up and glanced at Jill then stepped forward. "What? Did something happen? Did they find your sister? Is it your dad?" He looked around on the floor. "Is the baby okay?"

Jill was both touched and unnerved by the numerous ways he was concerned for her. She was also embarrassed by her obvious failing to hide the emotions she had tried to tuck away as she'd approached the cheery cottage after her walk. And it was cheery. Faded, silvery cedar shingles, thickly painted white trim, and the flowers all pinks and reds topping the fading green. How dare she bring her gloom to such a place?

Laura set Shiloh on the floor and made sure she was content. "The baby is *fine*." She stood back up and put an arm around Jill. "What happened, honey?"

Jill moved to the table, sitting down hard. "It has nothing to do with Evie. And, no, we hardly slept last night, which probably explains why I . . ."

"Why you what?" Grant's look of concern wasn't fading.

She put her elbow on the table and rested her forehead in her hand. "Why I just made a complete *fool* of myself."

"Well, who did you run into?" Laura stepped to her and brushed her hair out of her face. The touch felt nice, foreign.

Jill shook her head and groaned. "It doesn't matter."

"What can we do?" Laura slid into the chair next to her.

"Nothing." Jill lifted her head. "You've done so much already. You didn't even really know me before all this, and I'll never be able to thank you enough." She left it at that. She knew the Thorntons were exchanging looks, but she stood and picked up the bowl of batter. "So do we have blueberries?"

After breakfast, Jill and Shiloh found a hammock in the backyard and fell asleep, Shiloh tucked into her aunt's side.

* * *

"Well, Dad, what would you do?" Scott looked at his father, who was nodding his head, nearly asleep. "Yeah, you were always a great listener." Scott looked up in time to see a familiar figure heading his way. He'd noticed him earlier, playing Frisbee with his kids up the beach.

"Hello, Grant." Everywhere else he was Bishop Thornton. But not at the beach.

"Scott." The man offered his hand over the edge of the boardwalk, a little winded from play. "As soon as I spotted you and your dad out here,

I had to come over." He waved a hand as Scott turned toward his father. "No, don't wake him up. Let him sleep." He motioned Scott farther down the boardwalk. "You up here for the weekend, then?"

Scott followed him down a few planks and sat on the edge. "Yeah, got here Saturday morning. I saw your kids last night. They helped with a few fireworks."

Grant nodded, looking around. "Beautiful weather. Hanging on for a little while, anyway. We got here last night, and the kids and Laura came out to the beach after we got everything unpacked."

"Squeezing the fun in, huh?"

Grant chuckled. "Yeah, I guess. We were going to come up for the three-day weekend, but we'll be staying into the week now. Actually, I could use your help. I need to administer a blessing and would love another set of hands. Are you up for that?"

"When?"

"Oh, after lunch should be fine. Jill is back at the house sleeping right now—"

"Jill. *Parish*?"

Grant frowned at the way Scott said her name. "Yeah. She's had a tough time. My wife and I brought her here to keep her safe—"

"Safe?" Scott repeated, startled. "Safe from what?"

Grant nodded. He sighed and moved to sit on the boardwalk next to Scott.

Scott had to keep his keening emotions in check as Grant filled him in on all that had transpired since Friday, when he'd left Jill a crushed rose and a piece of chocolate in the offices of Brasher Books. Since he had seen her with bags of baby supplies at the minimart. Since he had asked to start over and she'd said . . .

I'm sorry, but I just don't have that kind of time.

He blew out a breath and rubbed his hands over his eyes. "I . . . I really don't think it's a good idea to include me." He was sure it was a really *bad* idea to include him. "Does she know you're asking me?"

"No. I just saw you and felt I should ask. I didn't realize you two knew each other enough that it would matter." He frowned again. "May I ask why it does matter?"

Scott lowered his gaze and fingered the weathered wood of the boardwalk. Bishop or not, Grant was still someone he would go to for direction. The man had been the one who had encouraged Scott's move to Portland to try to find his life. *Hm. Maybe Grant's not the guy I want to talk to after all.* Scott sighed. "I hurt Jill's feelings a long time ago—years ago—and had the nerve not to recognize her when we met again." He shook his head as Grant let out a low whistle. He *had* hurt her. He hadn't meant to. He'd agonized over it, actually, but that didn't matter, did it? He felt Grant's eyes on him.

"You didn't happen to run into her early this morning, did you?"

Scott nodded. "Yup, that was me." He looked up with a weak smile. "We sort of surprised each other."

"Hmm. That's too bad."

"I'd hate to upset her any more."

"Listen, that girl has been put through the wringer in the last forty-eight hours—"

"Fifty-six, actually." He thought of work on Friday.

Grant ignored him. "And got about three hours of sleep last night, staying up with the baby. Maybe it's not as bad as it seems."

"Mm-hm." It was. "I'm sorry I can't help. I can call someone from the ward if you need me to."

"Thanks. I'll let you know." He scrutinized Scott a moment, pushing his glasses up before he continued. "She could sure use a friend right now."

He agreed. "I'll let you know if I think of anyone who qualifies."

Grant chuckled sadly and nodded his head. "All right. Tell your mom hello. I'll come see your dad later. And you know you're welcome to stop by."

"Thanks. I think we'll be hanging out down here today."

Grant slapped him on the shoulder and walked away then jogged to pick up the errant Frisbee and rejoin his kids in play.

Scott stared out at the sea. *What would You have me do?*

He heard the squeak of the screen door and turned to see his mom coming down the long boardwalk, holding a tray. He stood and took it from her.

"Thank you, Scott. Oh, he's asleep." His mom reached a hand and pressed it gently on his dad's shoulder. She hushed her voice. "Was that Grant Thornton?"

Scott nodded.

"We've been blessed with wonderful connections, haven't we?"

Scott nodded again, knowing his mom was referring to Grant urging Scott to find work in Portland and move in with his brother, among other things. But guilt pushed the image of a younger Jill to the forefront of his thoughts. He set the tray down on the small weathered table.

"Thanks, Mom. You didn't have to bring it down."

"Oh, I wanted to. It's so nice to have you here, and your father loves to be out by the water. Sit down, and we'll have a snack." She took the other chair and poured out some lemonade. "The Thornton kids are getting so big. Did they say how long they would be here?"

Scott shook his head. "I'm not sure. Grant said they just got here last night and something about staying a few days."

"Oh, I'll have to call Laura and invite them over. We have so much room here, and your father loves company. You wouldn't mind, would you?"

Scott didn't say anything, just watched the Thornton kids dig a moat around a large pile of sand.

"I do wish you could stay longer, Scott. Are you—"

Scott suddenly stood. Jill Parish was running with the baby on her hip, running and calling to Grant, Hobbes keeping up at her heels.

He urged his feet to remain planted on the wood planks beneath him.

* * *

"Bishop Thornton! Grant!" Jill fought the sinking sand and ignored it filling up her shoes. Shiloh gripped Jill's shirt in her fists, hanging on as Jill maneuvered down the sand dune. She didn't know babies could get so heavy. "Grant!" He turned and, upon seeing her expression, rose from the beach chair under the umbrella and jogged her way.

"What is it?"

She swallowed and slowed, trying to catch her breath. "It's my dad. They—" She took another gulp. "They went to his house. I tried to call you. Laura's still shopping, and I only have your number."

He patted his shorts, looking for his phone, and grimaced. "Oh, it's in the bag. Your dad wasn't there, was he?"

She shook her head. "No. No, he wasn't, and they got away before the police made their rounds. Someone saw the car though."

"The license plate?"

She shook her head again. "No. But it was an old Impala. Blue." Her hands were shaking, even as she held Shiloh. "They left a note, tied around a rock they threw through the window."

Grant narrowed his eyes.

"It said that . . . that they would find Evie and she'd pay for what she'd done." Her voice broke. "Or we'll all pay."

Grant placed his hands on her shoulders. "It's all right. Let's look at what this means. They didn't find your dad, and they haven't found your sister.

And the police know what the car looks like. These guys aren't professionals. They'll make a mistake, and it will end."

She nodded but didn't believe him. "I told my dad to come here." She could feel her emotions give in to her fear. "I shouldn't have told him that. I'm sorry. I just don't know what to do." She pulled away from him. "He said he would come, but I don't want to give you all this trouble. I don't want to be causing all this—" She shook her head at her crumbling resolve. "I just don't want my dad to get hurt."

The strength of her fear of losing her dad took her by surprise. Her grip on the baby tightened as she tried to regain her composure. Grant lowered his head to look her in the eyes.

"Your dad needs to come here. It's safe here."

"But . . ."

"No *but*." He turned away, and she followed his gaze. Her mouth went dry as she saw him wave to the standing figure on the distant boardwalk, the figure who was watching them intently with his hands on his hips.

Scott hesitated, said something to the others on the walk, then jumped into the sand and ran in their direction. Jill shrank back, pulling Shiloh's head closer to hers. "What are you doing?"

Grant looked at her as a father looks at a child he wants to listen. "I told Scott Gentry what happened—"

"You *what?*"

"Now, Jill, I know there's an issue with you two, but right now, we need all the protection we can give you, even if that means one more priesthood holder in the know."

She didn't have more time to protest because Scott arrived, panting from the jog. Jill glanced at him then turned her eyes down to Shiloh. An ocean wind picked up, and the baby nestled closer into Jill.

"What's happened?"

Jill kept her eyes down but was caught by the worry in his voice. She watched the sand as Grant relayed the news of her father.

"What can we do?"

She turned her eyes to him. He addressed Grant but glanced her way.

"I haven't asked Jill yet, and I hate to ask you, Scott, but maybe Jill's father could stay at your place?"

Jill's eyes grew large. She turned and pulled the bishop's arm so he turned with her. She spoke, and he had to lean down to hear her.

"Bishop, if this is some kind of YSA match-making scheme, you are so mistaken—"

"Jill, I hardly think I'd take advantage of this particular circumstance to play cupid."

She studied him a moment then shook her head. She was losing her mind. "I'm sorry. I'm not thinking straight."

"No, I'm sorry. I would have run it by you first, but we're thinking on our feet here and Scott's mother is always extending invitations for our overflow. It was the first thing that came to mind."

Scott spoke up behind them. "I'm sure she wouldn't mind."

Jill and Grant both turned.

"I'm sure she'd be happy to help. I'll talk to her about it. My dad could use the company." He glanced at Jill again. "If Jill doesn't mind, that is. But," he shifted his weight, "I was going back to work tomorrow. When is your father coming?"

She jolted at being questioned directly and stammered. "He's . . . he's leaving this afternoon." She bit her lip. Work. Books. Cubicles. Him. It was so far away. She turned to Grant. "I'm so sorry."

He placed his hands on her shoulders. "None of this is your fault. Stop apologizing. Now, we'll all work together to make things right." He turned his head to Scott. "Jill's father can stay with us, Scott. I just thought it would be more comfortable—"

"No. He can stay with us. Mom was just saying how big her place is and she needed to have people over. I just wasn't sure about leaving her with . . . well, the situation. But I'll call work, see what I can do."

"I'll vouch for you if you need it."

Scott shook his head. "There's a lot I can do from here. Maybe I can offer to take on a few extra assignments."

Jill's mind reeled helplessly. How was he suddenly involved in this?

"You said Laura was still shopping?"

Jill took a breath. "She was still gone when I left the house."

"Did you tell your father not to tell anyone he was coming up?"

"He said he was going to let the bishop and the police know. But that was all."

Grant nodded. He didn't let go of her shoulders, and several seconds passed. It was calming, like a paperweight keeping her from scattering off in the wind. "Now, Jill, would you like a blessing?"

The question threw her. She blinked and swallowed. "I um . . ." She glanced at Scott, who looked away, trying to mind his own business. She hadn't had very many blessings. A baby blessing she obviously didn't remember then her baptism. She had timidly asked her dad for one before she left for college, and he had timidly given it to her with the help of their home teachers. Then her roommates had insisted she have one when she came down with a bad flu. She remembered the warm pressure of hands on her head, of the spoken words in her behalf. She kissed Shiloh's cheek. Her voice was small. "Okay."

Grant didn't remove his hands as he looked into her eyes. "Would you mind if Scott assists me?"

She glanced at Scott in surprise, but he looked down at the sand, digging in his toe. Then he raised his eyes to hers. He took a deep breath and shook his head, looking out at the ocean.

She lowered her eyes to the ground. "If you think it would help." She felt Scott turn his gaze to her.

Grant nodded but said, "Do *you* think it would help?"

She couldn't stop the small bob of her head, and she pressed her lips together. She inhaled and moisture came to her eyes. "Of course it would." She blew out the breath and kissed Shiloh's cheek again then turned and walked slowly back to the house, aware of the two men following her and hearing Grant shout instructions to his children as he walked away.

CHAPTER 6

I'm not worthy of this . . . I'm not worthy of this . . .

The mantra ran through his head all the way to the Thornton place. Laura pulled up in the minivan as they reached the porch.

"Hello, Scott. I didn't know you were here." Laura Thornton greeted him as she exited the driver's side and pulled a large package of diapers out of the backseat. "How are your parents?"

He followed Grant to the car and grabbed a couple bags of food. "They're great. Mom said she would call you. I just came to, uh . . ."

Grant spoke quietly to his wife. "He's come to assist me with the blessing."

Laura raised her eyebrows and nodded. She glanced beyond them to the empty doorway. "Is Jill inside? She's not still napping, is she?"

Grant frowned, and Scott grabbed another bag, leaving Grant to explain what was going on to his wife.

Scott let himself into the familiar cottage. When he'd returned from his mission to his parents' new home on a strange coastline, he'd been introduced to the Thorntons at church, one of the long-time visiting families with a vacation home in Pacific City. It had been comforting, knowing his parents had a rotation of strong LDS members throughout the year who were so close at hand in such a transitory community. The family had helped more than a few times. His mom had sent him over with plenty of batches of cookies, pies, and cakes to express her thanks.

He looked around, not seeing Jill but hearing the baby jabber in one of the back rooms. He walked over to a group of frames on a wall in the front room. A collage of years of memories. He found one picture and swallowed, shifting uncomfortably.

Scott turned at the soft sound behind him. Jill was just standing up, having set the baby on the floor to crawl around. She folded her arms over her middle but didn't look at him. The screen door squeaked open, and Grant came in, arms full of groceries, and held the door with his foot for his wife and the dog. They were in quiet midsentence, and it faded as they set the bags down on the huge table.

Once they'd put the groceries away, Grant motioned for them to sit with him in the front room. Laura excused herself and went back outside.

Grant blew out a breath. "I need to apologize. To you, Jill, and to you, Scott."

Scott lifted his head in surprise.

Grant folded his hands in front of him. "If there are ill feelings between the two of you, then maybe . . ." he rubbed his chin thoughtfully, "I didn't mean to press you into this." He lowered his eyes and sighed.

"Grant?" Laura opened the screen door and poked her head inside. "Excuse me, sweetheart, but I think the van has a flat tire."

Grant lifted his head. "What? How?"

"Well, I can't be sure, but I think it might have something to do with the big nail stuck in it and the high-pitched whistling sound it's making."

Grant rose to his feet. "Excuse me just a sec." He strode to the door as Laura backed away, and they both disappeared, the screen door banging shut behind them.

After a strained silence, Grant reappeared at the door. "Hey kids, I'm gonna have to take the van over to Cloverdale and get a new tube in this thing."

Scott sat up. "I can help you change a tire."

Grant shook his head. "You could if I had a spare. I've got to get it in before it loses too much air. I know the place; I just hope they're open today. I apologize, Jill. It shouldn't take long. Laura's coming with me to keep an eye on it as we go." He looked at the two of them, hesitating. He began to say something then paused. Then he said, "We'll be back as soon as we can. The kids will probably be coming up soon for lunch." He hesitated again then nodded and left. The screen door bounced closed again.

Scott stared at the door from the La-Z-Boy. Slowly, he looked to see Jill's response. She watched the door as well.

"There's a lot of construction in the neighborhood. Every once in a while a nail shows up," he said.

Jill nodded. She turned her attention to the baby, her face expressionless. Jill reached her fingers and wriggled them. The baby batted her fingers then crawled away to the corner of toys. Jill folded her arms across her middle again and stayed perched on the edge of the sofa, her jaw tense.

He couldn't blame her for not looking at him. But they were here, and she wasn't yelling at him, and he might not get another chance like this. He carefully opened his mouth. "I—"

Her eyes darted up to his, and he froze. She lowered them again, and he took a breath. "I didn't forget you." She closed her eyes, but he pushed on. "I couldn't."

Her brows wrinkled just a little, and it encouraged him. She was listening. Which was good because now that he'd started talking, he wasn't sure how to stop.

"I . . . lost . . . your phone number, everything . . . before we even left Costa Rica." He would not tell her how. He would lie if she asked. "I was really . . . ashamed that I couldn't even remember your last name." He winced at the slight shake of her head. "I got home and told my dad. We got online, and all I could look up was 'Jill from Oregon,' and one of the teachers said they thought you guys were from Salem—"

"Lebanon."

He paused at her response but quickly continued. "So, I just . . . I had no chance." He felt guilt from all those years rise his throat. "But I tried." He lowered his forehead to his hands and rubbed hard. "I didn't want you to think I . . ." He shook his head and waited, not expecting anything. "I didn't want that for you . . . on top of everything else." He rubbed at the sting of his eyes and quickly stood. He turned and faced the collage of pictures. "I didn't forget you. I just . . . gave up trying to find you." *I prayed for you. Hard.*

But it had been a kid's prayer. A prayer of remorse and worry and a hard lesson learned. A lesson his dad had made sure he understood.

You can't abuse those feelings, son. You need to be so careful. There are big problems in this universe, and you never know how your actions are going to set those problems spinning.

The baby made some scraping sound, and he looked her way. He leapt in an instant to pull her fingers away from the electrical outlet. The movement startled her, and her lower lip pushed out.

"Oh, sorry. No, don't cry." He patted her hand and picked up a toy. "Look, you like the kitty? Look at the kitty." The child wrapped her other hand tightly around the key chain, and he felt her pulled from him as Jill picked her up and held her close, shushing her.

He stood and put his hands in his pockets. "I'm sorry. I didn't mean to frighten her. Those outlets usually have those child-proof plug things in them. Here." He walked quickly to the kitchen and pulled open a few drawers until he found the right one, hurried by the whimpers from the baby. After rummaging through dice and paperclips, tourist pamphlets and half-empty packages of gum, he spotted a broken mug of twistties and several of the plugs he was looking for. He grabbed some and made his way around the room, plugging in the few open outlets. He stood and turned.

"Is she all right?"

He watched the baby, unable to fully look at Jill, but she nodded. The blue plastic cat with the key ring dangling from its head slipped out of the baby's fingers and dropped to the floor. He bent down to get it and, after a loud knock to his head, was immediately sorry.

"Owww."

Jill drew in her breath through her teeth and rubbed the spot on her head that had collided with his. She lost her balance, and he reached out to grab her arm, and they both landed on their rear ends. The baby crawled off Jill and retrieved the kitty on her own.

He fought the laugh that naturally came to him, but it helped to see her fighting it too. He gently let go of her arm and nodded to the baby. "What's her name?"

Jill leaned forward and covered her face with her hands. "Shiloh." She sighed. "Shiloh Parish . . . I think." She lifted her face and watched her niece. "I don't even know if she has a middle name. My sister left without telling me anything. She just left, and I have no idea if she's coming back or who these people are or—" Jill placed her fingers over her mouth.

Scott touched her arm, and she didn't pull away. She dropped her hand.

Sobered, they watched Shiloh fruitlessly grabbing at some books just out of her reach. When Scott looked at Jill again, she was staring vacantly at the floor, pulling at the area rug beneath them. He watched her fingers for several quiet minutes. He imagined them typing over keys, playing the rhythm of words she heard in her head. So it startled him when she spoke.

"I remembered what you said. It helped."

He furrowed his brow. He hadn't remembered much and that had really screwed things up. Carefully, he asked, "Which?"

Her voice was soft, sad. "About my friends. How it was their choice to get drunk. They were doing it to themselves, and it wasn't my responsibility." She crossed her arms over her knees, watching the baby now. "When I got home, I tried it with my mom."

He drew his head back in surprise.

She shrugged and nodded. "It helped." She went back to pulling the rug. "Eventually." She lifted her eyes. "It helped *me*, anyway."

Something lifted the weight off his lungs. The gratitude in her eyes. He had done something that helped? His mind raced back. For a moment he was dumbfounded. It struck him how they were sitting here on a beach house floor talking about something he had said eight years earlier, something that wasn't the thing that had haunted him, that had made him hate himself, made him look differently at the way he treated girls.

He watched her eyes draw away. "How did I not recognize you?" He shook his head.

She bit her lip before she answered. "People can change a lot between the age of sixteen and twenty-five." She held her hands out to Shiloh, who crawled her way. "We grow up."

He watched her profile, the way her softness was now defined, her light brown hair resting on her shoulders and smooth along her heart-shaped face. She had grown up.

Shiloh stopped in her progression and turned to crawl up his legs. He held her hands and lifted her to her feet. She breathed heavily, the way his nephews did when they were excited about a new trick. She lifted a foot and pawed at the air, her eyebrows raised in wonder.

"There you go. Now the other one."

She planted the first foot and lifted the other. After she took the step, she smiled and pulled at his hands to sit down.

"Good job." He reached over and handed her a soft book. She stuck a corner of it in her mouth.

He turned to see Jill wiping a tear away from the side of her nose. She caught his look and shook her head. "I haven't seen her smile before."

He turned back to the baby between them, feeling a deep determination to make this child smile as often as he possibly could, as often as he was given the chance. He reached and touched Shiloh's nose. "She has a pretty smile. Like her aunt." He didn't look up, just let the words go without expectation. He saw Jill's fingers working at the carpet again. *I'll make her smile again too. I'll find that look of wonder.*

He swallowed. "Jill, I'm sorry. Please forgive me?"

The words seemed inadequate, but right then, there was nothing he wanted more.

* * *

Her hand stilled on the carpet, and she felt his eyes on her. Her breath was caught somewhere between her shoulder blades, and her stomach ached.

Will I? She tried to swallow, and it hurt. She stared at the place where Shiloh had stepped, where she had grasped his fingers and smiled. Jill closed her eyes. *Don't I have enough going on?*

Yes. So let this hurt go.

Warm tears trickled down the track on her cheek. She drew a soft breath and met his apprehensive gaze. For eight years, she had hung on to this pain, quietly, in the back of her memories.

Let it go.

"Okay." The word was so small. But huge.

Scott exhaled but kept his smile of relief contained. Slowly, he reached his hand out. She thought she couldn't possibly take his hand, but then she felt her fingers slip around his, and he tightened the grip.

"Thank you." He wiped at his eyes with the back of his other hand. He blinked at her and shook his head, letting out a small laugh at himself.

Jill watched him, wondering. It was so long ago . . . She felt the warmth of his rougher hand against hers, watched his smile widen at Shiloh, who kicked their hands with her toes as she rolled on her back. She thought he would let go of her hand, but he didn't. He just tickled Shiloh's tummy with his other fingers.

A hearty giggle sounded from deep inside Shiloh's little body, and Jill gasped with a smile. Scott looked at her, grinning, and then his eyes were searching hers.

Her smile faded with the erratic beat of her heart. She turned her attention back to the baby. "I should make her a bottle." She pulled her fingers from his and stood. Walking to the kitchen, she wrung her hands then pressed them on the counter in an attempt to calm herself. He said he was sorry, that he hadn't forgotten; he'd only made a mistake. And she believed him. But that was years ago. He was a boy who had broken her heart. Who was he now? She really didn't need her heart broken anymore.

She looked out the big window, and relief filled her as she spied the kids trooping back from the beach for lunch. She pulled the formula and a clean bottle down from the cupboard then filled the bottle with warm water.

Scott got up from the floor and picked up Shiloh. "Maybe I should call Grant and tell him they can come back to the house now."

Jill hid her smile again. She'd been thinking the same thing, unable to shake the idea of Grant playing matchmaker. It certainly wouldn't be the first time he'd have been guilty of it as bishop of a singles ward. She watched Scott out of the corner of her eye. Shiloh showed him pages of the book and made a few soft sounds. He nodded and answered her with soft sounds of his own.

Jill shook the bottle, her mind racing. *I don't have time for this . . . I don't have room for this . . . I'm not—*

He brought her the baby, and as Shiloh reached for Jill, Jill's finger slipped off the tip of the bottle, and it sprayed Scott full in the face.

Shiloh giggled and clapped her hands, and Jill muffled her laugh as Scott blinked, the look of shock fading from his expression as amused suspicion replaced it. Just then, the kids burst through the door.

"Mom, we're hungry."

"What's for lunch?"

Scott reached for a towel over the oven door handle. "Trust me, you don't want to know."

* * *

"Amen." Her whisper joined the two men's, and she opened her eyes to run her finger along Shiloh's relaxed features. Jill had held her through the blessing, and the baby had fallen asleep with a full belly and soft words. Nobody said anything for a few moments, and Jill even felt the sound of her breath would break the peace in the room. Grant squeezed her shoulders.

"Thank you, Sister Parish," he said quietly.

She turned her chin toward her shoulder. "Thank *you*." She looked at Scott, who nodded.

Grant excused himself, shaking Scott's hand and patting his shoulder on the way out. Jill stood and laid Shiloh down in the crib next to her bed. The blessing had promised her strength and direction. It had mentioned that she would feel loved. Loved. Had she ever truly felt loved? She pulled Shiloh's blanket up and then straightened. She gazed out the window at a scrubby pine tree. She guessed she had felt loved at times. But there was something . . . something that prevented her from letting it take hold or sink in. She'd always thought she was stronger that way. But she hadn't felt very strong lately. She turned, and Scott held his hand toward the door. She walked past him, sensing his closeness. He shut the door behind them.

"I think you should meet my parents."

She turned, the peace rushing out of her. "Why?"

He gauged her startled reaction. "Because your father will be staying with them, and my mom would probably appreciate knowing a little about him before he arrives."

She flushed and looked away. "Oh. Of course."

He checked his watch. "I left my mom pretty abruptly. Would you like to come back with me now?"

She swallowed, glancing back at the closed door. "I guess now would be a good time, while Shiloh's asleep."

They walked quietly along the road. Scott furrowed his brow at a blade of beach grass he'd pulled as they walked, twirling it in his fingers. He cleared his throat and shot the grass like a small javelin in front of them. "Are you and your dad close?"

She thought about the question. "No. Not by normal standards, I guess. We barely talk." She pushed her hands into her jacket pockets. "But I'm closer to him than anybody. He tried. Out of all of us, he tried."

"You tried. You still are."

She conceded with a nod. "I tried because of him." She wasn't sure of this discussion. She changed the subject. "Do you like working at Cape & Moore?"

She caught his look, the one that said he didn't want to change subjects, and she ignored it, waiting for his answer. *Are you a patient man?*

He swept a larger rock out of the road with his foot. "Yes. It's busy. I didn't think I would miss school so much though."

"You *miss* school?"

He smiled at her surprise, his eyes reflecting the pale light of the sky. "Yes. Crazy, I know. But I was teaching my last year, had a couple of my own classes."

She could picture him in front of a classroom, BYU coeds eager to raise their hands and ask him questions after class. She wondered that he was still single.

"What did you teach?"

"Am. lit. Literary genres. I TA'd an advanced writing class for a couple semesters."

She wrinkled her nose, and he laughed.

"You didn't like advanced writing?"

"No. It was difficult . . . writing what they wanted."

"Ah. You were one of *those* students."

"One of *what* students?"

He just shook his head, smiling. "What didn't you like? Give me an example."

She thought a moment. "It was just really hard for me to write analytically without basing a lot of my theory on my beliefs in the gospel, which, of course, my hardcore liberal women's rights professor had a hard time relating to."

"She didn't grade you based on your opinions, did she?"

"No. But the look that came with the grade was not . . . encouraging. And she would remark to the class how we would never be writers if we didn't have an edge, if we didn't *push the boundaries of conservatism and shun the old ideals of moral finger-pointers who would bind our voices and our breasts in the name of religion.*"

Scott blew out a breath. "Whoa."

"Mm-hm."

"What was the paper on?"

"The downfall of the Greco-Roman Empire as a comparative to modern America."

"Sounds fun."

"Yup."

"Sounds conservative."

"Yup. You can't tell me there aren't a hundred papers turned in every semester at BYU with the same theme."

Scott stopped and nodded. "Maybe more often using the Book of Mormon, but sure. Not so often at OSU though?" He gave her a half smile.

She shrugged. "Not all the professors were like that. But in my next paper, I dissected the 'Proclamation to the World.'" He raised his eyebrows, but she furrowed hers. "I'd had enough rejection of family values and examples of immorality in my life. I was not going to explore them for my own *enlightenment.* As far as I know, choices to reject or ignore those good things were the only forces that had ever bound my voice or my breasts."

His silence punctuated her words, and she slowly raised her hand to cover her mouth. She felt the blood rising in her face, and she shook her head. "I'm sorry."

He fought a smile and spoke out of the side of his mouth. "No. That's all right."

She wished he would look away.

He cleared his throat, and she watched his eyes fill with compassion. "But in a way, don't you think those things you've gone through, even though you didn't choose them, created emotions and grounded convictions that come through in your writing? Because of the hurt . . . and confusion you endured . . . you're able to reach deeper and touch others with your words in ways somebody who has not suffered can't?"

She turned to him, cocking her head to the side in question. "How—?"

He dropped his eyes to the ground and kicked at a tuft of grass growing along the road. "I've been reading your book."

"I asked you not to—"

"I know. But after this morning, I had to go back and reread."

"Why?"

"Because before . . . I didn't know you."

"And now you do?" She searched him warily. Before this morning, she was just some woman who had snubbed his attempts. Now . . .

"Yes. I mean, of course I don't know you as well as—but I know more about where you come from, where you were once."

He knows where I was once. The truth warmed and frightened her. How many people in her life could say that? She wrapped her arms around her body as she sensed the danger of letting him get closer, the risk of getting hurt.

She swallowed and straightened her shoulders. "So now you're a biased reader who thinks my writing is wonderful because you feel you owe me?" She gave him a small smile, but she meant what she said. If her friends and coworkers had all been correct in their glowing reviews of her writing, she should be a bestseller by now.

"I don't think your writing is wonderful."

Her heart dropped, and she hated that she cared what he thought.

"I think it's soulful and poignant and funny. I think it's genuine."

She stared at him, soaking in his words but trying not to.

He began to walk again, and it took her a second to make her feet move.

"And now," he continued, "it's in the hands of a mainstream publisher."

Reality cleared her head. "I wrote it for an LDS market. It's too churchy, too steeped in vocabulary and dialogue written for an audience who knows what *Relief Society* and *elders quorum* and *patriarchal blessing* mean." She threw up her hands. "The *spirit world*, for heaven's sake."

"Exactly." The corner of his mouth came up.

She gave him a look of exasperation and shook her head. "I had to explain a few things to my coworkers. My expectations are not high."

He nodded. "That's probably good." She furrowed her brow, and he laughed. "On the other hand, people are curious creatures." He smiled at her. "Maybe you could include a glossary in the back."

"Mmm, and a brief history of the Church."

"And the Articles of Faith."

"And, of course, a statement for those who would insist we aren't Christians."

"Or that your bosoms are bound."

She giggled, and he laughed again, running his hand over his hair. He reached for the handle of the door suddenly looming in front of them.

He paused. "Um, before we go in, I think I should tell you . . . I used to be engaged to the Thorntons' oldest daughter."

Jill's mouth dropped open, and she tried to blink her eyes back inside her head. Her pulse quickened without reason. "Why . . . why should I need to know that?" Was the porch tilting?

"Because . . . my mom has not ceased to bring it up since it was called off two years ago." He pushed the door open and stood aside to let Jill in.

CHAPTER 7

Jill attempted to recover from the peek into Scott's past as she looked around. This house was much newer than the Thorntons' cottage. She walked into a large living space with high ceilings, pale wood floors, and walls the color of ripe wheat, all trimmed in white. A set of door-height windows made up the far and surrounding walls and were topped by another set of windows half that height. She stepped out of her shoes at a low bench in the entry and her gaze was drawn to a large portrait of a beautiful woman with blonde hair and a confident smile, relaxing in the arms of a handsome, tanned man with sandy brown hair that had been bleached in the sun. They were on the beach, with a piece of sculpture-like driftwood and the blue sea and sky behind them. A picture of perfection. These were Scott's parents. So unlike hers. Intimidation stirred, and she wondered, as she always did upon seeing happy couples, parents, if their children knew how fortunate they were.

Scott touched her elbow, leading her farther into the house. The open kitchen was to her left, with white cupboards, stainless-steel appliances and light fixtures, and warm brown, pebbled granite countertops. A bead-board island topped with a butcher block stood in the center. The broad beachfront room was divided into dining and entertainment spaces. The mission oak table sat beyond the kitchen to the left, and canvas upholstered furnishings took up the larger right portion of the room with views of shore, rock, sea, and mountain. The mantel of a corner fireplace held blue-sky photos in white frames, with windblown faces, silhouettes in front of the waves, figures kneeling at sand castles, and tan arms wrapped around tan shoulders. Every angle displayed a portrait of promise. There was no fear here.

Jill cleared her throat, rubbing her arm. "This is beautiful."

"Thanks." He glanced out the windows. "Will you excuse me? I'll be right back." Jill gave him a nod, and he opened one of the door-height windows and closed it behind him.

Jill stepped to the window and watched him walk across the large silver deck and down a long, gradually descending boardwalk. It led to a smaller deck with Adirondack chairs and a low table.

A blonde woman stood to greet Scott, rubbing his back and beaming up at him. Then Scott stepped around her and grasped the back of one of the chairs. To Jill's surprise, the chair turned, pivoting on the spot, and Scott pushed it behind his mother, who walked up as she continued to smile and talk.

A wheelchair.

Scott's mother opened the door, giving Jill a quick smile, then turned and held the door as Scott pushed the chair through. In the chair sat an older man with white, short hair combed neatly back and gray stubble dotting the masculine bone structure of his thin face. He did not give Jill a quick smile. He didn't look at her at all.

"Mom, this is Jillian Parish . . . from Lebanon. She's working in Portland at a neighboring publishing house." Scott's smile was a nervous one. "Jill, I'd like you to meet my parents, Roger and Hope Gentry."

"We are so pleased to meet you, Jill." Hope stepped forward with her hand gracefully outstretched.

Jill took the soft hand. "Thank you, Sister Gentry."

"Oh, call me Hope." She held an arm out to the sofa area. "Scott tells me we're going to have company."

"I'm sorry. I didn't mean for any of this—"

"No, don't say another word. We love company, don't we, sweetheart?"

Scott wheeled his father to a wide space between the sofa and the other seating around the low conversation table. A wide shallow bowl held an array of seashells, blue-green sea glass, smooth stones, and a glass ball. But Jill's eyes were drawn to Scott's father, who made a low sound that rose sharply as his head nodded.

Scott reached over and patted his father's arm. "We hear you, Dad."

Hope shook her head and laughed softly. "He knows we have company." She put her hand on his knee. "This is Jill, sweetheart. She's visiting Scott."

"The one I told you about, Dad." Scott lowered his eyes then slowly brought them up to Jill's. This was Scott's father, the man in the portrait? She searched Scott for answers.

Hope drew her attention. "Scott tells me you're an old friend?"

"I . . . well . . ."

Scott broke in. "I said we were friends once, Mom." He looked back at Jill. "It's been a long time."

"Well, a friend once is a friend at last, isn't that right?" His mother smiled at them both.

Jill noted Scott's eyes had become the shade of the sea glass. She nodded. "Yes." She turned to Hope. "Yes, that's how it goes."

"And any friend of Scott's is welcome. I hear you're a writer? That sounds exciting."

Jill smiled. "Well, it wasn't very exciting until a few days ago. I'm just a secretary at Brasher Books. I've only written a few things. Nothing published except for an article in the *New Era* when I was in college."

"Oh, well that is wonderful. We'll have to look it up."

Jill shook her head, suddenly wary of sharing something with Scott's mother that she had already shared with thousands. "It wasn't anything big, really."

"Well, it's an accomplishment, anyway."

Jill smiled again.

"And now you have a book being looked at. Have you always wanted to write?"

Jill swallowed, glancing at Scott, who watched her intently. "I . . . wrote in my journals . . . to kind of figure things out, keep track of my thoughts. I was addicted to my journals. The writing kind of started there. As I got older and read more books, I thought maybe I could do that too."

Hope nodded. "I'm terrible at journals, but I take my pictures." She gazed at the mantel and the walls. "Not everyone knows the story behind each one, but I remember, and the subjects do." She reached to rub her husband's arm. "It's a way to . . . prove you've lived somehow, isn't it?" There was a small tremor in her voice.

In the silence, Jill realized this poised, sunny woman had been shattered. The photos and portraits were not images of perfection but reminders of what it was to be whole. Jill glanced over the faces again.

Hope inhaled deeply and brightened. "Now, your father needs a place to stay, and we have plenty of room. Is there anything in particular I need to know about what he likes to eat?"

"I'm sure he'll appreciate anything . . . but he can cook if it's too much of a bother . . . or I can come and . . ."

Hope was shaking her head. She patted Jill's arm. "It's no bother. I love to cook, and look at my humble army of two to feed. And when Scott or his brother and sisters aren't here, well, I still cook too much and give it away, so don't worry about that. And you're welcome to join us anytime, though I'm sure the Thorntons will want to have their share of you. Are you a close family friend?"

"Um, no, actually." She glanced at Scott, wondering how much he had told his mother, how much she should share. "I know them from the singles ward, of course, but we were kind of . . . thrown together this weekend."

Scott smiled slowly at her, and she knew he must have withheld the major issues.

His mother sighed. "Well, good for all of us, then. You know, Scott and their oldest daughter, Kayla—"

"She *knows*, Mom."

"Oh. Well, let me show you around, and then when your dad arrives, you can make him feel comfortable."

Hope led her around the airy house, the guest room, the laundry, the bath. Scott followed, pushing his father, seemingly content to hang back and let his mother do the talking.

"Scott, why don't you take Jill up to the captain's loft?" She took the handles of the wheelchair from him and gently pushed Scott aside. She winked at Jill. "It's the best room in the house."

Scott hung his head and pressed his fingers to his eyes as his mother wheeled his father back to the main rooms.

"Would you like to see the captain's loft?" he asked apologetically.

"With a name like that, how can I say no?"

He smiled and nodded, leading her up a curved stairway above the entry.

Most of the house was angular, but the room in front of her was a semicircle, the ocean-facing wall a bow of windows lined with a long, curved seat. The flat roof of the first floor extended out beyond the windows, creating a shallow terrace overlooking the beach. A door to her left led outside. Two twin captain's beds were pushed against the flat wall behind them. A table between the two held a lamp, a large conch shell, and a pair of binoculars. One of the beds was rumpled, and a laptop sat on a pile of files on the floor. A pair of wire-frame glasses waited on the laptop.

"My brother and I sleep here when we come."

She took in the vast view. "I don't blame you."

Scott stood next to a telescope nearly as tall as he was. He looked up at the ceiling, and she followed his gaze, drawing in her breath. A semicircular window bowed upward into the sky.

"That must be incredible on a clear night."

"It is, when we get one." He rested his hand on the telescope.

She continued to survey the room and found more photos on the wall above the beds. Four black-and-white eight-by-tens hung in black frames, portioning off four young faces peeking out at her. Jill pointed to the first picture on the left.

"This is you?"

"Mm-hm." He pointed to the girl in the second picture. "My sister, Amy." Then he went to the picture after his own and said, "My brother, Trey, with the ears. You've seen him in the ward. And that's Leia, the baby. She's at the Y."

"How old are you here?"

"Um, fourteen, I think? My voice hadn't changed yet."

She smiled at the thought. Then she wrinkled her brow. "This is in California?"

He nodded. "Yup."

She looked at him, and he turned to the ocean-filled windows. She asked, "You said your family moved here during your mission?" He nodded again and gestured to the cushioned window seat. She sat, taking in the view behind her. He sat next to her and propped his leg up, leaning against the glass.

"My dad—he was in construction management. Successful . . . Monterey, Seaside . . ."

She nodded, understanding how that could be lucrative.

"When I left on my mission, I thought I had it all. I knew who I was, that I was doing the right thing, that my family would be blessed . . . I had a girl waiting for me." He rolled his eyes and shook his head. "I was going to convert everyone in the Missouri Independence Mission."

"What happened?"

"It all turned."

She watched him curiously, wanting him to fill in the blank between then and now, cautious about welcoming the distraction from the ever-present tangle in her stomach caused by the very events that had led her to this place.

"About six months into my mission, my girlfriend wrote me *the letter*. I hadn't gotten into a single door in Kansas City yet. And then," he leaned his head against the window, "my dad was working on a project up on an unfinished second story. He suffered a stroke." He turned his troubled eyes to her. "I wish you could see who he was." He looked over his shoulder at the ocean. "I wish everyone could."

Jill listened, unable to look away.

"I got the news, and it was unbelievable." He swallowed hard. "No way could it have happened because I was out . . . I was doing the Lord's work, and my family would be *blessed*, so I waited. I waited for the miracle recovery. But it didn't come."

"Did you stay out on your mission?"

He nodded, looking down at his hands. "Yeah. I did. I think I stayed out because I was afraid to come home. I stayed out because a part of me still believed that while I was on my mission, something had to happen, something had to make it better. I worked harder . . . prayed harder."

He turned and looked out the window again. "When I came home, and I saw my dad . . . nothing my mom had told me prepared me for that. I couldn't even tell if he knew who I was or that I was . . . significant. Mom kept telling me he did." He shook his head, and his voice dropped. "But it was hard to believe her. I was very angry."

Jill nodded. She knew that feeling. It was a completely different circumstance, but she knew that feeling. The feeling that you are nothing to a parent and not understanding why.

He had faded away in thought, and she wanted to bring him back. "What made your mom move up here?"

His eyes drew to hers again, and a small smile came to his mouth. "Her brother is a realtor in Washington. He urged her to sell the business and property, our house in Cali while she could, and move up there, where property values aren't quite so costly. Amy had already settled in Roseburg with her husband. My mom and the younger kids took a road trip up the coast, stopping at different places along the way, including here. By the time she got up to Washington, she knew where she wanted to be. She knew where she wanted my dad to be."

Jill looked out the windows. She understood completely. But it had to have been a shock to Scott. "I'm sure that was a lot of change to come home to."

"It's nothing compared to what you've been through."

She turned to him, feeling unsure of how he knew so much about her past and spoke of it as though she'd just confided in him days ago instead of years ago. . . unsure of the way he seemed to regard her now, as if he were seeing her up close for the first time. The heat rose in her face. Shouldn't she argue with him? Move away?

"My dad was my best friend, Jill. I think he might be proud of the part he played in finding you. Because he was the only one I told. He was the only one who knew how much I wished I could find you. If things hadn't happened the way they did, I wouldn't be here."

She swallowed the emotion pressing over her. "Here?" she asked, her voice suddenly a whisper. She couldn't accept it. Something horrible had happened to his father, and Scott was suggesting it was for her? So Scott could find her? She wouldn't want it that way. That she and Scott were both here in Pacific City was mind boggling, yes, but nothing more than a coincidence. Lots of Portlanders had beach homes, and it was a holiday weekend—

"Maybe it's grace," he said quietly, still holding her gaze.

Her heart skipped once. "What?"

His voice remained gentle as he quoted her book. "'What is grace but drops of heaven placed in our way to get us where we need to be?'"

Her heart pounded. "That's not fair." She knew he knew it wasn't fair, using her own words. She could tell by the way he wanted to smile but didn't. She shook her head, fighting the familiarity of him, the directness of his speech. "You can't be suggesting your father's stroke was a drop of heaven?"

He leaned his head toward her, conceding. "Maybe I shouldn't have said that. It would be like him, though, to want credit." He did smile then, and she felt herself return it.

Their heads were close together now, too close for Jill to think clearly. She should pull away. Turn her head—after all, the view—

"You, on the other hand . . ."

Her thoughts dissipated. "Me?"

She watched his eyes take in her features. He paused at her mouth before meeting her eyes again. "Maybe . . . this is the miracle."

She managed to give her head a small shake. He was so close now, close enough for her to see the fair whiskers shaved close on his chin and around his mouth.

She swallowed, unable to breathe. She didn't need this. Any of it. She didn't need a miracle. The scent of him pulled her closer. His hand slowly lifted toward her face.

"Jill," he whispered.

She didn't need to breathe, didn't need to think. Only feel—

No. Not again. She pulled away, inhaling deeply, bringing her hand to her forehead.

"Is something wrong?"

She heard his concern and blinked her eyes to focus on the room around her. Is something *wrong?* Wasn't *everything* wrong?

"Reality," she said in a faraway voice.

His voice was near, soft. "I thought we were discussing that."

She considered his sincerity. She nodded. "Yours."

"Some of it is ours."

She lowered her eyes. "I have to go. Shiloh is probably awake."

After a moment, he stood and offered his hand to help her up. "I'll walk you back."

"No. I . . . I'd like to think on my own for a bit." She had to clear her head. She stood and steadied herself with one hand on the telescope. "Thank you, Scott, for telling me about your father."

He nodded, and she could see the worry in his eyes that he'd said too much. That he'd crossed a very delicate line. She wasn't sure he hadn't.

She dropped her hand from the telescope. "I'll be over later, when my dad gets here."

He raised his head and gave her a small smile, covering his chagrin. "Right. Will you stay?"

"For a little while, until my dad is settled. I haven't seen him since Christmas, and he didn't even know he was a grandpa. He'll want to spend some time with Shiloh." She started to move away.

"Jill?"

She stopped.

"I'm sorry for everything you're going through." He held her gaze, hesitating, then said, "I'm really glad you're here."

She swallowed, needing to turn away, needing to withdraw into her own worries, her own troubles and leave him on the outside. But everything was changing. He'd invited himself in. He'd crashed into her cautious existence, but he wasn't some overconfident, thoughtless boy from a perfect world. He was something else entirely.

Her lips barely moved, forming her thoughts into words. "I was wrong. I was wrong about who you were. I thought . . ." She looked around the room. "I thought you were from this different place and I . . ." She shook her head. He reached for her hand and touched her fingers. Her thoughts wavered again.

If only he hadn't quoted her book.

Her fingers intertwined with his. "I'll see you later."

He nodded.

She wrinkled her brow, pulled her hand away, and walked quietly down the stairs. She slipped her shoes on and hurried from the house, trying to breathe the way she had before he'd stolen her keys. Her phone began ringing as the cottage came into view, and she answered as she wiped away her tears.

"Jill, this is Detective Okada. I found out how your sister got to Portland."

She halted. "How?"

"Delta Airlines flight 201 from SeaTac International."

"She . . . she flew?" People flew all the time; of course they did. But Evie had seemed destitute. Jill had assumed she'd found a ride or taken a bus.

That's when she remembered the money.

* * *

Jill paced back and forth in front of the sofa as Grant and Laura watched her. "You think she took the money?"

Jill nodded, grasping her hands. "I just can't imagine, from the state she was in, that she could have afforded to fly with her own money. She paid with cash. She tried to pay me for the baby stuff with a hundred dollar bill, and there were more in her pocket, but Shiloh didn't even have pants . . . nothing. I think she stole the money from Neil. I think that's why he's after her."

"Would that be enough to tick him off this much?"

She glanced at Grant and nodded her head. "If it was their fix money." She felt sick. "I don't think this is about love . . . or even taking Shiloh."

"Did you tell Detective Okada?"

She nodded. "He agreed."

"Are they working with Seattle police?"

She nodded again. "I feel like I should go home. It's the only place she knows to find me."

"But her boyfriend knows that too."

Jill paced then stopped and held out her hands to Shiloh, who was sitting on Laura's lap. The baby reached up, and Jill held her close. "If they find out where we are . . ."

"Does Evie have any other way she can contact you?"

"I gave her my cell number before I drove to the store that night. She may still have it." At this point, Jill wasn't sure of anything.

She turned her head to the sound of a car on the quiet road. Her heart hammered, and it made her angry. Of course, the car passed without incident.

"When will your dad be here?"

She turned back to Grant. "Six. Seven. What if someone follows him?"

Grant looked a little unsettled, but he straightened himself up. "They don't know where he is, and they don't know what car he drives."

"But they could find those things out." She hated the paranoia in her voice. "Lebanon is a small town."

The phone rang. Laura went to the kitchen to answer it.

"Listen, Jill. I'm sure your father will be careful. Let's think about this. So far, all these guys know is that Evie stole the money—we think—and that she and the baby were at your place. They found your dad's house and then hightailed it out of there. You said it . . . it's a small town. Nowhere to hide."

"So where are they?" People like that always found a place to hide.

He pressed his mouth closed.

She answered for him. "The *big* town. They're looking for Evie in Portland."

Laura came in and noted the lull. "That was Hope. She's invited us all to dinner." She looked between the two of them. "I thought it might be a good night to stay together, so I accepted."

Grant raised his eyebrows at Jill, waiting for her response. When she gave none, he folded his hands in front of him and sighed deeply. "Jill? How is your faith doing?"

Jill rested her head against Shiloh's. The question should have unnerved her, yet the question itself was like a cool cloth pressed to a feverish cheek. She took a deep breath. "It's gotten me this far, hasn't it?"

He smiled. "That's right." He slapped his hands together. "I'm going to round up the kids and have a little refresher course on safety and strange cars." He stood and reached for Shiloh. "Come on, little one, let's go play with the people who only *think* they have problems—like not getting a second cookie. Or having to take a shower. Or having to throw their dirty clothes *in* the hamper." He left the room.

He left Jill standing in front of the wall of photos. She gazed over them then focused on one shot. She leaned her head a little closer. Scott. Swinging in the hammock with a smiling brunette.

"Aren't those great?" Laura asked. She smiled and leaned against the back of the sofa. "I love looking at them. Every time we come, I take a few minutes to go back over every picture. It makes me feel part of something big. Something good."

Jill looked back at the photos. She didn't feel a part of anything, except a part of trouble for this family. She studied Scott's sun-touched face.

"Want to help me make some brownies?"

Jill nodded. Brownies would be good.

Twenty minutes later, Laura slid the pan into the oven and set the timer. She took the empty mixing bowl and held out the batter-covered spoon to Jill.

Jill hesitated then took it and sighed after the first lick. "Thanks."

Laura grinned and gathered the dishes to the sink. "I was thinking about your book. About grace." She quoted, "'There but for the grace of God, go I.'"

Jill ran her finger over the edge of the spoon, nodding. "Do you know the story behind that phrase?"

"Wasn't it a priest or someone who said it? A martyr or someone?"

"It's undocumented, but the story is that a preacher named John Bradford said it as he watched other prisoners led away to be hanged, acknowledging God's hand as the only thing saving him from the same fate."

"Oh, that's sad."

Jill licked the brownie batter from her finger. "Yes, it is. What's sadder is that he was burned at the stake."

"For his beliefs?"

Jill nodded. "But what *is* documented is his peace with his fate. His belief was that he would be accepted by his Lord."

Laura shook her head as she squeezed out a dishcloth and wiped down the counter. "The hand of God. You know, we can see it so much if we stop and look. How often do we say, 'Oh, whew, glad it turned out okay,' and continue on without a thought of how God works in our lives. I mean, look at us, with you here at a time when you need someone. And your dad and Scott . . ." She continued to shake her head.

Jill lowered the spoon. Laura moved to the sink and turned on the water to fill the basin. Jill watched the bubbles foam as Laura added the dish soap, considering.

"So." Jill attempted to focus on the remaining dark brown gloss coating the spoon. "Your daughter was engaged to Scott?"

Laura turned off the water and picked up a sponge. Jill watched her out of the corner of her eye with far too much interest.

Slowly, Laura nodded. She plunged the brownie bowl into the steaming sink. "Yes. Scott told you about it?"

Jill turned the spoon around in her fingers. "He only said they were once engaged and that it was called off."

Laura wiped out the bowl and rinsed it. Jill finished off the batter on her spoon and walked over to the sink next to Laura, washed her hands in the soapy water, and began to dry the dishes.

"It was . . . a difficult thing. I don't think either of them expected the breakup. I admit, being the mother of the bride-to-be, I probably have a skewed sense of what happened."

She stopped, and Jill waited, not wanting to pry too much but wanting to know more. Laura looked at Jill. "They are both great kids. They were good together. We were happy with their plans." She shrugged. "I think that's what made it so hard for Kayla to call it off."

Jill almost dropped the bowl. "*She* called it off?" The words were out before Jill could think to stop them.

Laura chuckled at her response. "Yes. She did."

Jill wanted to ask why. She wanted to know. She hated that she wanted to know.

Laura turned back to the sink. "I'm sure you can ask Scott about it. I don't think he minds so much anymore."

Jill set the bowl down and reached for another dish with greater care. "But you're such good friends. He seems so comfortable here."

"We love Scott. I think he feels that. What happened didn't change that. We let him have his time, of course, but between his parents and us here so often, he's a dear friend we didn't want to lose. Of course, it helps that Kayla lives across the country now." She gazed out the window over the sink. "You know, I don't think he . . ."

"What?"

She looked back down at the dishes and continued washing. "Well, you can ask him about it. I'm sure he'd do a much better job." A smile grew at the corner of her mouth. "I have a feeling he'd be willing to share it, if *you* were the one doing the asking."

Jill swallowed and flushed. "What do you mean?" She busily dried the measuring cups.

"He doesn't open up, that one. Not easily."

Jill frowned. The Scott she remembered was very open. He had been in Costa Rica . . . to his regret. And he'd been fairly forward before she *reminded* him who she was. And he had opened up today in the loft.

The puzzle kept her mind busy enough that she had no more questions about Kayla or the engagement.

Later, Jill stood out on the front porch with a freshly bathed Shiloh on her hip. After strengthening herself with a brownie, Jill had freshened up too and was trying desperately to appear calm. The door of the old white BMW swung open. The car's paint was dulled, and gray rust-preventative patched a few spots near the undercarriage. She had always wondered why her father hadn't taken the time to finish up this old car while he was always slicking up old cars for other people. Still, she knew the engine in it was as clean and maintained as it had been thirty years ago.

Her father straightened and looked at her. He looked at both of them. He gave a small nod, and she stepped off the porch, knowing they were being watched from just inside the windows. The Thorntons were giving them some reunion space.

"Dad."

"Jillian." He reached out one arm and patted her back then leaned in and gave her a quick kiss on the cheek. She smelled his aftershave, and it brought back the same torn memories it always did. He reached a finger but didn't quite touch the child in her arms. "This . . . ?

"This is Shiloh, Dad. She's your granddaughter." Shiloh watched him steadily, warily.

"I'd know her anywhere."

The simple statement tugged at Jill's heart. "Shiloh, this is your grandpa, Jeremy Parish. Can you say grandpa?"

"*M-ba.*" The sound was more of a breath. Shiloh dropped her head onto Jill's shoulder, chewing on her fingers.

Jeremy grinned. "There you go. There you go, Shiloh."

Jill smiled at the eager light in his eyes. He turned to her. "She looks like you."

"There's a little Evie in there too, Dad. A little of you."

At Evie's name, Jeremy pressed his lips together, but he looked back at Shiloh and gave her a nod. He held out both hands. "Will you come see me? Come see Gran—"

Before he could finish, Shiloh had stretched out and was in his arms, much to his surprise. She looked back at Jill and reached out to touch Jill's arm then turned all her attention to her grandpa.

Jill felt . . . left. She shook the feeling away, seeing her father's rare joy, but still, she put her fingers up to Shiloh's hand and felt better when Shiloh closed her fist around them, babbling and looking over this new person with surprising ease.

Jeremy pulled his gaze away from the baby to meet hers again. "Gosh, Jilly, you look so beautiful. How did I ever have anything to do with such pretty things, huh?"

Jill drew in a breath and released it quickly. "Thanks, Dad."

She was surprised again as he widened his arm and drew her in next to Shiloh. "I just love ya, honey. I'm glad you're okay. I'm glad you're both okay."

He patted her back, and she nodded, overcome by his words. She wanted to say something in return but couldn't find it. He stepped back, smiling timidly.

She took a deep breath and returned the smile. Finally, she said, "I hope you don't mind, but we're having dinner down the road with a bunch of people you don't know."

He nodded. "I'm just fine with that." He breathed in and looked around. "It's been a long time since I've been to the beach. Might as well make a real vacation of it."

"I'm glad you feel that way because you'll also be staying at their house while you're here."

His brow lifted in surprise. The screen door squeaked open behind them, and the Thorntons came out to meet Jill's father.

CHAPTER 8

The phone call with Calvin Reid was not going the way Scott had expected. True, he was new to Cape & Moore, but surely he'd proven himself enough in the last few weeks to be allowed to bank on some personal days. It wasn't helping that he was calling his boss on a holiday.

"You can have tomorrow, Gentry, but I need you back in this office Wednesday morning."

"Thank you. But I need more time. It's a family—"

"I don't care if your grandmother is being awarded the Nobel freaking Peace Prize. We're both meeting with the big man Wednesday morning—" Scott heard the squeal of kids and a dog bark in the background. Calvin was distracted but only for a moment. "Let's cut to the chase, Gentry. You know they hired you to replace me when I retire. There are half a dozen snot-nosed kiss-ups vying for your spot, so if I show up on Wednesday and your beachcombing hindend isn't standing in front of me, I'm taking one of them to the meeting, and they'll be the one Moore remembers. Understand?"

"Yes, sir." Scott pushed hard against the terrace railing, watching the small group make their way across the sand toward the house. "Can I say something?"

"Shoot."

"For the record, I'm not beachcombing. My family is involved in a crisis. What can I do to get a few more days? I'll work from here, take on extra projects—" He spotted Jill. "I'll even take over queries . . ." Scott waited. The queries via e-mail were probably the most dreaded job in the company. Cape & Moore preferred working with authors' agents, but the company was small and was open to direct queries from hopeful authors. Sorting and answering twenty to thirty queries a day was a daunting task, even if something stood out. Mostly, it meant dealing with entire first chapters pasted into the subject box or long bios about how someone had been writing since they were born. He wondered how many more vampire-fairy-werewolf love triangles, guaranteed *New York Times* bestsellers, and million-dollar promises he had just offered to endure.

"Please, sir. I'll come in on Wednesday morning for the meeting. But I need more time."

Finally, Calvin said, "Be here Wednesday morning. Then do what you gotta do."

"Thank you, sir."

Click.

Scott lowered the phone to the railing. The group had reached the boardwalk. A man, Jill's father, he guessed, held Shiloh and smiled as he took in his surroundings. Jill looked careful. Her face lifted. She spotted him, setting his heart pounding. He hadn't meant to lose his grip on his feelings for her. He'd meant to be cautious and give her the distance she obviously needed right now. But she'd opened up to him. Not much but enough to bring back old feelings. The way she watched him, the way she listened. The careful laugh. He'd found himself sharing what he had kept to himself for so long.

And then he'd gone and tried to kiss her.

Idiot.

He held up his hand, and a smile touched her mouth, only a hint of the beauty she released when her smile lit up her entire face. She brushed her hair behind her ear then looked away, nodding at somebody's question.

He'd take that. He turned and went inside, leaving the captain's loft.

As he made his way downstairs, he could already hear warm greetings and introductions taking place. He heard the sharp up sound of his dad's welcome, and as he opened the glass door out to the gathering on the deck, he saw Jill's father reach over and give his dad a good pat on the shoulder as he took one of his hands in his.

"I tell you what, Roger, you are one lucky man. What a place. What a place." His dad's head nodded as if in total agreement as he stared down at the wood. Sounds of amusement faded as Scott approached.

His mother reached for his arm. "Scott, you need to meet Jill's father. Jeremy, this is our oldest son, Scott. Scott, this is Jeremy Parish."

Jeremy stepped over and timidly held his hand out. "Scott. Jill tells me you've been a great help."

Scott glanced at Jill, who was taking a breath as if to protest. He beat her to it.

"Oh, I don't know about that." He raised his brow at her, and she dropped her eyes with that small smile still on her face.

"She said you helped give her a blessing."

Scott turned to see sincere gratitude in the man's face, and Scott wondered if the man knew about Costa Rica.

"You don't know how much that means to me." Jeremy held his hand a little longer until Scott nodded. Jeremy broke out in a wary smile. "And now you're opening your home to a complete stranger."

"Well," Scott's mother cut in, "let's get this food all set out, and we'll talk, and then we won't be strangers anymore." This declaration set everyone in motion.

Jeremy reached to take Shiloh back from Jill. He addressed Scott. "You've seen my granddaughter? Isn't she beautiful?"

"Yes." He reached and touched her curls. "And she does this." Scott pinched his fingers in the air toward Shiloh, and her eyes widened. Then his fingers dove for her ribs, and the hearty giggle erupted. Her laughter spread.

"Jeremy, bring her over here, and we'll belt her into this booster seat," Hope said. "Shiloh, would you like some *strawberries*?"

Scott turned to find Jill watching her father and Shiloh with worry. "Hey." She pulled her eyes away to look at him. "Are you all right?"

She searched his face, and the worry didn't go away.

He lowered his voice. "I'm . . . sorry about earlier. I didn't mean to—"

"No. No, it's not that." She lowered her eyes, and he thought he saw a blush. "I heard from the police." Jill explained the news and her theory about the money. "My dad's being brave. He's always been very good at . . . hiding the bad stuff."

Scott watched Jill's father. He frowned. "He looks like he's a proud grandpa." He looked questioningly at Jill.

She pressed a smile. "Well, he doesn't have to hide that part, does he?"

"No. No, he doesn't." He watched her, a little too long maybe, and she straightened, setting her mouth, reminding him of how she held herself at church. Jeremy Parish wasn't the only one good at hiding the bad stuff.

She changed the subject. "We should get something to eat before it's gone."

Scott chuckled. "I think my mom made enough food to last the week."

Jill nodded at the Thornton kids. "Not with *those* boys."

Scott frowned at the disappearing food and reached for Jill's arm, pulling her to the table and bringing a smile to her face. He caught a curious look from her dad but focused on filling his plate.

* * *

The grown-ups had moved into the sitting room. Jill was observing her father in a social situation and couldn't get over how easy it looked for him. He'd always been well liked, and she had vague memories of going to somebody's house and hearing laughter around her dad, but she had been very little, and after Evie was born, visiting stopped. Watching him now, it was like getting to know her father all over.

The three men sat next to each other, the wheelchair in the middle. When there was a breakout of laughter, her dad would reach over and pat Roger's shoulder or grab and shake his knee, like they were old friends laughing at old jokes. Shiloh practiced walking around the table, with adult hands reaching close to her once in a while as she made the slow, wobbly circle.

"Scott, how old is your father?" Jill had chosen to sit at the window seat to the right of the fireplace, and Scott leaned against the mantel. They were close enough to hear but far enough away to not be heard.

"Forty-nine."

She held in a gasp of surprise. "How old is Grant?"

"Um. Forty-six, I think. How old is your dad?"

"He'll be fifty-seven in October. He was thirty when he married my mom. They were nine years apart."

Scott nodded in thought.

She watched the three men. "It's interesting what life can do to a body." Her father's dark curls had given way to a little gray. His face was lined with care, and he held himself as a man much older, with a touch of protectiveness, as if expecting a strike at any moment. And he was thin, but she knew he took care of himself as he always had. Still, she could tell life was vibrant inside him, and she wondered at her father's resilience.

Her eyes moved to the man in the wheelchair. *Forty-nine.* Anyone who didn't know would guess Roger Gentry was in his midseventies . . .

Scott spoke quietly. "That portrait in the hall . . . that was taken my senior year." He turned and acknowledged her poorly hidden shock. "The year we went to Costa Rica."

She didn't know why she was surprised when she saw pain in his eyes. He wasn't hiding it. Not from her.

A sharp sound came from the back door, and they broke their gaze.

"Scott, come play with us." One of the kids was swinging what appeared to be a small ball being swallowed by a rainbow-colored snake.

Jill watched a smile smooth out the worry on Scott's face, and he gave the kid a nod. He held out a hand to help her up. "You want to play foxtail?"

She wasn't sure. "What's foxtail?"

He grinned, looking suddenly clever. "A *distraction*."

Out on the beach in her bare feet, Jill stood swinging the foxtail around by its long, tricolor nylon tail. The tail was stitched so it partly enclosed a hard, brown leather ball the size and weight of a baseball.

"Like this?" she shouted. The ball swung in an even vertical circle next to her.

"Yes. Now let go as it swings up."

She swung a big loop and let go, watching it fly like a comet straight up in the air then curve in a narrow arc to the side, its tail flying behind it. A couple of the kids laughed. She looked at Scott. "It didn't work."

"Nope." He was chuckling and shaking his head as one of the kids ran to retrieve the comet and toss it to her again. She let it roll in the sand and picked it up.

"Try it again, but aim, and let it go a little earlier."

"Like bowling?"

He shook his head. "More like pitching in softball."

"Oh." She held on to the last third of the tail like he'd shown her then spun it around and around and let go.

One of the boys dropped to the sand, laughing, as she searched the sky but saw nothing. She spun around in time to see the foxtail land twenty yards behind her.

"Okay." Scott was fully laughing now. "Maybe we can try it like bowling."

She had the thing in her hands again and was determined to get the hang of it.

"Just let it go—out in front of you."

She frowned and aimed at Scott. She spun the ball. *Like bowling*. She took a couple steps then bent her right leg and let go. The comet shot straight and fast, and Scott jumped out of the way, grabbing for the tail as it passed by him in a blur.

She heard groans come from the kids. She set her hands on her hips. "What did I do now?"

Scott picked up the foxtail, smiling sympathetically. "That was a lot better."

"Yes, it was."

"But there's supposed to be some arc to it. Like this." He spun and aimed at one of the kids, letting it go in a perfect rainbow through the air. Brady, the oldest Thornton boy, leaped, his arm outstretched, and grabbed the tail toward the red end.

"That's a point."

"For who?" she asked.

"For the catcher."

"Then how does the thrower get points?"

"He doesn't."

Jill's mind worked. "Well then, you don't want your thrown foxtail to be caught."

"Well . . ." Scott's smile widened.

"So don't you win by making it hard to catch?"

One of the kids spoke out of the side of his mouth, "Maybe *you* do."

"I think the point is," Scott said patiently, trying not to laugh at her affronted expression, "to master the throwing for your opponent and get your own points by catching it as high up on the tail as you can. The farther from the end of the tail you catch it, the higher the points you get. But you can't catch the ball itself."

She looked at him with her hands on her hips. "Okay." She held her hand out toward Brady. "Let me catch this thing."

She finally had the hang of foxtail, sort of, and was thoroughly out of breath after playing for more than an hour. The sky had started to fade into evening. She hadn't laughed this way in a long time. It felt good, like a new way of breathing. One of the kids threw a wild rocket to Scott, and it headed her direction instead. He ran hard, but she could easily take a few strides to beat him there. She went for it.

"I got it," he called as he saw her run.

"No you don't." She leaped for it and heard him grunt. She laughed as she felt the nylon tail slide through her grasp and halt, caught, then screamed as his arms wrapped around her and she went flying into the sand. She squirmed, laughing, and he reached for the tail, but she held it out and then awkwardly swung it away.

"Aagh." He stretched for it then collapsed at her hip.

"I win."

He jerked his head up. "What?" The kids were laughing in the distance, and he crawled up to her army style. "How do you figure that?"

She was still catching her breath and laughing as she saw mock disbelief and delight come and go in his face. "I think there are bonus points for interceptions."

He was speechless, but his eyes danced with the smile that wouldn't leave her face. The corner of his mouth drew up. He nodded his head. "Okay, Jillian Parish from Lebanon, Oregon. You win."

And suddenly, she couldn't breathe because she knew he would never forget her again. She pulled herself onto her side, and he drew back a little as their noses almost touched. His expression changed, and he searched her face.

"Oh no." One of the kids groaned, and Scott smiled.

"Oh no, they're gonna do it."

Jill bit her lip, grinning, realizing her heart was skipping and leaping in her chest.

"Oh man, don't look."

Jill sobered and dropped her eyes, letting the sand escape her grip. She sat up and looked out at the sun, an orange ball engulfed in flame, caressed by a thin cloud. Her heartbeat slowed, but each beat echoed beneath her throat.

"Oh man." Tyson, one of the younger boys, kicked the sand in disappointment.

A laugh slipped through Jill's lips, and she peeked at Scott, who glared at Tyson. He rolled over and got up, a sly grin on his face. Grabbing the foxtail from where it lay in the sand, he gave it a strong whirl and sent it soaring far beyond any of the kids. They turned and ran after it, yelling as they went. Quickly, Scott pulled Jill up.

"Come on before they decide we need a bigger audience."

She gave an anxious laugh, and they trotted up the beach, away from the kids and the picnic. He pulled her to a stop when the kids were dots and the blazing sun floated just above the water. He held her hand, caressing her fingers with his thumb as he looked out at the rose-colored sky and the gray waves. Slowly, she looked away from him and watched what he watched. The silhouettes of seagulls rocked on the far waves. Dark shapes of pelicans coasted in the air, meeting the round-peaked monolith out in the sea. Foam rushed the shore, and the breeze told her she was living. Moments passed.

"I think you're the miracle, Jill."

He hadn't turned to her to say it; he'd just spoken to the horizon, but his words sent a tremor through her soul. She didn't want to believe it. She suppressed the warmth his conviction kindled because she was no miracle. She was only a problem. A battered rock disrupting a smooth current, trying to be still enough not to bother anyone. Trying not to crumble. She felt his gaze turn to her, and she suddenly couldn't fight so hard. *Trying to be loved.* She lifted her chin, raising her eyes to his.

He breathed the words again. "You're the miracle."

Slowly, she shook her head, but she wasn't fighting the warmth anymore, not from his hands, not from his words. She'd been alone so long. He searched her upturned face, her steady gaze, and then he smiled and met her lips, nestling his nose next to hers, returning her kiss.

Jill let him pull her in as the warmth wove through her veins like liquid embers. This kiss was not to escape or distract. They were not teenagers in another world, though she found familiarity in the way he leaned his head. The rough of his shave was new. The strength in his arms and sureness of his mouth was new. And so warm. Oh, this could be so easy. So, so easy.

But nothing was easy. Not for her. It never had been, and if the past few days were any indication, it never would be. "Scott." She caught her breath.

"Hm?" He nuzzled the place in front of her earlobe, and she shuddered.

"Why . . . what happened . . . with Kayla?"

He pulled away, his brow furrowed. She made a mental note to kick herself later. He looked out at the water. The waves were beginning to rush higher up the beach, coming in for the night of high tide. The dusk light only emphasized the intensity in his eyes.

He took a deep breath, as though he were thinking about where to start. "Paige . . . the girl who was waiting for me on my mission, she wrote that . . . she'd found someone she knew really loved her." He continued to hold her, firm but gentle at once.

She swallowed. "Implying that you didn't?"

He nodded. "And then when I came home and met Kayla . . . it just seemed natural. I was so lost, and she was great. We were friends for a long time. Our families became close over the years." She watched him search the horizon. "Everyone talked about marriage and so . . . marriage." He turned to her. "I thought it was right." He looked down, and his brow wrinkled. "She called it off a month before the wedding."

"Why?"

"She said . . . she didn't think I loved her enough." He raised his gaze to her and brushed his fingers along her face. "She said that everyone deserves somebody who is passionate about them." Jill held his gaze for a long time, feeling her heart pound, fighting the voice telling her she didn't deserve anything like that. She closed her eyes. His lips touched her cheek, the places where her tears fell when she cried. "I think they were both right," he said softly.

Jill opened her eyes. "Why?"

"Because I never felt like this."

She was torn, rushed to a dizzying height and tethered by an undertow of uncertainty. She shook her head. "What about . . . everything? The mess? This morning—"

"This morning I was a jerk."

She breathed out a laugh. "I wasn't what you'd call *stable*." He smiled, but she continued. "I'm still not. I'm still—"

"I don't care. I mean, I *do* care. But I want everything that comes with you, Jill." He pressed his lips to hers, and the undertow eased its drag. She wrapped her arms around him and felt lifted.

"I found you," he whispered. He held her tightly, and she nodded. He pulled back just enough to see her face. He ran his hands over her hair. "You let me find you."

She felt the meaning of his words. Miracle or not, she had allowed this. She had allowed this chance of utter joy and utter misery, along with everything else, when she had first reminded him of their past. When she had stopped hiding. "I wish . . ."

"What? What do you wish?"

"I wish I had known you wanted to find me."

He gathered her up.

This kiss was the reunion of souls.

* * *

She nestled against his shoulder as they walked along the place not yet touched by water, where the sand was dry and growing colder on their feet. Scott watched the sun, partly obscured by clouds, sinking into the sea. Jill shivered, and he pulled her closer.

He felt the chill himself but made no effort to hurry. They would be back soon enough. He eyed the lights at the middeck of the boardwalk, as well as those up at the house. The kids had gone inside, and they were approaching the site of the fireworks he had set off for his dad—was that just last night?—and the scene of his lashing this morning. Shaking his head, he took a deep breath. "You're a fighter, Jill, aren't you?"

She looked up at him, clearly surprised at his words. "I don't know. I've never thought of myself that way. Most of the time I'm just scared. Especially lately."

"Well, no one can blame you for that." He paused where the black bits of charred wood had smeared down toward the water with the tide. He buried some with his foot, sweeping sand over the top. "This morning was a long time ago, wasn't it?"

She covered a yawn and nodded. "It started out awful. I'm sorry."

"Don't be. I'm glad you said what you did. I deserved it."

She nodded, smiling. "I was ready to crack you over the head with a piece of driftwood."

"You've had a rough time, and I've just kept adding to it."

The light from the boardwalk reflected in her deep eyes. He smiled, and he could tell she was feeling it—the wonder.

She gazed at him. "I keep thinking if we step up on that deck, this will all go away . . . like Cinderella and her pumpkin. Back to . . ." She didn't finish.

"You have Shiloh and your dad up there. And I won't be going anywhere."

Her eyebrows lifted. "You're staying?"

"If the slipper fits." He grinned at her grin. But it didn't last long. He touched her chin. "It will be all right."

"Why is that so easy to believe in moonlight, with waves rolling in and out?" She blinked slowly as he shook his head. "A boy comes to sit by you at the edge of the water and stops your crying, makes you laugh, and tells you not to let it bother you, and you believe him. Then he says it again at a different water's edge, in a different world."

He watched her carefully, remembering with her. "And do you believe me now?"

She thought then nodded. "You were right then. Regardless of anything else, you were right. I couldn't give up, couldn't let it overcome me." She sighed, and a little smile tugged at her mouth. "You know, I used you as much as you used me."

He protested with a laugh. "I didn't use you." Her smile told him she didn't quite believe him.

He touched her hair. "What happened to the curls?"

She sighed. "Oh, they're gone for now. I let them visit every now and then."

"I kind of liked them." He grinned. "Especially when they were wet."

She stared at him with wonder again. "This is so strange."

"Good strange?"

"Crazy strange."

"Stars and planets aligning strange?"

She laughed and shook her head.

"Wait, I've got it," he said. "Little drops of heaven strange."

She tilted her head back to look at the stars, and he caught her as she lowered her gaze again, kissing her until she stopped shivering. Changes had taken place in his life before, big enough to blast away what he thought was reality, his own strength, even his faith. This time, though, the blast was an awakening.

This time, he would rebuild. This time, he would come out stronger. Stronger for her.

Pounding sounded from the windows at the house, and they both laughed at the kids' gestures and faces behind the glass.

"Come on, Cinderella. We have a few more hours until midnight. We better get you back to the ball."

As they stepped up onto the deck, Jill's phone rang. Scott tensed, but she answered absently, smiling up at him.

"Hello?" After a moment, her grip on his arm tightened painfully, and he watched her face grow pale as she listened to whoever it was on the other end of the line. Then she whispered hoarsely, "No, please. I don't know where she is."

CHAPTER 9

"C'mon, Jilly-pill, I know you know where she is. Is she with you? Where are you, Jilly-pill?" The voice on the other end changed from sweet to threatening. "Do you have my girl?"

Jill didn't know if he was talking about Evie or Shiloh. It didn't matter. "How did you get this number?" Her voice was smaller than she would have liked.

The voice laughed. "Where are you? It's windy."

She slapped her hand over the phone mic and turned into Scott's waiting arms, focusing on the caller instead of Scott's concerned face. "Please, just leave her alone. I'll . . . I'll get you the money. I'll pay you back."

The silence gave her hope.

But the low chuckle that came seconds later did not. "Yeah, listen, Jilly. That's a great offer, but I doubt you could do that. I've seen your place."

Dread shuddered through her, and Scott's hand hovered near the phone. She closed her eyes and turned away from him. He lowered his head to listen next to her ear, and she was hit with the understanding that she was not alone in this. She reached and squeezed his hand.

"Where is she hiding, Jilly? Where's my little girl?"

"Can't you just let her go?" She knew the question would fall flat.

"How's your *dad*? Did he get our *note*?" The voice was friendly again, punctuating the *t*.

"Please . . ."

"Who's Marci Snyder?"

Jill froze.

"Doesn't she work in that big office building with you? Jilly?"

"I don't know where Evie is, Neil. Please believe me. She left."

Scott pulled the phone from her and hung it up like a punch to her gut. He frowned over the phone, pushing keys as she gathered all she had just to breathe.

"Do you have the detective's number on here?"

"Yes, Detective Okada. What . . . what are you doing? Why did you do that?"

He glanced up at her. "Was it helping?"

"What?"

"Being on the phone with him. Was it helping?" He glanced away. "Detective Okada? This is Scott Gentry. I'm with Jillian Parish. Yes. Yeah, she just received a phone call from Neil." He looked at her but continued. "Yes, her sister's boyfriend. I just texted you the number. Yes, here she is." He handed her the phone.

Her head spun. She stared blankly at the phone that had just brought fear back to her small grasp on security.

"The sooner the better, Jill."

She raised her eyes to Scott's and took a breath. "Detective?"

"Jill, can you tell me what he said? It was Neil Bradshaw?"

"Yes, I knew his voice . . . He kept referring to Evie or Shiloh as 'his girl.'" She relayed the upsetting conversation. Her hand came up to her forehead. "He asked about my friend Marci . . . He knows where I work . . ." Her voice tightened up. "I don't know what to do."

"Did you let him know you have Shiloh?"

"No. I only told him I don't know where Evie is."

He was silent for a moment as he finished processing the information. "Is there anything else?"

"Should I call Marci?"

"I'll handle that."

Good. She didn't want to explain everything. Her panic level was teetering. She gave him Marci's phone number.

"Jill, you need to call me if he contacts you again. I have a hunch he will. I know it might be difficult, but you need to talk to him, get him to drop any hint of your sister's whereabouts or what their plan is."

She bit her lip. "Okay." *Might* be difficult? "Do you think Evie could have taken another plane somewhere else? Somewhere far away?"

"It's possible. Any ideas as to where?"

Nothing came to mind. No connections.

"Think about it. I'll have the airlines check again for departing flights. How's your dog?"

She blinked at the abrupt change of subject. "Oh . . . Hobbes is good. Hobbling." She gave a weak chuckle at her attempt and felt a kiss pressed to the top of her head. It was all surreal.

Detective Okada assured her they would do what they could and hung up. Scott's arms wrapped around her waist from behind.

"I need Shiloh."

"All right." He still held her.

This was new, this not being alone. She still had so much she wanted to know about Scott, but for now, she alarmingly had all she needed. The fear inside her growled menacingly, and if she let her thoughts linger too much on Evie, she knew the choking tears would follow. But instead, she focused on Scott's warm arms and thought of his trust in her and the link between them that had survived years for this connection *now*.

He whispered in her ear. "It will be all right."

She closed her eyes. The words resonated in her mind. She had never heard them that way before . . . had hardly heard them at all. She repeated the sound in her mind.

"Are you ready?"

She nodded. He took her hand and led her to the glass door, where warm, yellow light shone from within. She entered to cheerful greetings, some pointedly cheerful, and giggles. She caught her dad's curious expression and pressed a smile then canvassed the room. "Where's Shiloh?"

Hope smiled and stood. "We put her down in Leia's room. I'll show you."

Jill looked at Scott, who gave her a gentle shove. "Go. I'll tell them."

She squeezed his hand once more and then felt the compulsion to hurry, to see Shiloh. Hope led her away as Jill heard the question from her father. "Tell us what?"

Hope stopped in front of the room. "She's in here."

"Thank you." Jill rested her hand on the doorknob.

"Jill, your father is a good man. You've been through a lot together, haven't you?"

She hadn't really thought of it that way. It made them sound like they had worked together for something when, really, all they had done was survive. Had he shared that much with this woman?

"I didn't mean to pry. I only asked about your mother, wanting to know you better. Jeremy was brief, and I didn't press him, and I won't press you, Jill. It's just that . . . well, friends make things so much more bearable, don't they?"

Jill glanced at the pictures lining the hall. "I really haven't had many, actually." The words were out before she knew she was saying them. The long day was catching up with her.

Hope leaned her head to the side thoughtfully. She nodded. "There is a sort of protection that happens, isn't there? A sort of shell. People can be careless, judgmental. But there are those who will not judge. There are those who have felt it too." Hope's eyes glistened. Her voice became strained. "Those are the best friends. I promise. We only have to find them."

There, in her blue eyes, Hope held the pain Scott had revealed. Only these were the eyes of the woman in the portrait, her love taken from her, an echo of it still there until what earthly time only God knew. Abandoned, in a way.

Jill swallowed. She couldn't say anything, but understanding was passed and accepted there in the honey-gold hallway.

Hope reached and squeezed Jill's arm. "Your father is very proud of you. It radiates from him every time he looks at you. I wanted to tell you that. Did you know?"

Did she?

Hope didn't wait for an answer. "You know, life is so strange. You're either floating or falling . . . or fighting."

Jill raised her eyes.

Hope slid her hand into Jill's. "We have to fight a lot, don't we?"

Jill could only breathe, unable to get past the strain in her throat and the salt pools in her lids. What was floating? Was it what had happened out there on the beach? Or was that falling? So little control. She had little experience with either. She knew fight.

"I've kept you long enough. I'm sorry. I just wanted you to know you're welcome here. Your family is. You have a beautiful niece. I think she is a very fortunate little girl."

"Thank you." Is that what Shiloh was? Fortunate?

Hope smiled, gave Jill's hand another squeeze, and turned.

Jill watched her walk away then quietly opened the door, closing it softly behind her, and slid onto the bed next to the little girl. Jill wrapped her arms around Shiloh and pulled her to her chest. Shiloh sighed.

"Shh." Jill ran her hand over the baby curls. "It will be all right." Then the tears fell, warm saltwater soaking slowly into the comforter as her thoughts circled like the white gulls.

The alarm clock on the nightstand told her little under an hour had passed when Jill heard a small knock at the door. She got up carefully and stepped into the hall.

"I'm sorry, Dad."

He shook his head. "You don't need to be sorry. Do you feel better?"

She nodded and brushed her hair behind her ear. "Are you doing okay?"

"Yeah, I'm glad I came." He tilted his head to the side. "Scott is a good man. He told me about Costa Rica."

She met her dad's eyes.

"Don't look so shocked. Actually, it was a shock to Hope. She had no idea. Started grabbing tissues like they were candy on Halloween." He grinned at her gently.

She rubbed her eyes. "Ugh. This has been such a long day. How . . . ?" She began to tear up again and looked at the ceiling. "For years, I haven't cried. Now I can't seem to shut the dang things off. How are we . . . ?" She tried to shake it away.

Her dad put his hand on her arm. "We'll just take what comes. You're strong, Jill."

She grunted in disbelief.

"And you're tired. I think the others are getting ready to go."

Scott cleared his throat behind them. "May I show her something first?"

Jill and her dad turned.

"Scott." Jeremy held out his hand, and Scott took it in a firm handshake. "I think I'm going to turn in. It was great meeting you. I've already said my good nights to your parents." He turned to Jill. "I'm going to peek in on my granddaughter first though." He gave Jill a subtle wink and leaned toward her. "Take what comes, Jilly," he whispered then slipped into the bedroom. She watched him bend over Shiloh and take her little hand.

Scott held out his. "I know you're tired, but I want to show you something. It won't take long."

She ran her fingers through her hair and nodded, taking his hand. His grip formed around hers once more, and it fit; it was strong. He led her up the stairs to the loft.

"I'm not sure we'll get another clear night. Clouds are supposed to roll in tomorrow."

She lifted her gaze, and the scene nearly took her breath away. Scott left the lights off, and the stars hovered above them in a semicircle, a smile of lights winking as strips of high, thin clouds ushered past. A satellite blinked slowly in its orbit. After a few moments, she felt him watching her.

"Scott." What did she want to say?

"I just wanted to show you. We don't need to talk about anything more today." He laughed quietly. "I don't want to try. Do you?" He stepped aside and invited her to look through the telescope.

She shook her head and sighed. Exhaustion softened all the edges. She stepped forward and looked through the eyepiece of the telescope, finding the distant lights, considering the vastness of creation. "Which is the larger star?"

"It must be Saturn. You missed Venus. It sets earlier, but it's brighter and easier to spot."

She stepped away, and he took a turn. "It's interesting," he continued, adjusting the eyepiece. "Saturn and Mars are both on the brightest side of planets visible to the naked eye, yet Venus blows them both away in brightness—if you catch her at the right time."

He looked at her.

She swallowed. "I'm sorry we missed it."

He stepped to her, taking her hand. "Jill." He touched her face again, just along her jawbone. His thumb caressed her lips, and her eyes closed. She breathed his scent, amber and ocean air, then his lips touched hers. He kissed her softly, and any anxiety eased for the moment, replaced with an ache for his affection. Things disappeared as the kiss warmed and she pulled him closer—less important things, like finding a highchair, Hobbes's leg, the ruined copy of her favorite book, then even important things, like . . . Evie . . . even Shiloh . . . breathing. Scott let go too soon. "I feel like I'm taking advantage of you," he whispered in her ear.

"I don't care. If I were a different kind of girl—"

"Don't be . . . ever." His eyes searched hers in the darkness, and the things she'd just forgotten came painfully flooding back. He kissed her again then gently led her back down the stairs.

Someone handed her Shiloh, who was wrapped in a blanket, and after everyone had expressed their thanks, they walked back to the cottage in the night, Jill watching the stars more than her feet and someone guiding her with their arm through her elbow.

Heavenly Father . . . so many thoughts of fear and hopes and confusion and inadequacies and overwhelming blessings rushed through her mind . . . *dost Thou know the desires of my heart? Because I don't have a clue.*

CHAPTER 10

"Hello, Brasher Books, this is Marci at Mr. Hayward's office. How may I help you?" She turned around in her chair and checked her lipstick in the small mirror hanging on her cubicle wall. The circles under her eyes told her she'd had a little too much fun this weekend up in Vancouver. The concert had been incredible though, and her boyfriend had finally started hinting about a ring. She was only half listening to whoever was on the phone as that giddy feeling returned, the same one she felt when Todd had said, holding her hand out, *I've always liked an emerald cut. How about you?*

"I'm sorry, could you repeat the question?"

The male voice on the other line spoke up. "Yeah, I was told I could find Jill Parish at this number, but no one seems to be able to help me."

"I'm sorry, Jill is on vacation. Can I take a message for you?"

"Well, it's kind of important, a family thing, and I'd like to get a hold of her. Do you know where she went?"

"I can give you her cell phone number."

"I have that . . . Keep getting darned voicemail." He chuckled.

"Well, I think she'll be back next week, but she may check in. Give me your name and number, and I'll tell her to get a hold of you when she calls."

He paused. "Well, see, I'd hoped to surprise her. I'm only in town for a couple days. Did she go far?"

The light from her boss's office blinked.

"I'm sorry, but could you hold a second? I have another call." Without waiting, she switched the line. "Yes, Mr. Hayward? Mm-hm. Yes. No, I'll have to make copies of those before we send them out. Yes, sir. Spicy Italian, no mayo, no cheese, got it." She added no jalapeños to the order and made a face.

A pair of navy blue uniforms caught her attention, and she sat up as the police officers approached. She hung up the phone and slowly stood, eyes wide.

"Marci Snyder?"

"Yes. That's me." She looked from one to the other.

"I'm Officer McKay. This is Officer Kent." They held up their badges. She gave them a little nod.

"Has anybody tried to contact you about your coworker, Jill Parish, or have you been approached by any strangers?"

"Um." She swallowed and glanced at the phone, the blinking light signaling she still had an active line. "Is Jill in trouble?"

"Not at the moment. Her apartment was broken into on Sunday, and we believe it involves drug activity."

Marci furrowed her brow. "What? Oh, Jill wouldn't do drugs. She's a *Mormon*, for Pete's sake. I can't even get her to taste my half-caf caramel machiatto. What did the thieves want?"

Officer McKay shook his head. "Jill's innocent in this, but she is involved. She received a phone call last night from the suspect. He threw out your name."

"What?" She grabbed the desk and sat down hard. "But I don't do that stuff either!" She knew they were attracting attention from the other cubicles. "I had a few beers at the concert but . . . Who is this guy? Is Jill all right?"

"We think he got your name from her stolen laptop. Miss Snyder, it's important you answer our question. Has anyone contacted you about Miss Parish?"

She abruptly drew in her breath and turned to the flashing light on the phone. Carefully, she pointed her finger, nodding her head.

The police officer crouched down next to her. "Did you give him any information?"

She closed her eyes tightly, thinking back over the conversation. "I told him she was on vacation and offered to give him her cell number." Her shoulders sagged with shame. "But he said he already had it. He wanted to know where she was." She looked at Officer McKay. "Then my boss rang me." She looked at the phone. "He said he was family and that he was here in Portland." She watched the little blinking light, and then it stopped. She breathed out a sigh of relief. "He hung up."

"He may call back."

"Officer, what's wrong with Jill? Is she okay? Who is this guy?"

"She's fine, a little shaken up."

"Well, can I talk to her?"

He nodded. "She'd probably like to hear from you. But can you tell us anything you might have noticed over the weekend, anything unusual? Been aware of anyone hanging around?"

Marci shook her head. "I was in Vancouver all weekend. I didn't get home until late last night. Although . . ." She cocked her head to the side. "Friday was really strange."

"Friday?"

"Yeah. There was this guy. He actually stole Jill's phone . . . but then he returned it."

Officer McKay took out a pen and notepad. "Did she get his name?"

"Yeah." Marci frowned. "But I don't know if—"

"The name?"

"Scott Gentry."

Officer McKay lifted his pen off the paper. "Scott Gentry?"

* * *

"The Grateful Bread?"

Scott smiled at her. "Clever, huh?"

She inhaled as a customer opened the door with a bag of baked goods. "Mmm."

"You have to get here early for the bread. It goes fast." He held the door open for her, and she walked into a clean, airy bakery with pale pink walls and café seating.

Scott walked up to the glass counter. "I'll have a loaf of the challah bread."

The woman behind the counter nodded and began bagging a large hand-braided loaf of golden bread.

Scott turned to Jill. "Is there anything you'd like to try?"

"I'll get a loaf of the cinnamon bread for the Thorntons." She eyed the scones on a glass-covered silver pedestal. "Have you had these?"

Scott staggered back half a step with his hand over his stomach. "Really good. Really, dangerously good."

The woman looked at Jill after handing Scott his loaf with a smile.

"I'll have the cinnamon loaf and two of the blackberry scones," Jill said in response to the woman's gaze.

Outside, Scott put the packages in the trunk, and Jill ducked into the car. She turned to the backseat and handed her dad a paper-wrapped scone.

He blinked at her then smiled. "Thanks, Jilly."

"Blackberry. You like those, right?"

"Mmm. I'll share this with sad missy, here. She didn't like it when you left." He broke off a piece of the tender scone and popped it in Shiloh's pouty but open mouth. One solitary tear sat under her eye. Her grandpa patted her hand. Shiloh lifted her eyes to Jill's.

Pain, like a net, drew around Jill's heart, pulled tight and cinched closed. She swallowed, not speaking her thought aloud.

Are you lost without her?

A memory flitted through the space separating Jill and Shiloh. It had been an overcast day, and the ache came flooding back.

"Mommy?" Jill held her hands around the gash in her knee. It hurt, like sharp rocks. The blood was coming fast, and she was scared. What if it didn't stop? She looked at the overturned tricycle, and the tears squeezed out. The boy had said she was too big for a trike. But she loved her trike. She didn't want to be too big.

She tottered through the open garage and up the steps. "Mommy?" Sissy was crying—a sound like one of Daddy's cars trying to go, only it was small, like sissy was far away and up high. Jill followed the sound, hurrying, wincing. "Mommy, I fell on my trike." She sniffled and wiped her face. Her fingers were dripping red, and fear shuddered through her. She limped to Mommy, who was asleep on the couch. Jill shook her shoulder with her balled up fist. "Mommy, I fell, and it's bleeding." She sniffled with a sigh. "And Evie is crying." She looked toward the swing. It wasn't swinging anymore. It needed to be started again.

She shook her mom again. "Mommy, please be awake. It hurts really bad, and my fingers got blood on them." The crying hurt her chest because she was trying to be a big girl. *"Mommy."*

The bottle of Mommy's drink was on the floor. Mommy said it helped her feel better. She said it helped the owies go away. There was some in the glass. Jill picked up the glass, drawing in her breath at the prints her fingers were making. She looked around for a towel to wipe it. She used her shirt, and that was better. She would help sissy after she got the medicine.

The burn hit the back of her throat and went up her nose, and she coughed, gasping. The glass slipped from her hands and hit the edge of the table. It broke with a ting-crash sound, and then—

Nothing. No yelling, no fixing, no helping, no mad Mommy. Only Evie crying her car cry and Jilly being afraid. Very afraid. Because she didn't want to be a big girl.

"Evie. It's okay." Jill stood frozen, huddled, shivering with her cries. "Don't cry." She reached a shaky finger to touch her mommy . . . to try again. "Mommy, help."

Jill wrapped her fingers around Shiloh's.

"Jilly, you all right?" She dropped her eyes with a nod and turned to the front as Scott opened his door and slid in.

"It's cool out there. I hope it doesn't rain."

She nodded again and focused on the white paper bag in her lap. Shakily, she reached in and pulled out the other scone. Staring at it, she held it out. "Here."

"Isn't that for you?" Scott glanced at her dad, who was already chewing a mouthful and giving Shiloh another bite.

She shook her head and held it closer to him. He hesitated then took the scone, watching her. He broke it in two pieces then gave her back one. Sincerity rested in his eyes.

"Thank you," he said, nodding to her. "They're good."

"Have some, Jilly."

She couldn't help but smile at her dad's words spoken through a mouthful of food. She noted the beginnings of concern in Scott's brow and accepted the half scone. She took a breath then quickly popped a torn piece into her mouth. Cream, flour, and sugar, and the smooth taste of butter, followed by the pop of blackberry, all melted in her mouth. She closed her eyes and chewed.

"Better than chocolate?"

She swallowed and opened her eyes. She shook her head, and he chuckled.

"Close," she conceded. She looked down again, feeling his gaze on her. She hadn't fooled him. "Dangerous though."

She felt his smile. How? How could she feel it?

She had woken up this morning in that place between dream and awake, and it had taken her far too long to sort out the real from the not. So when Scott had called early to ask if they'd like to see the dory boats at the public beach, drive up to Tillamook to tour the cheese factory and get some of their famous ice cream, then spend the rest of the day on the beach and have dinner, it had taken her several seconds to retrace, evaluate, remember, and say yes.

And part of her had wanted to run the other way.

"So what is it about chocolate?"

"You're still reading my book."

He gave her a sheepish smile.

She brushed her hair out of her face and sighed. "I don't know. It's . . . sweet and creamy . . . melty. You can drink it. The bite is firm but giving. It can be dark and rich or light and smooth." She peeked at him, and he looked at her in a sideways glance, biting his lip. She cleared her throat and watched the scone in her hand. "It can fit your mood, but if you don't have a choice, it still works."

"Works for what?"

"Whatever ails you. Comfort. Courage." She shrugged. "It works."

He chuckled and nodded then gratefully left it at that.

They drove under overcast skies past more homes—some closed up for the gray winter—a grocery store, and shops. Jill gazed out the window as worry settled in around her like fog. And when Scott reached over and put his hand on hers, it sent the fog swirling. His fingers curved around hers. His hands weren't large, and his skin was a little rough, except when he touched her face. But they were always warm. She glanced at him, but he just drove quietly, letting her think . . . or worry.

Her phone rang. "It's Detective Okada." Her brow wrinkled. "Hello?"

"Hello, Jill. How are you holding up?"

"Fine."

"What can you tell me about Scott Gentry?"

"What?" She glanced at Scott, who looked at her curiously. She cleared her throat. "Why?"

"We traced the cell phone Neil Bradshaw used to call you from last night. It was reported stolen to the service provider this morning, and its service has been cancelled."

"But he was able to call me."

"Yes."

"What does that have to do with Scott?"

Scott turned his head as he drove into a public parking area near a wide beach access and pulled into a parking spot.

"We're here with Marci Snyder."

"Is she all right?"

"Yes, but we believe Neil tried to get information from her this morning." A shiver ran down Jill's spine. "She told us you had an unusual day at work on Friday."

Jill rested her forehead on her fingers. "Yes, it was odd." She looked up to find Scott watching her intently, her dad leaning forward, waiting to catch any news.

"Miss Snyder tells us Scott stole your phone?"

Jill sat up straight, suddenly alert. "But that didn't have *anything* to do with . . . He was just trying to . . ." She looked at Scott. His brow furrowed, and he rubbed her hand in both of his.

"He was just trying to what?"

She sighed. "To ask me out." The detective waited as she paused. "He left me his phone then called it from mine." Scott grimaced.

"And that worked?"

"Not exactly. I was annoyed more than anything."

"Well, I'm running a check on him. Will you be seeing him again?"

"I'm with him right now." Scott smiled slowly, and she couldn't help the lift at the corner of her mouth. "Detective, Scott being here is pure coincidence—"

Scott murmured, "I don't think so."

Dang, he was persistent. It emboldened her. "His parents live here and are good friends with the Thorntons. Neither of us had any idea that we would meet here. We have witnesses to that. Stealing my phone on Friday was a stupid thing, but I know he has no connection whatsoever with Neil Bradshaw or drugs or anything." She glanced at Scott, and he nodded with conviction, though she detected a bit of worry. She turned back to the phone. "My dad is staying with the Gentrys, and wouldn't Scott have told Neil where I was and that I have Shiloh? And it's not as if we're strangers. We met after his senior year, when he lived in California, not here or Seattle or—"

"All right, Jill, all right. I'm still running a check on him, but you're right. It makes no sense for him to hold that information . . . unless he's putting on a show."

Jill swallowed and squeezed Scott's hands. "He's not," she insisted. "He's helping us."

I know it. He's helping me.

"Be careful, Jill. Watch for anybody who seems to be paying too much attention to your movements. Stay close to the people you trust. Neil Bradshaw has a record of drugs, violence, and theft—all misdemeanors, of course, in three states. Not enough to really keep him in jail until now. It's adding up, along with a collection of his used aliases. I'll call you when the airport gets back to me about your sister."

"What about Marci?"

"She's not to be alone until we get this figured out."

Jill withered. "Can I talk to her?"

"Sure."

"Jill? Are you all right?" Marci's voice was high with excitement. "I didn't even know you *had* a sister. I'm so sorry about your apartment. Is it true? Scott Gentry is there at the beach?"

"Yes, he's here. We're . . . getting to know each other. In the middle of all this mess."

"That's so romantic."

Jill breathed out a laugh. "No. No, really, it's not. It's just a mess, but I . . ." She looked down at their hands. "I trust him."

She heard her dad clear his throat. "I've got to go, Marci. Please, be careful. Don't be by yourself."

She hung up and sighed.

"Am I in trouble?"

She smiled at Scott. "Should you be?"

Jeremy laughed from the backseat. "Why not just send flowers and a note?"

Jill looked behind her. "Thank you, Dad."

Scott bowed his head, nodding and red around the ears.

He got out and opened the trunk of his car. Jill followed and took a quick inventory. Diaper bag, stroller, backpack, sun hat, jacket in the bag, blanket.

"You know, we're only going to be out here for an hour, tops." Scott picked up the stroller. "Actually, we'll only be *in town* for fifteen, twenty minutes. It's not that big. Then we'll head up to Tillamook."

Jill bit her lip, nodding. "I just haven't been out with her like this before."

Jill hoisted the diaper bag over her shoulder as her father lifted Shiloh from her car seat. "Ready to go, Shiloh? Hey, that sounds like a song. 'Ready to go, Shiloh, we're ready to go, Shi-loh.'" He bounced a little dance as Jill stared with a half smile on her face.

"Did you want your purse, Jill?"

She nodded and took it from Scott.

"Keep an eye on that," he said. "You wouldn't want somebody to steal your phone."

She glanced at him sideways. "Or my keys."

He smiled and asked, "Stroller or backpack? Or would you like me to push the backpack in the stroller while your father continues to carry Shiloh around on his shoulders?" They both watched Shiloh pull at her grandpa's curly hair and reach down for his nose.

Jill paused. "I haven't seen him so happy . . ."

"Ever?"

"No. But it's been a long time."

His hand wrapped around hers once more. "And you? You seem to be struggling with it this morning. Not that I blame you." He leaned close to her ear. "Is it me?"

"Yes, Scott. Out of all this nightmarish chaos, you alone are the cause of my reeling emotions this morning."

He raised his eyebrows playfully. It was the reaction she wanted from her sarcasm, but her words weren't entirely false. She straightened her shoulders, remembering the way she rose to his defense with the detective. She hadn't felt so sure of anything for some time. "I do trust you. I just . . . need to stay focused on priorities."

He nodded, searching her face. She looked away at Shiloh. Her voice was quiet.

"I could use a good friend though."

Scott looked down at their hands, her grip tight in his. He looked up at her, understanding in his smile.

"I think I can do that." He brought her hand up and kissed it then dropped it again. "It's what I asked for, isn't it?"

"What?"

"At Walgreens. A chance to start over."

She flushed and looked away at the memory of her harsh words. She mumbled, "We'll always have Walgreens."

He laughed. "C'mon." He closed the trunk and flung the backpack over his shoulder, pulling her hand. "Your dad seemed pretty excited to see the dory boats. Let's see if we can still catch a few."

A small crowd had gathered at the top of the beach. Only two boats were left sitting at the surf's edge. The crew of one of the boats called out and pushed as a particularly large wave came in. The small fishing dory rocked, and the men braced themselves and began to dig in against the shifting ground, pushing against the power of water and gravity. After a few low waves, one man gave another shout, and the men clambered aboard as the engine fired up.

"Whoa!" Jeremy shouted as the bow of the boat lifted into the air against an incoming wave. The men held on and moved with the vertical lift, making it look easy. The engine growled and the captain stood tall, leaning into the next wave.

"How do they get past it?" she asked. The boat seemed to make no progress as another wave lifted the bow high again and the men were drenched in seawater. The blue and gold state flag rippled erratically in the ocean wind on the boat's tall mast.

"This is why people come to watch. The fight."

The captain made quick use of the moment between waves, gunning the engines, but another tall wave lifted and actually seemed to push the boat back this time. Jill was able to make out the smile, though, on the captain's face under his knit hat when he turned his head. The two men behind him sat to adjust to the boat's angles, nodding in answer or encouragement.

"Come on!"

"Go, go, go!"

The crowd around them shouted, calling through cupped hands as the next wave gathered itself for another shove. Everyone seemed to lean forward as the wave slammed into the front of the boat and continued underneath. The crowd whooped in delight, and after a few more waves, suddenly, the boat was out past the surf, into open water, a white water bug skitting its way out to the massive Haystack Rock. Seagulls swooped and settled in its wake.

"See? Easy." Scott smiled, and Jeremy clapped Shiloh's hands together. "Wait 'til you see them come in. *That's* the easy part. Just gun it full bore toward the beach and slide up onto the sand."

"I guess that would be easy with a flat-bottom boat." Jeremy was grinning like a little boy. "Do they bring in a good catch?"

Scott shrugged. "It depends." He nodded toward the restaurant to their left, built right at the top of the beach. "We'll eat dinner at the Pelican. You're guaranteed a fresh catch anywhere in town, but here we can eat right on the oceanfront."

Jeremy peeked up at Shiloh. "Do you like fish, Shiloh? Hmm?"

Both men turned to walk toward town. Scott halted when Jill didn't follow, still holding her hand. "What is it?"

"I feel like that boat."

He looked out where the struggle had taken place, considering her words. She observed the way his mouth curved over his grown-up chin. It had been one of the first things she'd noticed about him when he'd shown up at church and his name was read, knocking her senses into pandemonium. Of course, she'd shown nothing at the time, even when Scott had locked eyes with her. Even when Trey Gentry had looked at her pointedly then leaned over and whispered to his brother.

Scott turned and leaned toward her. "What kind of friend would I be if I didn't remind you the boat made it out to open water?"

She nodded, and he touched her hair. He pulled her to follow her dad. "We're between waves now. We have the whole day to spend together. C'mon, let's get a kite for Shiloh." He gave her a mischievous smile. "And maybe some chocolate."

He looked away and didn't see the small shake of her head. Between waves. What would the next battering bring? Something told her it would be beyond chocolate's magic.

CHAPTER 11

Evie looked into the restroom mirror. The dark hair color she'd chosen was harsh against her pale skin, but she did look different. She leaned forward and applied more black eyeliner. A woman entered, holding a little boy's hand. The woman glanced her way and pulled the little boy closer, directing him into a stall, a reaction she'd gotten used to before she had her baby. But after Shiloh had been born, even when she was pregnant, women hadn't pulled away from her. Maybe they hadn't been friendly, but occasionally, she got at least a quick smile.

She leaned toward the mirror again and put on lipstick. Her chest ached, and her thin hands wouldn't stop shaking. She was fine, she told herself. She threw the lipstick into the bag she'd bought at the thrift store and grasped her fingers. It was better.

It was better this way.

Her lip quivered, and she bit it. This was better for Shiloh. Rubbing the ache in her chest, she picked up the bag and left the restroom.

"Hey there, Reece. Like the hair."

She halted at the tone, at the sound of her mother's name. A couple of the guys she had met last night leaned lazily against the front of the bank building.

She moved past them. The one named Chris pushed himself away from the wall and joined her, moving in a little too close. The other followed. She could feel him on the backs of her shoes.

"What are you guys up to?"

"Ah, that's the question, isn't it?" He held up a paper in front of her, and she hesitated too long, reached for it too slowly, because her own face stared back at her from the wrinkled page he snatched away. "I told Gage here this looks a lot like that little mouse we met last night."

She kept walking and turned her face away, hiding the fear churning in her stomach. *No. Not yet.* She should have dyed her hair sooner. She grimaced then glanced at him. "What am I, a poster child?" She grabbed the paper successfully this time and scoffed. "Yeah right." She crumpled up the paper and headed for a trash can, but Gage reached around her and grabbed it back.

He smoothed it out, and she pretended not to care.

"Everlisse. That doesn't sound much like Reece."

"Get that all by yourself?" She put her head down and walked faster.

Gage's arm came casually around her shoulders as he kept up with her pace, but she felt the tension in him and knew the gesture was not a friendly one. Knew it too well.

"So what made you decide to dye your hair?"

She glanced up at his green and purple Mohawk. "Are you kidding me?"

He ignored her and leaned down to her ear. "What kind of name *is* Everlisse?"

She had never been good at this. These lies and taunts. Neil was. *Do it like Neil.* She pulled her arms around herself. "How would I know? Sounds like something from a fairy tale."

Chris chuckled. "Yeah, it does." He gestured for the paper, and Gage passed it to him under her nose.

She saw the arms draped around her shoulders in the photo. A graduation gown. Jilly. She had called the police? She squeezed her arms tighter around her. She hadn't expected that.

"It says here that there's a reward for any information we can give the police."

She forced a laugh. "And you guys are going to walk into the police station. Something tells me they'd probably be happy to see you." She shrugged out from under Gage's arm, trying to keep her hands steady. "Listen guys, I'm meeting a friend, so if you don't mind—"

"What'd you do, Everlisse? How'd you get your face on a wanted poster?"

Her heart stammered as she shook her head. "You guys are crazy." She turned and noticed a guy barely glance in her direction as Chris grabbed her arm. Blazer over a hooded sweatshirt, baggy jeans, scruffy beard. It might work. Out of desperation, she called out. "Trent!"

The guy in the blazer lowered the newspaper he'd just pulled out of the machine and frowned.

* * *

He'd been watching the girl out of the corner of his eye. The guys she was with didn't look friendly. She was a mess as well, but still . . .

Her smile was desperate as she held his gaze, and he fought the urge to look around for whoever Trent was. He cleared his throat, stood up straight, and gave a small wave. The guy who'd grabbed her released her arm, and she hurried forward. Yes, she was definitely hurrying toward him.

"I'm sorry I'm late. These guys were giving me a hard time."

He looked at the guys and narrowed his eyes. They seemed to be backing away, the taller one looking him over suspiciously. He looked down at the girl. She shivered, and her eyes were scared as she watched him.

"That's all right." He folded up the paper. "I was just going to read until you got here. Ready?"

She gave him a jerky nod as her eyes glassed over. He took her arm and gently led her away, around the corner. He looked back a few times, and when he saw no sign of the two thugs, he led her into a coffee shop and sat her down.

"Can I get you something?" Her hands were shaking, and she seemed to wilt into the chair.

"Why did you do that?" Her voice was touched with fear.

He shrugged, keeping his tone casual. "It looked like there might be trouble if I didn't play along." The fact that he was a curious psychology major was only a small motivation. He asked again, "Can I get you something?"

She shifted in her seat and glanced toward the counter. "Coke?"

He nodded and went to the counter, keeping an eye on her. He brought the drink back and sat down, waiting until she had sipped enough cola to breathe.

"Are you all right?"

She shrugged, keeping her eyes down. She bit her lip and looked out the window then furtively glanced around the coffee shop.

"Did you know those guys?"

She shook her head and took another drink. "We met for a minute last night at this place, but . . ." She shivered again.

"Here." He took his blazer off and draped it around her shoulders. She didn't say anything, just stared at her drink. She looked like she might cry, so he played with the straw wrapper, twisting it around his finger instead of looking at her.

"Thanks."

He looked up and nodded. She wore so much dark make-up he couldn't really tell what her eyes would look like without it. Sad. Pale. She reminded him of a waif or an urchin from *Les Miserables* or any Dickens movie he'd seen, from her tight-knit hat right down to her fingerless gloves. He'd worked with a few runaways at the shelter. But she wasn't a child. There was something old—no, *lived*—about her.

"Is your name really Trent?" Her eyes were wide again.

He smiled. "No. Close though. It's Trey. People who don't know me well sometimes call me Trent. I don't know you though, do I?"

She shook her head and took another drink.

"What's your name?"

She looked away. "Reece."

He nodded. "Do you go to Lincoln High?"

She laughed and swallowed her cola before she choked on it. "I'm twenty-two." She bit her lip, and he suspected she was lying.

"College, then?"

She studied him out of the corner of her eye then shook her head. She lowered her eyes and spoke to her drink. "I'm getting away from here. From everything." Her chin quivered, and she wiped her gloved hand under her nose.

He was careful. He leaned his head to the side. "Are you running away?"

She thought about his words, studying him. She nodded. "But not in the way you think. I haven't lived at home for a long time. I was here, visiting my sister, and now it's time to . . . make things better."

"Better how?" He was beyond mere curiosity; he felt compelled to keep her talking.

She shook her head and pulled at her hands. "Any way will be better." The glassy look returned to her eyes, and she turned to the window. A thin drip of black ran down her sallow cheek. She wiped it away with a shaky hand. "I have to go now. You've been so nice."

"Do you know where you're going?"

She nodded at the street.

"Would you tell me?"

She looked at him, steadier now. "Why?"

He shrugged gently. "In case someone, your sister, wants to know. Someone here would know. Just in case."

Slowly, she shook her head. "Nobody can know where I'm going."

His concern rose. "Why?"

She blinked her glassy eyes, and another black stream slipped down her face. "Because," her voice was a whisper, "then I might hope somebody would find me."

He swallowed hard, somehow knifed by her words. She wiped her tears again and stood up.

He stood quickly and took the blazer she held out for him.

"Is there anything else I can do?" Should he let her leave? "I can take you to the bus or the airport. Do you have a car?"

"I'm taking a taxi to the airport."

"Please, just let me drive you." He needed more time, more information. Maybe he could talk her into coming to the shelter. It wasn't the nicest place, but they tried to keep it safe. "Taxis are pretty expensive."

She looked down at her grasping hands. To his surprised relief, she nodded.

* * *

Evie glanced at Trey as she gripped the bag in her lap. He was driving her to the airport. She still didn't know why she'd said yes. This was better though, and she wasn't really afraid of him. He was one of those men she would watch out of the car window, arm in arm with some girl their age, talking, smiling. Those men who probably didn't use, who went to jobs and took those girls out to dinner, proposed and got married and became good dads. Dads who wouldn't let anything bad happen to their wives or their kids . . . But she usually watched those men from the car, behind the glass.

He reached for his phone, and her grip tightened, along with her stomach.

"Hey, this is Trey. I won't be able to meet you until later. No, I'm driving a friend to the airport."

He smiled at her, and his eyes were kind.

"Yeah, I'll give you a call when I get back, see where you guys are. Okay, bye." He hung up, and she breathed.

He looked at her again, and she felt another question coming on.

"So you were visiting your sister?"

"Mm-hm."

"Does she live in the city?"

She nodded.

"But you can't stay there?"

She shook her head, staring in front of her.

"Listen, I volunteer at a shelter near here. There's room for you. Food. Until you get back on your feet."

"I can't stay here." She looked down at her fidgeting fingers. "It would be bad if I stayed here. Really bad."

He furrowed his brow, watching the road. He sighed. "Reece, I feel like I'm aiding and abetting here, and I don't like that feeling."

"I'm not a criminal." Sort of.

"I don't mean it that way. I just wish I knew once I dropped you off that I wasn't making things worse for anybody, including you."

"You aren't." She said it with conviction because it was true.

"Do you and your sister not get along?"

She played with the buckle on the bag, wondering again at his questions, why he asked so many, why he seemed to care.

He ran his hand through his hair and blew out a breath. "Father in Heaven, help us," he mumbled.

Her eyes widened. She looked ahead, wondering again.

"You know, sometimes, things can look pretty bad. Really awful bad, and we jump too soon or give up or run away." He glanced her way, and she bit her lip. "But most of the time, if we're just still, if we stay and hang on, we find the help we need. Or it finds us."

"I found help."

"You did?"

Evie nodded.

"What kind of help?" He sounded suspicious, and she wasn't surprised.

She pressed her fist to her chest. "The kind in here." Her voice had come out hushed.

"And that's the same help telling you to leave now?"

She dropped her fist and didn't answer him. That help was barely a thread, a see-through fiber of hope she found early that morning while Neil was stoned. She had left her hope at Jill's—with Shiloh. "You seem like the kind of person who wants to save people."

He smiled in that understanding way again. "What if I am?"

"I don't need to be saved. I . . . I don't matter. I'm . . . saving someone myself, so . . ." She braced herself against the pain in her chest. "So stop asking me questions."

He was quiet, and she worried that she had angered him. But he didn't sound angry.

"So this leaving . . . this is an act of heroism?"

She breathed and could feel her lungs push against the tightness there. Could someone be a hero and be so messed up? She pictured Shiloh, looking up at Jill while she fed her a bottle. The nice apartment. The bookcase. The warm bath and food. How she had fallen asleep and burnt the dinner and lost the baby.

She shook her head and another tear dropped. "I don't think I can call it that." She sniffed and sat up, looking at the approaching exit. "But it's as close as I'll ever be able to get."

Trey pulled up to the unloading area but then pulled away.

"What are you doing?" She reached for the door handle.

"I'm going to park, make sure you get in all right."

She chewed on her lip, watching the gate raise as he pulled a parking stub from the machine. The car wound up and around the garage until he found a spot. He parked and got out without a word as he waited for her. She gathered her bag and got out of the car. They entered the busy ticket lobby, and she was immediately more at ease and more anxious all at once. She located her airline and took a few steps then stopped.

"Please, don't come with me. I meant what I said. No one can know where I'm going."

He pursed his lips and tapped his car key against his leg. "All right. I'll wait here."

She looked around and found a grouping of chairs around a corner, out of sight of the check-in area. She pointed. "Sit there."

He watched her steadily.

"Geesh, just sit, okay?"

He finally nodded and left for the chairs. When she saw he was seated, she hurried to her airline, glancing behind her. After waiting in the winding line several hand-wringing minutes, she finally stepped up to the counter.

"Name?"

"Alisa Johnston."

"ID?"

Evie handed the card over, knowing it would be accepted.

"Thank you, Mrs. Johnston. Will you be checking any luggage?"

"No."

"You're cutting it close. Here are your boarding passes. Make sure you hang on to them until needed as you have three changeovers. Do not leave your possessions unattended. Once you have gone through security you cannot return to this part of the airport. Do you understand?"

Evie nodded.

"Thank you. Have a nice flight."

Evie tucked her boarding passes into her bag. She found Trey where she left him, still surprised he would wait.

"Everything go okay?"

She nodded.

"Is there anything I can say to talk you out of this?"

She shook her head. "I don't know you. I've already told you things—" She looked away. "I wish . . ."

A thought flashed through her mind. She watched the people milling by, and her eyes caught on a little girl reaching up to hold her mama's hand. She swallowed. She stepped to the chairs he had left and bent over a small table, fishing around in her bag. She pulled out a receipt and pen and shakily wrote. She folded the paper up several times and put the pen away.

Holding the note in both hands, she looked again at the little girl then at the note. "If I give you this, will you promise not to read it or do anything for . . . a week?" The shake in her voice wouldn't go away.

His eyes were on the note. His jaw was tight. "Twenty-four hours."

She shook her head. "Three days. Final offer."

He studied her then gave a nod and reached for the note. She pulled it away, breathing, the pain in her chest pushing the tears out like pressure in a syringe. "I'll believe you if you promise." She searched his eyes.

Without looking away, he said, "I promise."

She saw what she was looking for and handed him the note. He grabbed her hand, and she turned her wrist down, not wanting him to see the needle marks under her sleeve.

"You have to know that you are cared for and loved by *somebody*."

She raised her chin and swallowed back the tears, steadying the tremor through her body. The words hurt because they were truer than anything else she knew. "I know." She slipped her hand out of his and looked at the note then lifted her eyes once more. "Thank you, Trey. I won't forget your name."

* * *

They walked to the security lines, saying nothing more. She left him and moved quickly through the line. He was frozen, feeling helpless as the note burned in his fingers. He pressed it, as if he could squeeze the information out. She glanced back at him as she put her boots and bag in a tray. He nodded and hoped his smile appeared encouraging. She went through the metal detector, gathered her things, and hurried up the ramp.

He looked down at the note. His heart pounded in his chest, and a light sweat broke across his forehead. Steadily, he pulled at the corner of the paper and paused, measuring consequences. He glanced up at the crowd of people moving on to find their gates.

He held his breath then made a decision. His fingers couldn't open the folds fast enough. He fumbled then read the meager writing.

> *I wish I had met someone like you a long time ago.*
> *I think it would be good to know you were checking in on them.*
>
> *Jillian Parish 185 Fulmer. phone is 555-6025.*
> ~~*Tell them I have that I*~~ *My little girl's name is Shiloh. Kiss her for me.*

His hand went to his head, and he stepped back. He looked up, searching . . . frozen in place. She leaned against the wall, her mouth open, shock on her face and the pain of betrayal in her eyes.

He gulped air and stepped forward. "Reece!"

She turned and disappeared, running into the crowd, swallowed by it. He ran. "Reece, wait!"

He felt hands on his chest, firmly pushing him back. "No, wait. Reece! I have to get to her. Please." He jumped up and couldn't see anything but bobbing heads and carry-ons. "Reece! I know your sister!"

"Sir, if you don't back away, we'll have to take you into custody."

He ran his hand through his hair and backed away. "But . . . I shouldn't have let her go."

The security officer gave him a sympathetic look and pointed to the glass doors leading out.

He looked down at the note and paced a few times, backing away enough to satisfy the officer. After taking a few deep breaths and failing to loosen the knot in his chest, he pulled out his phone.

* * *

Jill leaned back in her chair and stretched. They had eaten dinner out on the deck of the Pelican Pub, the only patrons braving the brisk wind coming up off the breakers. The day had been long, and despite her hesitation to do so, Jill had enjoyed it. They'd bought ice cream cones at the cheese factory and taught Shiloh to say "moo," which sounded more like "ooo," and "numm," which she was very good at and repeated every time she smacked her lips to Jill's scoop of "Udderly Chocolate." Then they stopped at the airplane museum, and her dad had taught Shiloh all about prop engines. Scott pulled off at Netarts Bay, and they had walked the docks, watching tourists pull up crab pots full of doomed crustaceans. Scott had brought a few kites from his parents' house, and they'd found one shaped like a butterfly for Shiloh. They'd spread out a blanket, and after getting the butterfly and a brightly colored box kite anchored in the sand and flying above them, Scott taught Jeremy and then Jill how to fly the stunt kite, pulling the twin strings, one held in each hand, and guiding the kite as it swooped and whirled, working with the wind. The action exhilarated Jill, and more than once, her laughter carried in the air, moving around her. And she hadn't meant to bring the kite crashing down on Scott as he dove into the sand, arms over his head. She really hadn't.

Now Shiloh sat on her lap, still working at the crackers that had come with Jill's chowder, squealing as Scott threw fries to the gulls. Jill clapped along with her.

"You look happier," Scott observed.

Before Jill could reply, her phone rang. She furrowed her brow. "Unknown caller."

Scott leaned toward her, concern on his face. He nodded, and she took a deep breath.

"Hello?"

Silence. All she could hear was the surf, the seagulls, and Shiloh's babble.

"You at the beach, Jilly?"

Her heart plummeted, and she threw her hand over the mic.

"Is that my girl?"

She hung up, shaking. She tried to get a breath.

"Jill?"

"He knows. He knows we're at the beach." She looked at his blue eyes, searching for the flecks like air she needed to breathe. "He knows I have Shiloh."

He furrowed his brow. "He knows we're in Pacific City?"

She shook her head, pulling Shiloh closer. "He heard the sounds. He asked if I was at the beach, and then . . . he heard Shiloh." She threw her head back. "*Why* would I answer with her in my lap?" She scooted her chair back and stood. "We can't stay here. My dad." She found him out on the beach, talking to some of the dory men. "He can't stay here. If they see him at your parents' house . . ." She looked around then started gathering their things. "We have to go." She pulled the diaper bag up, but it was stuck. She pulled again, and the chair moved with it. She pulled again and again, the frustration rising, turning to panic.

Warm arms drew around her. "Shh. Jill."

Slowly, her heart calmed. "It's stuck," she whispered weakly.

"I see that. But your arms are full. I'll get it."

She nodded, and he held her a little longer.

"Why? Why did this happen?" She leaned her head on his shoulder. "And why won't it end?"

"I don't know. But we'll figure it out, okay?"

She took a deep breath.

"Ma ma?"

Jill felt a small finger pressed to her cheek. "No, sweetie." She kissed the finger. "Jill."

Shiloh looked around at the ground. She lifted her hands and jabbered a question.

Jill followed her search. "What do you need?

Shiloh reached to the ground. "Da da da da."

"Did you drop something?" Jill bent down, peering under the table. Then she straightened. "You want to see Hobbes?"

Shiloh let out a string of syllables.

Scott smiled. "That might be it."

Jill stroked Shiloh's head and kissed her. "Okay, let's go see Hobbes."

The phone rang again, and they froze. "I can't do this again." Scott took Shiloh from her, and she read the number. She didn't recognize it. She shook her head at Scott.

"I'm right here."

She answered, not letting her eyes leave his gaze. "Hello?"

"Hello, umm, is this Jill Parish?"

"Yes. Who is this?" Her heart was no longer pounding; it pulsed like an out-of-control strobe light. She leaned on the table.

"This is Trey Gentry. I—"

"Trey?" She looked at Scott. He held out his hand for the phone. She didn't argue.

"Trey? This is Scott . . . It's a long story." He looked up at her as he sat down. Shiloh reached again for her crackers. "You what? Her sister's name is Evie . . . Are you sure?"

Jill slowly sank back down into her chair, leaning toward Scott, reading his eyes.

"Okay, but . . . go easy, things are pretty rough."

She blew out a small breath at his understatement.

He shook his head. "Another time, bro." Scott handed the phone to Jill. "I'm not sure, but I think he found your sister."

"But, how—?"

He nodded to the phone. "She said her name was Reece."

Jill gaped as her stomach rolled.

"Jill?" The worry in his voice turned to fear.

She shook her head, shook away the dread. She breathed in deeply. "Reece is my mother's name."

Carefully, Scott asked, "Do you want me to talk to him?"

She shook her head again and put the phone to her ear. She took another breath. "Trey?"

"Jill, you need to listen to me and then ask questions later, okay?"

"Okay." She sat still as Trey recounted all that had happened, very still, up until he told her about opening the note and finding Evie watching him. His voice broke, and he sucked in his breath.

"Jill, I'm so sorry. I just thought . . . if there was anything in there that would help me help her . . . I just thought she was a runaway. We've been able to help a few . . ."

She rubbed her forehead, her emotions a mix of relief and anguish.

"I thought maybe you had offered to keep the baby," Trey continued. "You had the little girl with you at church on Sunday. I didn't know . . . I just didn't know . . ."

And now Evie was gone. He hadn't alerted airport security. He had called Jill. And Evie knew he would. Evie knew and now might run harder.

"It's okay, Trey." She blinked against the tears, fighting to keep her composure, telling herself this was somehow good. But all she could feel was emptiness.

Trey said, his voice low, "She was right here. She was so scared, and I had her right here."

Jill held her hand over her mouth; she couldn't assure him again as she broke under the weight of emotion brought by his words. *I had her right here.*

* * *

Scott glanced in the rearview mirror as he drove back from the restaurant. Jeremy stared blankly out the window and held Shiloh's hand as she slept. Scott peeked at Jill. She'd broken down after the phone call with Trey, sobbing softly into her hands, barely able to tell them what had happened. She was calmer now, but he guessed that calm could slip at any moment. She quietly spoke on her phone to Laura.

"Thanks, Laura. We'll be there soon." Jill ended the call and looked at Scott. "She's packing up my stuff."

He nodded. "We'll leave as soon as you're ready. We'll head back to Portland, and you'll stay at my place—" He put a hand up at her protest. "I don't give a *rip* about conventions right now, Jill. We have an extra room for you and the baby, and your dad can have my room. I'll sleep on the couch. Or I'll make Trey sleep on the couch. Heaven knows he'll do it, he's so torn up." He made a sound of frustration, pounding his hands on the steering wheel. He caught her flinch and reached over, gentler now. "I'm sorry. I'm sorry for this nightmare you're going through."

She leaned back against the seat. "I have to find her."

"I know." After a few moments she added, "At least she had Trey."

He nodded. He'd been thinking the same thing. Trey and Detective Okada were now working with airport security, trying to locate Evie. Despite Jill's gratitude for the role he'd played in getting them one step closer to finding her sister, Trey was pretty crushed that he hadn't tried harder, hadn't acted on his gut instinct to somehow keep Evie there.

Jill and Scott were quiet, each of them thoughtful, unsettled.

Jeremy spoke from the back. "I'd like to come back here. Maybe stay."

Scott glanced in the rearview mirror, and Jill turned around.

"You mean, permanently, Dad?"

"Yeah. I think I'll look into it, after we get Evie, and after that no-good waste of creation is behind bars."

Scott raised his eyebrows. Jeremy seemed so . . . meek. But there was a little fight in him. Scott looked at Jill, who had turned back to face the front, her fingers playing with the hem of her shirt.

"He had a little to do with creating Shiloh, Dad."

"Hmph. Very little. His only redeeming quality. As far as I'm concerned, he'll be stripped of that connection when he meets his Maker." Jeremy shifted in the seat. "If he ever makes it that far," he murmured.

Scott hid a smile. Jeremy had shown and said very little about his lost daughter. Jill had said he hid things well.

"So you think we'll find her, Jeremy?"

"Darn tootin'."

Scott glanced at Jill, hoping Jeremy's positive attitude would catch on, but her head was bowed, her brows drawn together in worry.

He reached over and touched her hand. "Hey."

She lifted her eyes to him, and they were still a little red from crying at the restaurant. She shook her head. "I just keep thinking of what I could have done . . . to make her stay."

"She's a grown girl, Jilly," Jeremy said.

Scott agreed with him, but he knew the words didn't help.

She lowered her eyes. "I suppose you would just tell me not to let it bother me."

He frowned at the road ahead, making the turn into their neighborhood. "What kind of worthless advice would that be?" He pulled into the Thorntons' drive and faced her. "Let it bother you, Jill. Being bothered is better than feeling *nothing*. Just . . . don't let it drive you away from yourself and the truth."

She watched him, her eyes filling with some complex emotion he couldn't place.

"I'll get Shiloh in the house. You two talk." Jeremy maneuvered the baby out of the car and left.

Scott turned off the car and faced Jill.

She swallowed. "How do you know?"

"Know what?"

She looked scared but not fragile. Not breakable. Her soul seemed to search his. "How do you know me?"

He gave a small shake of his head as she made the slightest move closer, her fearful eyes softly drawing in his. He smelled the sea air on her skin and in her hair. That space inside him opened up again . . . only for her.

She shook her head. "I don't understand why you're not running away. You don't know what you're getting yourself into. This isn't just about me. It's about Shiloh and Evie and who knows what else. How can you know you want any of that?" She lowered her face, turning her eyes down. "How do I know you won't"—she furrowed her brow—"I mean, I wouldn't blame you if you—" She didn't finish.

He lifted her chin with his fingers, and her eyes drew up to his again. "You think I'm going to brush all this aside? There's more than just chance at work here. You may not believe that yet, but I do. Someone said courage is grace under fire. I know you're a fighter, Jill. If you believe I know you, then believe that."

CHAPTER 12

Hope pressed a folded tissue to the corners of her eyes. "Is it really that awful?"

Scott sighed and pulled her to him. "I thought you should know. You need to understand why I need to get her out of here."

After dropping Jill off at the cottage, he'd hurried to his parents' house so he and Jeremy could grab their things and he could explain the situation to his mother.

"But surely he wouldn't find her here if all he has to go on is the *beach*?" She pulled away, taking his hands.

He shook his head. "It's not so much that, although Highway 6 *is* the fastest route to the coast from Portland, and that leads directly—"

"Here."

"Mm-hm. But, Mom, Trey had her sister right there, and she slipped through airport security. I have to help Jill find her. It's too close to let go."

As she held his hands, reading him, her look of worry relaxed. She patted his cheek then took his shoulders, a smile growing. "It's good to see it, Scott."

"What?"

"You . . . you look *alive*." Her eyes shone, and he felt his throat constrict. "I've missed that for you."

He swallowed hard. "I'm sorry, Mom. I'm sorry I wasn't there for you at the beginning with Dad and for so long after. I was too wrapped up in myself."

She was already shaking her head, her smile widening. "It doesn't matter. I knew you'd find a way through. You're like your father. I try to be like him, you know? He always found a way." She pulled him close and whispered, "Fighters, both of you." He suppressed the sob in his chest. "Let Jill know she's in my prayers, that you're both in my heart."

He squeezed his eyes tight then let his mom go so he could pick up his bags.

"Call me."

"I will." He turned for the door.

"Bring her back here. Please."

He looked at her over his shoulder. She beamed as the tears fell.

He nodded.

* * *

Jill picked up Hobbes as Grant drew Scott in, patting him hard on the back. "We'll be back in Portland day after tomorrow. We'll keep an eye on your parents."

Scott nodded. "Thanks. We'll be in touch."

Grant stepped to Jill, looking her in the eyes. "Be careful. Remember your blessing. You have the power to discern. You choose what to do with what comes."

"Thank you, Grant. For everything." She rubbed Hobbes's head, and he licked her chin. "Be good, Hobbes. Be steady." She looked up at Laura after she set the dog down, feeling the pang of leaving him, but Scott's apartment didn't allow pets, and it would be better this way until things were more settled. "Are you sure you'll be okay with him?"

"It's like he's one of us. Don't worry, Jill. He'll be fine with us for as long as you need." She pulled Jill into an unexpected hug. "We'll be praying for your family." Jill's heart stuttered at the affection, at the word *family*, and she was unable to say thank you again.

Grant held out his hand to her dad. "Jeremy, it was great to meet you. I hope we meet again under easier circumstances." The men shook hands, and Grant stepped back to put his arm around Laura.

"Thanks for taking care of my girl. My *girls*." Jeremy slid in next to Shiloh, and Jill and Scott got in the car. They began to ease away from the cottage.

Jill felt a lurch inside as Laura waved. Laura called out, "Just love her. The rest will come to you. Remember, *but for the grace of God . . .*" She waved again. "I'll see you when we get back home."

Jill nodded, unable to breathe. The car backed out, and the family became smaller, until they turned out of the neighborhood and onto the rural highway out of town and back to Portland. Jill shivered and rolled up her window. She watched Shiloh play with the soft book she would not give up. Her little finger pointed, and her full lips pursed.

"Djj dj dj djj dj."

Shiloh was her complete responsibility now. She had no idea what that meant or for how long. And if they found Evie . . . if they didn't. What had Officer McKay said about the state? No way was Jill letting strangers take Shiloh. She breathed out. "She might be going to Texas?"

"That's a possibility. Dallas International." Detective Okada had called with his findings at the airport. Despite Evie's attempt to keep Trey from knowing where she was going, with the time line, they had been able to narrow the search. But so far, neither of her sister's names had showed up on any passenger lists, and they were still running through security tapes. Texas was an option, as were several other big destinations. Just the thought made Jill's resolve waver. If Evie were to go somewhere like Texas, she couldn't pick a better place to hide. She would be a grain in an immense field of wheat. No, not a grain. Chaff, a bit tossed and turned where the wind blew. Big cities, little towns, miles of highways, turnoffs, thousands of all kinds of people. Jill folded her arms over her stomach, squeezing.

The ride was quiet. She found herself holding her breath at every passing car. They'd been e-mailed a picture of Neil and a couple of his cohorts. The state patrol would be on alert for a blue 1980s Chevy Impala on major highways from Portland to the coast. She had looked up photos of the car on the Internet and remembered her father's groan, knowing he was lamenting the modern version of the classic he loved.

The '61 Impala convertible. Comic book lines any superhero would be proud of.

The 80s models looked like a regular old car to her, so every dark vehicle they passed made her stomach knot until she could make out the color. With the fading light, that was getting harder to do.

"If the connecting airports had her picture, wouldn't they find her?"

Scott took a deep breath. "They're big. But there's a chance." He reached and peeled her hand away from her waist and rubbed her fingers.

She knew he wasn't saying the other *buts*. But Evie could change her appearance, change her plan, buy another ticket somewhere else using another name. All she had to do was walk off the plane, out of the airport, into a cab, onto a bus, and disappear. And right now, though she was more than a missing person, the police were not conducting a high priority manhunt. She was wanted for abandonment and suspected theft. "If they find her flight, they'd notice if she didn't make a connecting flight, right?"

He nodded and brought her hand up to kiss it.

How was he doing this? Where had they been three days ago? Now, he and his brother—even his parents—were as caught up in her life as she was.

And he seemed to want to be. He kept doing the right things, reading her the right way. As much as she hated that he and his family had been dragged into this, that she was so exposed, almost all her demons shoved to center stage of this tragic play, it was him. She wanted it to be him.

As if he needed any more tragedy in his life.

She bit back another apology. She knew she would just be told not to apologize.

"Get down! Get down!" Scott pulled her down, and she heard her dad scuffle in the backseat. Headlights zoomed past. "Shh—" He stopped himself and fumbled with the phone.

"Scott?"

"Stay down. They slowed."

Her heart strobed in her chest. Scott frowned, keeping an eye in the rearview mirror. They curved around a bend.

"Did they turn around?"

He was pushing keys on the phone. "I don't think we should find out." He pressed on the gas. "Detective, this is Scott. I think we just passed the Impala. No, it's getting dark . . . headlights and blue . . . Chevy. Yes. No. Well, I'm trying to put space between us . . . I saw brake lights, and then we went around a bend . . . umm, mile marker . . . thirty-one. Yeah, thanks." He hung up. The car continued to accelerate. "If they figure out it was us, they'll know we're headed back to the city."

"But . . . how would they know it was us?" She had to hope, to look for reason.

He shook his head. "I don't know. They'd be looking for, what, two adults, maybe three if they think of your dad, and a car seat, leaving the coast?"

They fit that description. "But we ducked?"

"Yeah, I don't know if that helped or made it worse. It's still light enough to see if you're looking."

"Scott, they know what I look like. And Dad."

He nodded, watching the speedometer. "They're sending a state patrol car."

"You're driving really fast." As much as Jill wanted distance between them and the other car, she gripped the armrest as they maneuvered another blind curve. She drew in a sharp breath.

"I'm keeping it under seventy-five."

"It's *fifty-five* here." They went over a rise, and Jill's stomach stayed behind. Her phone rang. She looked at the number, and the amount of tension in her body doubled.

Unknown caller.

She took a breath. She wasn't going to fall apart again. *Courage is grace under fire.* Did she believe that? Did she believe in grace?

She did. She wrote a three-hundred-and-twenty-eight-page book about it. Adrenaline rushed through her, and she no longer felt like cowering.

"What do you want?" She held on to the arm of the door as Scott made a turn.

"Hey, Jilly-pill. What are you up to?"

"I'm considering having my number changed, Neil."

"You enjoying the beach?"

"Yeah, it's great. Did I tell you we're in Astoria? You should join us, nice and rainy up here. It's fizzling out our fire though. The marshmallows are getting soggy." She gripped the phone as the car climbed a hill. She was sure they were going faster than seventy-five.

Neil chuckled. "Yeah right. Maybe we'll join you. Maybe I can see my little girl. Maybe sooner than you think."

She braced herself as the car crested the hill and bounced down on the shocks. "I hate to tell you this, but Evie is *gone*, Neil. Like, leaving-on-a-jet-plane gone. It's just like her too, playing the sad little stray, getting all the sympathy and money she could and then, poof. Gone."

"Oh, I think I can find her. I found you."

She covered the mic as a truck zoomed past. "That was really difficult. Get online lately? Pick up a phone book? Evie isn't in a phone book, is she, Neil?" She caught a warning look from Scott. She took a few breaths, trying to contain the anger she felt unleashing her tongue. "Anyhow, have you considered my offer?"

"What offer was that?"

"To pay you back the money she stole, so you could have your little *high* you're so miserably dependent on . . . you *weak, twisted addict*." She felt the swelling flood. "What are you without that, huh? You'll never know. You'll just keep ruining your *sorry* life and the lives of everyone around you!" Her body wracked in pain. "You don't care enough to stop. You don't feel anything. It's the fix . . . the fix you live for. It doesn't even love you back. It just takes and takes." She squeezed her eyes against the hurt, against the images. "You just take and take and never give anything. *Anything.* I hate you." She drew in a ragged breath. "I *hate* you!"

She felt her father's hand on her arm. Neil had hung up somewhere in the tirade, and she dropped the phone in her lap. She was crying again.

"I'm okay." She wiped her eyes, and her dad handed her a handkerchief. She cleaned herself up. "I'm okay." She wasn't, but she would be. She was horrified and embarrassed by her outburst, and she was pretty sure she'd just made things worse, but in some odd way, she felt strong.

Scott glanced at her sideways with a sort of pride on his face.

They heard sirens, and Scott slowed. Oncoming flashing lights passed, and she sat up, watching them disappear behind them as quickly as they had come. Another blaze of sound and lights passed. Two patrol cars. She watched the last one disappear, and then her eyes met Scott's. He held her there a moment, then he nodded, reaching for her hand. His grip was sure. She sat back in her seat, willing herself to breathe.

Not much was said during the remainder of the trip back to the city. Adrenaline left her and exhaustion wove its way through her senses. Scott's phone rang, and he spoke quietly. She was too tired to try to understand. He spoke with her father, and someone patted her shoulder a few times.

She became aware of increased traffic and the bleary lights of the city. The car stopped and the ignition cut.

Her door opened. "C'mon, Jill." Scott's voice was soft. She undid her seat belt, and he pulled her up. She got her feet underneath her, and he supported her to the door.

"Shiloh."

"Your dad's bringing her in." He led her through the door and up a flight of stairs then knocked, and another door opened right away. "Hey."

"Hey. The room is ready. Where's the crib?"

"In the trunk."

Scott led Jill down a hall and set her on a bed. He crouched in front of her and ran the back of his hand along her face. "Jill? You awake?"

She nodded in the dark.

"We'll bring your things in and set up the crib." He reached for a bedside lamp and switched it on.

She squinted and turned away.

"All right?"

"Mm-hm."

He moved to leave, but two steps from the door, she felt the urgent need to call him. "Scott?"

He returned and sat, putting his arm around her. "What is it?"

She leaned heavily, not caring what he thought of her as the panic subsided. "I don't know. I just . . . didn't want to be left alone."

Her father came in with a load and Shiloh. Jill held her arms out and pulled the baby to her. Trey followed with the crib and more bags. Jill closed her eyes and smelled Shiloh's hair, leaning into Scott again and listening to the others set things up. Shiloh stirred and began to whimper, pulling Jill out of her waking sleep.

"Her diaper bag?"

"Here."

She laid Shiloh on the bed and pulled out things to change her. Jeremy handed her a half-empty bottle. "Do you think she'll want this? It's cold."

Shiloh took a few draws then pulled it away and closed her eyes.

"The crib's ready."

Jill stood, and Scott steadied her. Then she put Shiloh down and covered her with a blanket. She softly ran her hand along Shiloh's face. Standing up, she focused on Trey.

"You helped Evie," she said.

He lowered his head, looking at the floor.

She stepped to wrap her arms around him. "Thank you."

He hesitated then rested his hands on her back. "I'm sorry," he said into her shoulder.

She shook her head. She stepped away, and Trey looked at Scott then left the room.

"Get some sleep, Jilly." Her father gave her a small hug and lowered his head to peek up at her. "We'll see what tomorrow brings, okay?"

She nodded, and he smoothed her hair quickly then left. Her bag sat at the end of the bed. She stared at it, unable to lift her eyes.

"The bathroom is just across from this room. Towels are in the cupboard. Can I get you anything?"

She shook her head. He stayed put.

She wiped a tear. "I . . . I'm sorry I'm . . . this way. I'm usually able to hold it together, you know?"

"Jill, you're human."

She nodded. "Do you think I made it worse?"

It took him a few seconds to answer. "Probably not. If anything, you just showed him you were tougher than he thought."

She pulled at her hands.

"I have a meeting in the morning . . . something at work. But I'll be back here as soon as I can, and we can make a plan, okay? Okada will call about anything that comes up." He stepped to her and took her hands. "Jill, they can't do much more about Evie. Not from here. They've got authorities on alert in the major airports."

Jill nodded, feeling the tears well up. "But it might be too late."

"They're focusing on Neil now."

She sucked in a breath. "Okay."

"We'll talk about it tomorrow." His hand came up to her face, and he kissed her cheek. Then he wrapped his arms around her, and she felt her consciousness fight to stay taut, but it was losing.

"I love you, Jill."

The words were so soft she thought she'd imagined them. But she drew in her breath and wrinkled her brow. She pulled away to look at him, and he looked carefully back.

"I know I should wait, but . . . I wanted you to hear it now. You need to hear it now. I love you. So . . . sleep on that and nothing else." He pressed a kiss to her cheek again, and his warmth spread from there to the tips of her fingers and down to her toes. She was dreaming. "Good night." He stepped away and closed the door behind him.

She didn't know how long she stood there, staring at the door, her hand on the edge of the crib, but sometime later, she pulled off her jacket and shoes, found the lamp switch, and wrapped the covers over her body, sinking into oblivion under Scott's words.

* * *

"He should be home soon."

Jill bounced Shiloh on her hip and looked over at Trey, who was studying at the table.

"Dee dee."

"Can I make her some lunch?"

He turned the page of his thick book. "Of course. Use whatever you need."

She left the bookcase she'd been studying without interest. Nothing could distract her. Reality was too blaring for her to be tempted by the titles on the shelves. The thought of her novel flickered. Rewrite.

She had struggled all morning, caring for Shiloh, aching for Evie, feeling the lift of the words she wasn't sure she had heard him say. Her emotions played Boggle with her priorities: shaking them up then trying to find answers in the jumble thrown down. Focus. Focus on what is important. There is no place for anything else.

But he'd changed everything.

"Ma ma, dee dee."

She walked to the kitchen and searched the fridge, finding the yogurt Laura had packed for her.

She glanced over at her dad on the sofa by the windows as she sat down at the table with a spoon. "What are you reading, Dad?"

He looked up from his paperback. "Oh, Clancy." He held up the cover. "Found it in the bookshelves."

The Hunt for Red October. "Not enough action for you here, huh?"

"This happens to other people."

She nodded. Her father read. Never anything too grand or deep, but he read. She thought it had probably saved him through some of the abuse. He had most likely hidden from reality there in Clancy, Grisham, L'Amour, and Patterson. He'd taken her to the library a couple times a month, offering her the same escape. She wondered, not for the first time, if he had been a different kind of man . . . her mind drew the same conclusion it always did. He would have left. He would have taken them with him.

Jill sighed and wished for the highchair at the beach house. Shiloh kept grabbing the spoon. "Is this a yogurt facial?"

Trey laughed, and it was a good sound. Hadn't she just laughed recently?

Keys jiggled in the door, and it opened. She breathed. Felt it. Scott scanned the scene and when he found her, the corner of his mouth came up in a cautious way. He locked the door behind him, and she pulled in another breath as he approached.

"Are you getting some lunch, Shiloh?" He leaned over and rubbed Jill's shoulder. "You look like you got some rest. How did you sleep?"

She nodded, watching him, feeling the flush come. Had it been a dream? The question had haunted her all morning. Shiloh reached for the spoon again, and Jill pulled it away just as Scott leaned forward to take the chair next to her.

"Oh."

He paused, yogurt from the spoon in Jill's hand smeared across his nose and cheek. Trey muffled another laugh, and Jill felt her own giggle bubble up, but she swallowed it.

"I'm sorry."

Scott shook his head, hiding a smile. "Thank you for sharing, Shiloh."

Shiloh pointed. "Dee dee dee dee."

"Mm-hm. Yum."

"Here, I'll get you a paper towel."

"No, you stay. I'll get it." Scott got up and wiped off the yogurt at the sink, his back to her.

Jill glanced sheepishly at Trey, who watched her, a little baffled but still chuckling and shaking his head. She raised her eyebrows. "It was an accident."

"I know, I know. I just . . . didn't think you had those."

She rolled her eyes, well aware of the reputation she had among the young adults of the ward. Scott came back and sat down.

"It's not the first time she's squirted me in the face with dairy products . . . or whatever this is."

A quiet laugh found its way up from her chest this time. Scott had brought over a fresh, damp paper towel and wiped Shiloh's face and a bit of her hair. Then he took the spoon from Jill.

"Here, Shiloh. Let the trained professional do it."

Jill balked.

"It's true. Right, Trey?"

"I don't know about the professional part, but trained, definitely." He answered her questioning look. "Our sister, Amy. Three kids. Holy terrors. Great spitters, each of them."

She smiled and watched Scott make a funny face with his lips as he fed Shiloh a spoonful of yogurt. "Amy kept a small umbrella hanging on the highchair."

She laughed, and it occurred to her that she'd laughed more in the last few days, even amidst all this turmoil, than she had in months.

Scott peeked at her, smiling. "I'd walk in and find her huddled behind this clear umbrella, splattered in something green, still holding the spoon and trying to get beans or whatever in the kid."

"My kids are all getting bananas. Who doesn't like bananas?" Trey shook his head and returned to his studies.

Her smile lingered as she continued watching Scott feed Shiloh, and he stole glances at her, grinning. Finally, he scraped the bottom of the container and gave Shiloh the last bite. He used the spoon to clean her face a bit then reached suddenly and kissed Jill on the mouth. He pulled back as she blinked.

"I love your smile." He got up and threw away the container, tossed the spoon in the sink, and left down the hall.

Jill felt eyes on her as she stared after him, resting her flushed cheek on Shiloh's silky curls. When she turned back, Trey moved quickly to look back down at his book.

After she collected herself, she asked, "What are you studying?"

He lifted his eyes. Blue but no flecks. She noted the similarities between the brothers for the first time. Same blond, same build. The ears, though, and something more boyish about Trey. Maybe that's why he wore the goatee.

The corner of his mouth lifted sardonically, but remorse hung in his eyes. "Psychology."

She nodded. "Perfect."

"Yeah."

Her dad sighed from the sofa.

* * *

She put Shiloh down for a nap, aware of the cold she felt after letting the baby go. She rubbed Shiloh's warm belly and watched her for a minute, her small body stretched out and peaceful. Comforting. How had she not known of this child who was now so thoroughly woven into her being? What would become of it all?

Heavenly Father, help me be part of her happiness.

She found Scott waiting in the hall after she closed the door. He had changed out of his work clothes.

"She's a good baby, taking this all really well."

She raised her eyebrows. "You think so?"

He nodded.

Jill looked at the closed door. "Sometimes I think I can see her worry, wonder where her mommy is." She lowered her eyes. "I'm not sure what she's used to."

"You're doing a great job. She knows you love her."

She looked up at the words, and he took her hands.

"We need to talk about what we're going to do next."

Her jaw tightened, knowing he was right but wanting to push it aside for just a little longer. It had all seemed suspended for the morning, hanging in the background like an old, filthy window everyone was tired of looking through but nobody wanted to clean.

He looked at her hands and lowered his voice. "Jill, you said you could use a friend."

She nodded.

"I hope I'm not . . . giving you too much to think about. That's not my intention. I just want you to know I'm here. I'll be here, but if it's too—"

She pushed up, returning the kiss from before. He stumbled back as she drew her arms around him. She didn't want him to apologize or offer to slow down or any other stupid thing he was thinking. She wanted to tell him she loved him and pressed her meaning into every move. He resisted momentarily but then returned her effort with great interest. Nothing faded, but it all slowly intensified. To heck with escape. This was facing life. This would be the scariest thing she had ever done. She had to feel this, wanted to . . . before they had to talk about a plan, before they had to face—

"A-hmm."

Scott pulled back a bit, looking down at her. The floor seemed to tilt. "A-*hmmm.*"

They both turned their heads at the sound. Trey came into focus.

"Sorry, man. I really gotta go." He nodded to the bathroom door they were blocking. He fought a smile.

Scott took a deep breath and ran his hand through his hair. He took Jill gently by the shoulders and moved her farther down the hall.

"Way to go, Scott," Trey murmured as the bathroom door closed.

Jill looked up when she heard Scott's soft chuckle.

His eyes lit. "I would have to agree." She smiled, and he traced the side of her mouth with his finger. "So," he appeared shaken, taken in wonder, "we're good, then?"

She never thought anyone would look at her that way. The words she longed to tell him were a weight on the tip of her tongue, and she failed to find the strength to send them into the air. She only nodded, sure and more alive than she had ever been.

He drew her up and kissed her until they heard a flush. Scott groaned. "I believe that's our signal to work out those other things."

"Appropriate."

He blew out a laugh and held her face gently. His eyes narrowed, but they were still lit up. "Cougar."

She grinned and bit her lip.

* * *

"Thanks, Detective. Yup. Bye." Scott hung up and rubbed his eyes. "All right. They must have pulled off somewhere after they spotted us."

"So it was them."

He looked at Jill. "Yeah, but there aren't any towns or rest stops in that area, so they think they just pulled off on one of the forest roads and parked in the woods with the lights off. They did find the Impala in Tillamook this morning, abandoned at a gas station. The station's cameras showed Neil and two guys getting out, and they left the keys. They bought some food and made a phone call then left. They walked out of surveillance, probably caught a ride with someone."

"They just left the car because we might have spotted them?" Jeremy asked.

"The car was stolen. But the person named on the registration didn't report it, only admitted it had been stolen when the police called."

"What?"

"Okada said this guy knew it was Neil, figured he'd get it back to him. He was pretty tight-lipped about it and anything else he was asked."

He turned to Jill and pressed his fingers into the table. "Jill, I think this is bigger than we thought."

"What do you mean?"

He pushed through his hesitancy, and she braced herself. "The Seattle police had an inside man on a big drug deal. It went bad when the middle guy didn't show up with the money." He waited for her response.

Then understanding hit. Her voice weakened. "How much money?"

He rested his hand on hers as it tapped the table. "A quarter million." The tapping increased under his fingers.

"You're saying," she swallowed, "Neil was the middle guy?"

He nodded.

"And somehow . . . Evie stole two hundred fifty thousand dollars?"

"I don't know. I don't know how much she took, but it was enough that Neil couldn't make the deal, so he took off, chasing Evie and you and now us. Actually, I'd say we're on the lesser end of things. I'm pretty sure the guys looking for Neil are a little more . . ."

"Connected," Jeremy said.

Scott looked at him and nodded.

"But that makes this Neil guy desperate." They all turned to Trey. He leaned forward, resting his chin on his thumbs. "She knew. She knew how desperate he would be. That's why she was so set against anyone knowing where she went. She figured it would put us in danger if we knew."

"Do you think she knew about my apartment?"

Trey shook his head. "I don't think she considered Neil would think of you so soon, if at all. I don't think she would have left the baby with you if she suspected he would move in your direction. She asked me to check in on you, that's all. It was naïve, but . . ."

Jill finished for him. "But she was desperate."

Trey nodded. "I saw it in her eyes. Forgive me, but your sister seems to be very . . . *small* to be taking on what she did. It was as if . . . she couldn't decide between fight or flight."

Jill's gaze trailed off at nothing in particular. "She never could."

Scott squeezed her hand, and she looked at him.

"She didn't have anything, only the clothes she was wearing," she said. "Where was the money?"

He shrugged and shook his head. "If it was in larger bills, she wouldn't need a suitcase. A couple hundred bills in her pockets or a wallet. Maybe she stowed it somewhere before going to your place. A locker at the airport."

Jill considered that. "So the police look for Neil now?"

He nodded.

"And somebody in Texas will have a picture of Evie from seven years ago, and my mother's name may or may not be on a flight itinerary from yesterday." She shook her head at how hopeless that sounded.

Scott glanced at Jeremy and received a small nod. He turned back to Jill. "Your mother's name was never on the flight itinerary."

"What?"

"Okada called your dad this morning when you were still asleep and didn't answer your phone."

Jill pulled out her phone and slumped. She'd let the battery die.

Scott continued. "A woman matching your sister's description was seen on a security camera exiting a Portland to Chicago flight and entering an airport restroom. The woman Trey described never came out, but they suspect she changed her appearance. A woman with the same bag came out and made her connecting flight—a connecting flight from Chicago to Kansas City. No passengers were reported missing on that flight."

"Chicago to Kansas City?"

"She's trying to get lost, Jill. She chose the longest flight to Dallas available."

"Why didn't you tell me?" She looked at her dad. He patiently gestured for her to keep listening. She turned back to Scott.

He pulled over a notebook and a pen. "Detective Okada crossed Neil Bradshaw's name and a few aliases he's used with Evie Parish." He paused, as if deciding whether to continue.

"Tell me what he found." Jill eyed the notebook.

He blew out a breath. "One of Neil's names was Mitchell Johnston. A Mrs. Alisa Johnston boarded the same flight Evie did."

Jill sat back in her chair. "Alisa?"

Scott nodded.

Alisa. Everlisse. When they were kids and Evie was little, only three or four years old, she had an imaginary friend who was pretty and brave, and Evie called her Alisa.

She looked at her father, who nodded his head as though he knew exactly what she was thinking.

Scott continued, watching her carefully. "Alisa Johnston didn't make her connecting flight from Kansas City to Dallas."

Jill leaned forward, breathless. "She got off?"

He nodded. "In Kansas City."

Jill's hand tapped the table again, her thoughts whirling. She turned to her father. "Dad, I need to ask you a favor."

"What do you need, honey?"

"I need you to watch Shiloh for me. For a few days." She kept her voice steady, despite the tightening of her chest.

He watched her a moment then nodded his head. "I can do that. You bet I can."

"Jill?"

Jill turned to Scott. "I'm going to find her. I'm going to Kansas City, and I'm going to find Evie. Please, don't try to stop me or talk me out of it." Her heart raced, but though it felt right, the whole idea of flying to a strange city scared the brave right out of her.

"I won't talk you out of it." He reached into his back pocket.

"You won't?"

He shook his head and dropped some folded printed pages onto the table. "If I did that, I'd have to eat one of these boarding passes." He pushed the pages toward her.

She pulled one to her. "These are—"

"Flights from Portland to Kansas City, where Evie didn't make her connecting flight."

"How . . . how did you pay for this?"

Scott cleared his throat. "We all chipped in some."

Her gaze moved between all three men, then slowly, she picked up the papers. "There are two tickets?"

He took a deep breath. "I thought . . . you might not want to do this alone. I thought maybe I could help. Kansas City is big, but I happen to know it pretty well . . ."

It took a few moments, then she remembered. "Your mission."

Scott nodded.

She stared at him, and he shrugged.

"Take it, Jilly," her father said.

She looked at the tickets again. Finally, she said, "I have to go."

Scott took her hand and squeezed.

"I have to go and . . . try. If I don't, I don't think I could . . ." She covered her mouth with her hand but then straightened and met Scott's patient gaze. "And I need you to come with me."

Scott smiled reassuringly. He nodded. "We leave tonight." He reached under his chair and pulled up a little cellophane bag tied with a gold ribbon. "This was for you in case you chose to go alone. A little added courage."

She leaned her head to the side and took the bag. A slight smile came to her lips, though her anxiety over what they were about to do eased only a fraction. "And now?"

"Now you have to share."

She couldn't help the short laugh that escaped her. She looked at Trey, her father, and Scott, overwhelmed. She could hardly get the words out. "Thank you." She tugged at the ribbon. "A little chocolate never hurts."

CHAPTER 13

They had a short layover in Salt Lake City then were off again. Haunted by the drifting pictures of Evie and Shiloh, her father, her mother, and the turbulent wake she left behind her, Jill started when Scott reached and pried her grip from around his hand. He stretched his fingers then took her hand again.

"I'm sorry," she said. "I haven't flown much. Takeoff makes me . . . worry."

"I noticed. What could you possibly be worrying about?" He raised his eyebrows and gave her a hint of a smile.

She breathed out. "I just . . . see the faces I'm leaving behind . . . anticipate that whatever can go wrong will go wrong. And what that would do to them."

He gave her a sympathetic look. "No faith?"

"Faithful people have died in plane crashes, Scott."

He nodded. "I know."

Of course he knew.

She shook her head. "I'm sorry."

"Let's just try to hope. All right?"

She nodded and stared at the flight magazine in the pocket in front of her. The flight to Salt Lake had been long and quiet. She'd even dozed, waking on Scott's shoulder, hearing the deep breathing of his sleep. She had thought they would talk, but he seemed content with her silence, only asking a few questions about how she had come to Portland and her dad's fixation with classic cars.

Now, though, she was wide awake. So was he.

"Did Okada ever tell you what came up on my background check?"

She lowered her eyes and smiled. "Four speeding tickets in the last three years, which doesn't surprise me after yesterday, and a citation for trespassing and defacing private property, which does." She looked at him questioningly.

He chuckled. "Let's just say one of my professors didn't have the sense of humor I thought he did."

"What does that mean?" She leaned her head back against the seat, looking at him, waiting for more insight as to how the boy she had known for a few days had grown into a man.

He looked sheepish. "It involved toilet paper in the upper hills of Happy Valley."

She couldn't help the upward curves of her smile. Insignificant problems with the law were refreshing. "I toilet-papered a house once," she said. "To welcome our new seminary teacher. It was probably one of the most rebellious things I ever did. And *fun*. He came out with a garden hose and drenched us."

He laughed, but she could see him thinking, watching her, and she knew from the way his eyes lowered he was going to ask a question. Maybe even a difficult one.

"How is it that toilet papering was the worst thing you ever did, and we are on a plane to find your sister, who is . . . ?"

He didn't have to finish. Her gaze drifted back to the magazine. "My mom . . . she had liver disease. Diagnosed during my second year of college. Dad had finally convinced her to see a doctor about her pain. I remember thinking that maybe she went with hopes of getting some prescription painkillers." Jill wrinkled her forehead. "'Stop drinking, and you can heal.' That's what the doctor said. 'Stop drinking, and you won't die.' There was a good chance. Dad was so hopeful, so supportive. He thought it might be a turning point. He still loved her, you know." Jill pictured her dad carrying her mom's limp body to the bed and tucking her in or helping her into the shower, reading by her side as she slept off her stupor, pouring out bottles when he found a chance, not showing the true hurt when more appeared. "He never gave up until the very end."

"Why did she drink?"

She looked at him. "I don't know. I asked Dad once. He told me that some things in this world can't be forgotten, and mom used the drink to try to forget. It scared me, his quiet voice. I've imagined it was some sort of abuse." She looked out the window at the dark atmosphere. "I don't try to guess what kind."

Scott didn't say anything, just ran his fingers gently over her hand. She blew out a breath and turned back to him.

"So she had a chance. She had me and Evie and Dad, and she could have lived. And she chose not to." She heard the edge to her voice. "Evie was only a junior in high school. She had already started hanging out with the druggies. It might have been easier, I guess, instead of fighting every minute of your life to choose what you knew was right over what you felt you deserved."

"Is that how it was?"

"That's how it *is*. Trying every day to fit into the normal world around you. Because when you live with an alcoholic, it's never normal. Even when it's part of every minute of your life. Evie's normal became getting high, being accepted by those who offered the high. She ran away with Neil after Mom died because Neil was her normal."

"And your way?"

Her eyes misted over as he searched them. "I'm still fighting."

He gently touched her face. "What is normal, anyway?"

She shrugged and let out a sad laugh. "A job, an apartment, a dog. A clean kitchen."

"Sounds boring."

She laughed again as he brushed his thumb under her eye. "I stayed *busy*. I just didn't know how lonely being busy was."

He nodded and continued to caress her hand, calming her as she fought the fear that this was too much for him, that she would scare him away. But his eyes were too full of sincerity to be thinking like that.

"I've never talked like this with anyone but you," she said.

"I'll take that as a compliment."

* * *

He'd had her all to himself for several hours, yet he'd only begun to ask the countless questions he had for her. The mood was not lighthearted, and he kept reigning in his thoughts, his questions, being careful, choosing so he wouldn't mar the beginnings of this *something* he knew could be bigger than anything he'd imagined before she'd come back into his life.

And yet, when she smiled, it excited that space in him, an accomplishment so trivial but so paramount. With all this turmoil, to make her really smile was something heroic. At least, that's how it made him feel. Like he had a super power.

He had seen her before, here and there—at church, coming out of her office building. She had seemed so together. Infallible. Trey had used the word *controlled*. That was before the revelation. Cougar. He would never forgive himself for the lapse. It no longer mattered, but he would be making it up to her for the rest of his life. Longer, if he could manage it.

Controlled. It was why Trey had suggested Scott shake things up. Then judge from there. It wasn't until the humiliation of his failure with the phone switch, the awful crash when those pages went flying, and seeing her pick up papers as she tried to hide the tear she'd fought, that he knew, whoever she was, he wanted another chance. And he'd hated the thought that he wouldn't be given one.

Incredibly though, he had. Looking at her now, he shivered at how far they'd come in such a short time. He wondered how much farther they had to go until the smile and the look of wonder would not be so hard fought. Something told him it would take much more than time. But he'd seen it when they'd played on the beach. Her energy, her joy . . . it would be worth this fight. He was sure of it. Why else would he have been put here in her way?

He pressed his finger to the center of her brow. She'd let it fall again with worry. "Tell me."

She raised her eyes and blinked slowly. He was grateful for the close confines of the seating and that their heads leaned toward one another as they talked.

"Shiloh."

He nodded. "Do you know what you'll do?"

"If we find Evie, will she understand? If she comes back, she's going to have to get help. I can't let her do to Shiloh what . . ."

"Your mother did to you?"

Jill nodded. "And then there's work. I suppose my dad could help out, but he has a life too, I think, and he's never wanted to live in Portland. I *want* him to move to the beach if that's what he wants to do. But how am I supposed to take care of Evie and Shiloh and leave them every day to work? How am I supposed to trust that Evie wouldn't just leave again? And I don't want to leave Shiloh. She's had enough of whatever her life was like before." She closed her eyes and rubbed her forehead. "I don't even want to think." Her eyes flew open. "But that's the other thing. I don't know *anything*. You should have seen me that first day. When Officer McKay mentioned child services, I panicked, thinking they would find me incompetent. They would watch me trying to take the tray off the highchair and check the no box."

He laughed and covered his mouth. She nudged him with her shoulder.

"But you want her. That's more than they could find in her own parents."

"No. No, Scott. Evie loves that little girl. I saw it. There's no faking what I saw. I know that, somehow, having Shiloh gave Evie something she never had before. Trey said she was doing this because she believed it would be better, and it was tearing her up. I believe him."

He spoke softly, considering her loyalty, her belief in her sister. "If we find Evie and that's how she feels about Shiloh, then we'll convince her that it will be better for her daughter if they were both surrounded by people who love them and that she needs to get real help with her addiction."

Her expression faltered. "We couldn't convince my mom of that."

"No. But maybe it's not too late for your sister."

She nodded, thoughtful. "Maybe she loves Shiloh enough." She turned to the window, the beginnings of a sunrise turning a dark world to gray.

* * *

"Do we even know what we're doing?" She looked down at the flyers in her hand. They had distributed them throughout the airport, bought a map of the city, rented a car, and were now hanging the flyers on a main street in the middle of Kansas City, Missouri. They had digitally darkened Evie's hair a shade, and Trey had added a little smudge of eyeliner around her eyes. Jill looked around her at the quiet street in the gray morning hours. "How big is this city?"

"About 450,000 people. A little smaller than Portland, actually."

Maybe it was the towering buildings stretching around her or the complete strangeness of this city, but she had difficulty believing him.

He touched her elbow. "C'mon, let's move down the next street."

As the city came alive with people, Jill watched them pass, drive, interact, and keep to themselves. Thousands of faces. Not one of them caring who she was or what she was doing there. She passed out the flyers, holding them up and speaking loud enough to at least draw a glance. Her throat hurt, and her hands trembled along with her voice because it was hopeless. Her eyes followed a group that might attract her sister. She stuck out her arm.

"Have you seen this girl? Reece? Or Alisa?" They nudged past, barely looking up, one of the guys running his eyes over her. "Look at the picture, not me." The guy shook his head, chuckling as he walked away with the others.

Her head spun. What if someone had spotted Evie but they were walking on some other block? What if they didn't see a posted flyer because their heads were bent down? What if Evie saw the flyer and it scared her farther away? Her fist tightened around the page in her hand, and she dropped her arm. A fresh wave of people came in her direction. What if one of them had seen her? Her chest tightened.

She stepped up. "Have you seen this girl? Please, she's my sister."

A couple looks of sympathy, and the flyer was taken from her hand. "Thank you. If you have any information, the number to call is at the bottom." The group moved on.

She found Scott talking to a police officer, their heads bent together over a flyer. He turned and gave her an encouraging look. She took a deep breath and stepped to the center of the sidewalk again but was knocked sharply around.

"Hey, watch it, baby."

"Oh, I'm sorry."

The broad young man looked her over. "That's all right. That's all right." His eyes darted to the few pages that had fallen to the ground. "Here, let me get those for you."

Despite his sudden politeness, everything about him made her tense.

"There you go, gorgeous. Who do we have here?" He pointed to the face. "You lookin' for her?"

Jill pushed down the spark of hope. "Yes. She's my sister. Have you seen her? She would have only arrived yesterday."

"A lot of time to get lost since then." His eyes came up. "She don't look like you though." He winked.

Her stomach twisted. "Have you seen her?"

He rubbed his chin, studying the paper again. "Maybe. I'm, uh, meeting with a few friends. Why don't I take you with me, and we can ask around?" He had already reached for her elbow and was brushing up against her, moving her away. She stopped, everything inside her telling her this was wrong.

"What's the matter, baby? You with somebody?"

"Yes, she is."

She breathed. The man released her at the sight of Scott and the police officer. He put his hands up. "Okay, I apologize. She wasn't wearing no sign around her neck." He winked at Jill and held up the flyer. "Mind if I keep this though? This is *your* number, right?" He grinned, chuckled at Scott, then moved on quickly under the watchful eye of the officer.

"It's not my number," Jill said quietly, as if needing to reassure herself of the truth. She wrapped her arms around her middle and closed her eyes as Scott took the stack of paper out of her hands. He rubbed her arms up and down.

"He was playing with you. If he calls that number, he'll end up having a little chat with the nice people down at the police station." He leaned closer. "You okay?"

She shook her head.

"You want something to eat?"

She shrugged. "I feel like if I stop, we'll miss the person who's seen her."

"I've spoken with Officer Dobbs here. He'll put the word out, have Evie's picture posted to every unit in the city. They'll check all the known hangouts."

She felt the tension ease as she saw the concern in the officer's eyes.

"We'll do what we can, miss."

"Thank you."

Scott pulled his arm around her. "C'mon. Let's sit somewhere and eat. You're exhausted."

She nodded and let him guide her away from the faces on the street.

* * *

She teased her food with her fork.

"Jill, we're in Kansas City. At least enjoy the barbeque." As soon as the words were out, he regretted them.

"This isn't a vacation."

He set down his napkin. "I know. I just . . . I think we're doing all we can."

"Are we? Isn't there more? Shouldn't I be visualizing her coming around every corner? Running into the good person who helped her yesterday, who knows where she slept and is meeting her in a few minutes about a job? Or hearing there was some raid and she was pulled out of the dregs and is in holding until someone can claim her? Am I supposed to hope for *that*?" She dropped her fork. "Shouldn't I be *fasting*?" She leaned onto her fist. "I'm sorry. I can't enjoy this, Scott." She gazed out the window, chewing on her lower lip, tension around her eyes. They scanned the people rushing by. "I thought I saw her twice. Something breaks inside me every time I find I'm wrong."

He wanted to touch her, to ease the tension showing on her face. "I know this isn't a vacation."

She looked down. After a few moments, she nodded. Quietly, she said, "I have no right. After everything you've done. After I've dragged you into this—"

"I came quite willingly."

"—after helping me . . ." She raised her luminous eyes and timidly reached for his fingers. "But my priority is Evie."

He nodded. "And mine is you." He wouldn't let her look away, and she didn't. Slowly, he leaned across the small table between them. "I love you, Jill."

He saw her struggle, breathe, wonder. He was making it worse. Cautiously, he sat back and tried to look as if he didn't expect an answer, that it was enough that she just knew. He looked at her plate. "Let's get a box for that. You may be hungry later."

She sat back and brushed her hair behind her ear with a nod. Her eyes drifted to the street.

Good. Good, Scott. Way to stay in the background. He had warned himself to do just that. This trip was not about them. He was support, backbone, encouragement. Not the spotlight. "Maybe we should go back to the hotel, get some sleep, let the police take it," he raised his hand at the alarm on her face, "just for a couple of hours. The evening crowds will be coming out by then."

He could see her fight, but fatigue won out. The only sleep either of them had allowed was on the plane. She nodded in defeat, and he signaled for the check.

As they exited the restaurant, he noticed a poster on the window. Jill saw it too.

"3 Doors Down. You like them," she said.

He nodded, reading the concert times. They were playing that evening at the Sprint Center, just a few blocks from their hotel. He stepped away, but Jill stayed put.

"Evie likes them too. I remembered when I had your phone. I hadn't thought of it in a long time . . . hadn't really thought of Evie for a long time." She lowered her eyes. "Not very sisterly of me, I know."

He rubbed her arm. It wouldn't be any use to remind her that Evie was the one who broke contact. A couple came out of the restaurant, and he pulled her out of their way, but she was reading the poster again. She stepped closer and ran her finger over the glass, over the time of the concert.

"I think we should go."

"To the concert?" That was the last thing he thought she would want.

"Maybe she'll be there. Even just hanging around outside. They were her favorite. At least in high school."

"Jill, it's a huge arena."

She nodded and bit her lip, looking hungrily at the poster. He held his breath then blew it out as he pulled out his phone. He dialed the ticket number and waited.

"Hey, I was wondering if the 3 Doors Down concert at the Sprint Center is sold out yet? Yeah, tonight for two. Mm-hm?" He turned away from Jill and lowered his voice. "How much?" He closed his eyes and swallowed. "And those are together?" He pulled out his Visa. "Yup, I'll take 'em."

After the transaction, he turned to Jill, pulling her to him and looking her in the eyes. "Is this doing more?"

She nodded, a tear escaping. "I know it's a big arena, but it's a big city, and at least this has some sort of connection with her, instead of just," she looked around them, "chaos."

He wiped her tear away and kissed her cheek. "We'll try."

"Thank you." She found his lips, and he was more than willing to accept her gratitude.

* * *

"Hello, Miss *Snyder*. Marci, right?"

Marci turned from the mailboxes in the lobby of her apartment building and was immediately filled with alarm. She recognized him from his picture. She looked around, trying to remain calm. "Hello."

"You're hard to get alone."

"What do you want me alone for?" She swallowed and fingered her keys. She'd heard you can gouge out an attacker's eyes with keys, though these seemed very short and so did her reach. "Do I know you?"

"We have the same friend. I was hoping you could help me find her."

"Oh? Who are you looking for?"

"Jill Parish. She's my cousin. I wanted to surprise her, but I'm only in town—"

"Oh, are you the one who called?" She gave him her best smile. "I am so sorry I lost you. My boss had me on the other line and blah blah blah." She laughed nervously and swallowed. "What was your name again?"

"You work with her. You know where she is, right?"

She nodded, peeking around him, not knowing if he was alone. "Yes, but I told you before, she's on vacation."

"At the beach."

"Mm-hm. Lucky thing." She pressed her lips together, feigning another smile.

"I think she's back."

"Oh? Well, why don't you try her apartment?"

"I did. Nobody home. The place is a mess though."

"Really? Huh. That's strange. She's kind of a neat freak. And she *is* supposed to be on vacation for the rest of the week, so I don't know why—"

He stepped to her, and she stood her ground, her eyes widening at his menacing grin. "I think if I were to hang on to you and let the right people know, we might get somewhere."

She blinked her eyes innocently. "Are you coming on to me?" He paused to chuckle, close enough now, and she threw all her strength up through her wrist, feeling the crack of cartilage as the heel of her hand rammed his nose. He cried out in pained surprise, and she readied her keys just as two officers in navy blue grabbed the man's arms and jerked them down, cuffing him. One read him his rights, and the other called in on his radio. She peeked around again and saw two strangers being shoved into the police car.

"Miss Snyder, we told you not to try anything." Officer McKay looked at her reprovingly.

She took a deep breath, calming the nervous stammer of her heart. "I was just giving you guys an opening."

CHAPTER 14

Jill's sleep had been deep and dark, beneath the surface of something she couldn't be part of, something shimmering, suffocating, undeserved. She heard the rush of surf then . . . the shower.

Several minutes later, a sliver of light met her eyes, and Scott emerged from the bathroom dressed in jeans and a dark T-shirt, towel-drying his hair. He grabbed a brush from his bag and turned to go back in the bathroom but paused to look in her direction.

"Are you awake?" His voice was soft enough that if she'd been asleep, it wouldn't have woken her. He had made her lie down as soon as they'd returned to the hotel room while he made phone calls and promised to sleep too.

"A little," she replied, inhaling the masculine, steamy scent coming from him and the bathroom. She had been tense, still feeling they would miss a link to Evie by leaving, still recalling his clear, unveiled words at the restaurant, aware of his closeness once they arrived at the room . . . but she had drifted off to the sound of his voice much more quickly than she would have thought herself capable of. She noticed his bed was slightly rumpled. She had insisted on the double room when he had insisted on paying for their accommodations. She didn't want to be left alone. Not ever again.

She reached for the lamp and switched it on, glancing at the clock, and dropped her head back down on the pillow. "Your hair is all spiky."

He nodded and held up the brush. "The bathroom is all yours. But can I tell you something first? It's good news."

She nodded and pulled herself up on her elbow.

He stepped to the bed and crouched down next to it. "They found Neil."

"What?" The words were simple, and yet she struggled.

"He went after Marci."

"What?" She felt sick.

"No, it was a setup. They knew he'd been following her."

"But she could've been hurt." She raised her eyebrows at his soft laugh. "She *could* have!"

"I know, I know." He moved her hair out of her eyes. "She broke his nose before the officers stepped in."

As he told her the details, Jill felt herself relax and let go of that one fear, that one chain around her psyche. Neil was going to jail for a long time. Too many trails connected him to the drug deal, too much evidence gathered, too many other people wanting him gone, including the bad guys who may still try to silence him. And attempted kidnapping had been added to the long list.

One less link to keep Evie from returning with her.

Scott smiled. "Feel better?"

She nodded. He brushed his finger along her face and got up to tame his hair.

She pulled herself off the bed and dragged her bag into the bathroom. "You smell good." She saw his smile in the mirror across the way as he brushed his hair, and then she shut the bathroom door.

She sighed into the steamy mirror. She had to wake up. Turning on the faucet at the sink, she splashed her face a few times, the water jarringly cold in the wet heat, until a shiver ran through her.

"Okay," she told the foggy mirror, "quick shower, find Evie, go home."

After kneeling in quiet prayer, Jill emerged from the bathroom dressed and made up, feeling energized and more sure. She put her things away and looked around for her shoes but paused.

Scott knelt beside the bed, head bowed in his own prayer. She lowered her head but not her eyes, hushed by his action and the Spirit pervading the room.

After a moment more, he turned to her and stood. "Hey."

His simple greeting summoned a rare, full smile to her lips.

"That's beautiful."

She flushed. "I think this is the right direction."

"The concert?"

"Yes."

He stepped to her and gently held her waist. "I hope so." He turned to the dresser holding their bags and pulled something from his. "I got you something." He faced her again. "My sister, Amy, said this was the one to get."

She thought he was giving her chocolate again. She was wrong. She pushed her hair away from her face and took the large paperback book in her hands. A chubby baby on a sunburst quilt smiled at her from the cover. *America's Best Childcare Series, What to Expect the First Year.* Looking back up at him, her voice caught.

"It's for you and Shiloh. And Evie." He looked unsure but expectant.

She didn't recognize it at first; it was a gradual thing, coming on second by second. She could breathe deeply, watching him, and she could feel the ache in her core, the awareness of her soul, the light that he was just above her. And it propelled itself, a bubble of certainty pushing up to break the surface, too strong for her to anchor any longer. To strong for any undertow. Just a bubble, pushing up and up, as if it had no other purpose but to burst into his atmosphere.

"I love you."

The words were a hush, foam on sand, but he heard them. She saw the wonder in his eyes, the rise and fall of life in his chest, the strength of his soul, everything—everything she loved in front of her, taking in her words with muted fervor.

She tried again, testing herself.

"I do. I love you." She reached a hand to his shaven face, the thrill of her words pulling up the corners of her mouth. What was this joy that had her suppressing a laugh? He searched her eyes, the hint of a smile touching his lips. She tossed the book on the bags and embraced him, inhaled him, pressed into him as his arms came around her and he settled his face into her neck.

They stood there for a moment, not wanting to break the clarity of her discovery. Finally, he pressed his lips to her throat, sending welcome tremors to her fingertips, and then he faced her. Her gaze moved from his eyes to his mouth and back again.

She hadn't forgotten Evie or Shiloh or any of it. It was all right there waiting for her. But she was not alone. He would not let her forget. He would not pull her away or distract her but urge her forward, next to her. The muted fervor deepened.

He whispered urgently, "That's all I need, Jillian."

And then he kissed her deeply, and she pressed into him, giving in to the moment until he lost his balance, falling into the media cabinet. She breathed out a laugh, which seemed to incite him. He stepped into her, his arms strong around her, making her feel amazingly feminine and wanted.

She reached up, leaning her head back with a smile, and again, he kissed her throat.

"This is what it feels like?" she asked the ceiling, breathing in this new awareness.

"I need to give you books more often."

She laughed and let her fingers slide over his face. He kissed them as they passed over his warm mouth.

"Is this better than chocolate?"

She nodded, smiling. They watched each other, catching their breath. "Is it really all you need?"

He nodded, gathering her up tightly. "For now." He grinned and lowered his voice. "We need to get out of here."

She nodded, feeling a rush of hope. "Let's go find Evie."

* * *

The confidence of her earlier elation didn't last. They had started an hour before the concert, handing out flyers. Most people avoided them. People out for a pleasant evening didn't want to be brought down by somebody's runaway sister. Inside, they'd walked up and down the aisles, skirting the perimeters and watching at different entrances. Evie's flyers were posted on every door. After the band had taken the stage, they found their seats and stayed put until most of the arena was standing, dancing and singing with the music, some making their way closer to the stage. Security tried to keep everyone in order, so Jill and Scott took turns leaving, scouting, until it didn't really matter where they were anymore.

The concert was winding down. And Jill had seen no sign of her sister.

"Hey, buddy, watch it."

Scott put his hand up. "Sorry. Excuse us."

The crowd pressed, and they had to yell above the noise.

Jill tried to maneuver around a large man with a beer in his hand.

"Where do you think you're going, sweetie?" His words weren't meant to be kind.

She turned away from his liquored breath. "I'm looking for someone."

"Oh yeah, sure. Hey! She's looking for someone. Just let her on up to the stage! Yeah right, you are." Somebody shoved him, and he spilled what was left of his beer down her shirt. He laughed. "Awww, I'm sorry. I guess that's what happens when you—"

"What's your problem?" Scott cut the man off when he stepped in front of his face.

Jill's assaulter was unfazed. "Your *girlfriend* thinks she can go wherever she *wants*."

"Yeah? And where's *your* seat?"

Laughter erupted. The pasty man shoved Scott in the shoulders, sending him into more people. Scott straightened himself up, receiving a few shoves from behind, and Jill grabbed both his hands.

"C'mon," she yelled and pulled him away, moving back from the stage and on to the next section. The man yelled something after them, but she kept Scott moving away. They found a break in the crowd, and he pulled off his jacket, dabbing her shoulder where the beer had soaked through.

"I'm sorry."

"It's not your fault." She took the jacket from him and continued to wipe her shirt as she glanced around. "I don't know." She sighed. "I don't know how to find her."

The first few chords of the next song brought her eyes around to his. The band was playing "Away from the Sun," Scott's ringtone. Jill leaned her head to the side, listening to the lyrics over the crowd. They were words of hopelessness, of being in the dark and wondering about ever finding a way out, back to those in the light.

"Your favorite?" she asked Scott.

He shrugged. He bent close to her ear now so he didn't have to shout. "It was how I felt after Costa Rica."

She pulled away and blinked at him. He leaned in again. "Then, with my dad, and . . . well, when nothing seemed to go right." His arms drew around her, and he pressed his forehead to hers.

"Do you feel that way now?" she asked.

He shook his head.

"Me neither." She didn't. Despite the desperation of their search, despite being soaked with beer, despite everything, a light burned inside her. And she clung to it.

He kissed her briefly. Then he turned her, and they continued their way to the other side of the arena, searching, trying to stay out of the way.

After an encore performance, the concert ended.

"I need to—" Scott gestured to the restrooms. "Will you be all right?"

She shrugged and nodded, disappointment drawing a curtain around her as the endless crowds moved past them and through the glass doors. "Hurry."

He nodded. "No lines."

She gave him a half smile, and he left her holding herself, looking around out the glass front of the arena. They were near a side entrance, smaller than the front entrances most people milled out. A white jacket caught her eye for no reason other than it was dark outside and the jacket stood out in the small crowd on the other side of the street. The wearer seemed to be calling to another group and laughing loudly under the street lamp. There was some shoving from his companions and more laughter. Then the group momentarily broke apart.

Jill drew in a breath and strode to the window. She pressed her hands to the glass. A small figure, bent in on herself, showed through the crowd for a fraction of a second. Jill glimpsed a knit cap, miniskirt, and boots. The group absorbed the figure again, as if she'd been a ghost just carried along. Quickly away.

"Evie!"

Jill rushed to the doors and pushed through, stumbling past figures in the way. Her heart beat erratically as she ran over the lawn and spotlights on the trees, ducking under their red-leafed branches. "Evie! Wait!" She paused at the street, too far away to be heard as the group rounded a corner. She couldn't wait. She threw out her hands in front of her and ran into traffic, hearing the screech of tires, the horns blasting through her, blasting her breath away. She hit the other sidewalk and ran under the street lamps. *"Evie!"*

She rounded the corner and saw them, slowing down in front of a gap between old buildings, a dark space near parked cars. They were turning down an alley. She pushed herself forward, clenching her jaw. She paused just before the alley, swallowing her breath, her heart. She turned the corner and the group noticed her immediately.

Three men turned at the sound of her footsteps against the gravel. Straightening up from their positions against an old car, they watched her deliberately as she moved forward. She needed to see. She needed to be sure.

"You looking for something, gorgeous?"

She searched beyond the men. "I . . . I'm looking for my sister. I thought I saw her with you."

The man in the white jacket relaxed his stance and shifted his weight toward her. "Heeeey, baby. You still lookin'? You remember me?" She glanced at the man, startled to see it was the same one who had bumped into her before lunch. His comment drew the rest of the group's attention, and more faces turned to hers in the slice of faded light from the street lamp far behind her. She searched them frantically, trying to find the one, afraid it had been a delusion.

"Evie?" she called to the group beyond.

"Nope, no Evie. I've got somethin' you might want though."

She ignored his advancing steps, breathing frantically, still searching the group. "Reece?"

The group seemed to still at the name, and the broad man who called her *baby* chuckled. "Now, why you wanna go and mess things up? Huh? You want to get messed up?"

Her attention jerked to him. He liked it.

"You knew she was here. You knew from the picture." Anger pulsed through her body. Nobody cared. She called again, "Evie, it's me!"

He laughed, and with his last step toward her, she found herself pressed against the alley wall. "Now, there's sorry ways of gettin' messed up . . ." He furrowed his brow and clucked his tongue. "Or," he reached a finger and ran it down her arm, "there's nice ways of gettin' messed up." Her heart stuttered as the two men behind him chuckled. He placed his hands on his hips, moving aside his jacket to show her the gun shoved in the waist of his pants. Her anger vanished as fear finally hit her. He cocked his head to the side. "Why you all alone, baby? Your boyfriend give you up like your sister?"

She stepped to the side, back toward the light, but he wrapped his thick hand around her arm. She fought to keep the tears away, to keep terror and despair from taking the hold they desperately desired. She forced the words from her burning throat. "Please, I'm just looking for my sister."

He nodded, watching her. "Any of you know her?" he addressed the faces behind him without taking his eyes off her.

She looked franticly behind him. His other hand wrapped around her other arm, and she struggled away. "No!"

"You scared?" He held her still. He was so much stronger than she had imagined, jerking her toward him. "I told you before I'll help you find her. You'll do somethin' for me, first."

She heard a faint cry beyond the faces. She gasped and shoved against him. "Evie! Don't let them hide you!"

He pulled with her shove and easily wrapped his arms around her, laughing. She could hardly get breath as he squeezed, but she smelled rank cigarettes and pungent body odor covered by his cologne. He pulled her toward the car, dragging her as she fought, and she was unable to get her hands up, pressed too close to him to use her knees or feet as weapons. She thought to reach for the gun, but he jerked her hard in warning.

"You don't want none of that, sweetness. I got something much better." One of his friends opened the back door of the car, laughing.

"No!" she cried to the blank, pale faces, but some had already turned away. He tried to shove her down, and she fought him, screaming. As his hand came over her mouth, she bit hard, and he swore. In one move, he lifted her against the car and reached back to strike her but paused.

The faint sound of running on gravel reached her ears. Suddenly, she was slammed from the side with the force of a truck and then fell down hard into the scraping gravel, rocks clawing into her hands. The hand that had gripped her was pulled away, and she scrambled to get up as movement erupted all around her. She crawled away toward the light, fighting to get on her feet.

Then she heard Scott. "*Run*, Jill—" His plea was cut short by a dull thud and grunt. She spun around. Silhouettes scattered, getting away, but the thick, heavy figure she had only just escaped was battering Scott as Scott lunged himself into more blows, slamming her attacker into the car. The two other men hovered, as if waiting their turn. He looked back at her. "*Run!*" One of the men grabbed him and slammed him into the side of the car, smashing the window.

A scream filled her ears, wet her eyes, emptied her of breath. He swayed dangerously, only to be picked up again.

"Run, Jill."

Tearing herself away with a cry, she ran out of the alley toward the street, footsteps sounding behind her. Her pursuer grabbed the back of her shirt, slowing her down, but she twisted, throwing her elbows and fists. Her elbow made contact, and she was free again. She ran until she reached the light and fumbled in her pocket for her phone. "Help! Somebody! Help me!" She waved at car lights leaving the arena and called toward the few lights in the windows of the buildings dwarfing her. "Help!" She dialed, her fingers clumsy as she looked behind her in the alley. The dark figure of her pursuer hovered indecisively. She held the phone so he could see it. "They're coming!" she shouted. The shadow moved away and started running down the street.

She watched the alley, trying to dial again. She'd left him. "Scott!" She held the phone to her ear, but tears blurred everything, and the phone shook in her fingers. *Scott. Heavenly Father, hear me.*

A loud, sharp siren pierced the cold, but she still heard the compressed shot echo off the walls in the alley, rocking her where she stood. A gunshot. Without a thought, she ran back into the alley. The flashing of red and blue lights coloring the walls followed her. She stopped short.

A small figure stood, swaying, and a knife dropped from her hand. *Evie.* The girl began to tremble, holding her side, and Jill ran to her, her eyes sweeping to two figures on the ground, one eerily still in his white jacket, the gun inches from his outstretched hand. The girl dropped into Jill's arms, and they both sank to the ground.

"Evie?" Jill pushed off the girl's cap and brushed away her hair, the flashing lights pulsating red and blue on her skin. She bit back her panic, thinking of the other figure still moving on the ground. "Evie, it's me. I found you." Tears coursed.

Evie opened her eyes. She raised a hand covered in dark, sticky liquid, and Jill tried not to think that it was blood—Evie's blood.

"Evie, what happened?" Confused, she looked at the knife and gun. A pool of blood spread beneath the man in the white jacket from the slash across his neck.

"I knew . . . you'd get away." Jill's attention was drawn back to her sister. "You had to . . . for Shiloh . . . I couldn't let him hurt Trey." Evie's hand dropped to her chest. "Not Trey."

Calls filled the alley, along with the pounding of sure feet.

Evie's hand moved to Jill's and rested there, so light, so fragile. "You'll . . . be good to Shiloh." Evie's eyes closed.

"Evie?" *Don't leave me. Don't leave me again.* Scott's body lay in front of her, his face to the ground. He struggled to move. "Scott? *Scott?*" *No. Not him. Not everyone. Not again.* She pulled Evie closer, rocking her. Wet warmth spread, cooling her hands in the night air, and she shifted Evie in her arms, lifting her.

"No." Evie's clothes at her waist were saturated. "No." Weeping openly, Jill scrambled to find the bullet wound, to press against it, to stop the flow of blood.

Evie gasped weakly. "Jilly?"

"Yes?"

"It's better."

Jill shook her head, then Evie's body began to shake, and Jill clung to her, even when the paramedics tried to pry her away, even when the convulsing stilled, even when they lifted Evie's body to a gurney.

Evie's hand slipped from hers.

In her mind, Jill stood in the middle of the room, surrounded by broken shards, pain cutting her knee and shattering her heart like the glass. She was trying to be big. *I'll take care of you, Evie. Mama. Shh. It's all right. I'll make it all right.*

But it wasn't—and she couldn't. She didn't want to fight anymore. She'd lost. What made her think she could win? *You're nothing. You get what you deserve. Nothing.*

She couldn't breathe in the flashing lights. She could no longer hear the chaos pressing against her ears. A medic pulled at her sleeve, his mouth moving.

God, where are you?

Her own arms wrapped around her were not enough.

And then someone else's arms wrapped around her.

Can a woman forget her sucking child? Yea, they may forget.

She shivered, closing her eyes against the sting of the tears.

Yet will I not forget thee. Behold, I have graven thee upon the palms of my hands; thy walls, thine afflictions, are continually before Me.

Behold, I am with thee and with those who will hear My voice and know Me.

With her intake of breath came warmth and sound. A low moan.

She threw herself in the direction of Scott, who was still being treated. He was awake enough to shake away the medics, wrap an arm around her, and hold her, no matter the pain, as she mourned so deeply it drowned out everything else around them.

CHAPTER 15

Jill traced her finger along his hand, knowing the lines, the curves, each hair. She took care to keep away from the bandage where the IV used to be.

"You better watch it. A guy could get used to that."

She looked at him, the bandage above one eye concealing stitches, the other eye's bruise still purple and blue. "Did I wake you?"

He shook his head and pressed it back into the pillow. "I've been watching for a while." He took her hand and brought it up for a small kiss. "You ready to go home?"

She nodded and breathed. Ready to go home. Ready to see her family. Ready to take part in the arrangements. "Evie's flying home with us."

He nodded and kissed her hand again before he looked out the window. She knew what he was thinking, but there was nothing he could have done—nothing that would have changed anything because she'd gone over it herself, wondering how she could have done it differently. But she still would have made the same decisions. He would have made the same decisions too. Evie would have made the same decisions.

She spoke just above a whisper, the only way to keep the pain low. "I hope she knew."

He turned to her. "Knew what?"

"How important she was to me. At the end . . . I hope she knew."

"She knew you were there. You'd come to find her."

She squeezed his hand, and the nurse came in with breakfast and release forms. Jill's phone rang. She took a deep breath and stood, walking to the hospital window.

"Hello, Laura."

"Hi, Jill. Grant says you're coming home today?"

"We'll be in tonight, eight thirty."

"Good. I can't imagine you want to stay there any longer."

"No." No, she needed to be home. "How is Hobbes?"

"Great. He's walking pretty well now. He'll be happy to see you, and I already miss him. We saw Shiloh and your dad this morning. They're so good together."

"They're good for each other," Jill said. That belief had given Jill comfort as she'd worried about her dad this past week.

"How's Scott?" Laura asked.

"Scraped up. Wrapped up. Refusing extra help." Scott looked up at her, and they shared a small smile as he stretched against the pain of his broken ribs. She felt the rise of emotion and shook her head, turning back to the window. Her voice quieted. "He's more than I deserve."

"Don't say that, Jill. I'm sure he thinks the same of you."

She turned. Scott reached for her hand, peering up at her in that way guys did. Jill nodded, swiping at a tear.

"Jill . . . I have something important to share with you. I think the sooner you have this, the better. You know how we forwarded your mail to our house?"

"Yes."

There was a pause. "Are you sitting down?"

Jill furrowed her brow and swallowed. "Is it bad?" She felt weak. Weaker.

"I don't think so, but it isn't anything easy."

Jill felt for the chair next to Scott by the window. He had stopped filling out paperwork and was watching her. The nurse bustled out.

"You got a letter. Honey, it's from Evie. It's postmarked Wednesday, from Chicago."

The air whooshed out of her, and her forehead fell to her hand. "A letter?"

"I'm sorry, but I didn't know if it could help at all, if it should wait until you got home, or if you wanted to hear it now."

Jill found herself shaking. It was a shock. But she had no qualms about Laura reading the letter. It was a relief, somehow. Like someone else would be in charge, would be strong.

"Would you like me to read it to you?"

Jill folded her free arm across her middle, and she half turned to Scott. "There's a letter. I want you to hear it with me."

"All right." He reached out his hand, but she climbed on the bed next to him and leaned carefully into his shoulder. He drew her arm through his and wove their fingers together.

She switched to speakerphone. "Okay."

There was a tearing sound and rustling of paper. Laura took a deep breath. "To Jilly." Her voice had a slight tremor to it.

I had to write because I couldn't just leave without saying something. You might know Trey by now. He helped me, and I think he thinks he let me down, but he didn't. Maybe at first. Tell him that. Tell him he's one of the best people I've ever known, even though that may sound stupid. But please don't think I want you to find me. I just want to explain.

I cleaned up, you know. I really tried because I remembered what you said about Mom and why I was so small and born too soon. I remembered that, Jilly. Neil laughed at me, but I tried really hard. And she's perfect. Shiloh is the one thing I did right. But since she's been born, it's been harder. I messed up sometimes. Once I woke up and couldn't find her, and I was afraid Neil had taken her like he always said he would, but then I found her in a drawer, shaking because she'd been crying so hard—just shaking— and I knew I couldn't.

I'm no good for her, Jilly. I love her so much, but it's better this way. I don't want her to be scared anymore.

Neil's been with another girl. I don't think it's the first time. I'm no good alone. Don't try to find me. Just promise you'll love her and give her what I can't. I know you can do it. You're so much stronger. I think she's like you.

You can't try to find me. I've been with bad people. Neil's involved with bad people. I'm writing their names on the back of this letter so you can give this to the police, and that will make things safer, I think. I put some money in a bank account for Shiloh. It's under the name Shiloh Jillian Parish. The deposit slips and everything are in the envelope. I was going to tell you about it, but when you didn't take the money for the diapers and stuff, I thought maybe you wouldn't take this money either. I still don't know if it was the right thing to do. I still don't know if you'll take it. But I know whatever you do, it will be the right thing.

I could never be like you. One of us knew Mom was wrong. I always knew she was wrong about you.

Kiss Shiloh. I feel turned inside out, it hurts so bad. I've given her up. But it's better. It's better for her.

Maybe you could tell Dad I did something good.

Everlisse.

P.S. Trey told me I was loved. I told him I know. I know you loved me.

Jill felt the world close in around her, suffocating her.

Scott gently took the phone and turned the speaker off. "Thanks, Laura. We'll call you when we get in . . . I will . . . Good-bye." He set the phone down.

He smoothed Jill's hair. "C'mon, Jill. Breathe. You've got to breathe, love."

She didn't want to. It would hurt. If she kept still, didn't let things in or out, it didn't hurt as much.

"Jill. For me. For Shiloh." He patted her face and shook her a little. "For *us*."

The faces flashed in front of her, everything. So much sadness in such a small window. It all became fuzzy.

"Jill, if you don't breathe *right now*, I'm going to have to give you CPR, and there are better ways to get a kiss from me."

She dragged in the air. It did hurt, burned against her tightened insides. She saw him, running after her in the sand. She held Shiloh, laughing as he tickled her. She saw her dad, walking with Shiloh on his shoulders. Quiet sobs escaped her, and she had to breathe again.

"Shh." Scott rubbed her arm, patted her hair. "Shh, that's better."

The pictures of Evie, proud to be in her arms, accepting her protection; of Jill, brave on her trike; of her dad, holding her mother on the beach, relishing the golden day with the woman he fell in love with.

The breath was softening the edges. *I know you loved me. I know . . .*

She sobbed again, quietly. Breathing was not the enemy. Neither was life. Not love. She inhaled deeply and relaxed into his embrace as he handed her a tissue. She cleaned herself up.

"Where is she, Scott? I mean, how do you think she'll be held accountable?" She'd given the question voice. It was not a new question, not to her. She waited for an answer.

"I . . . I don't know, Jill." He kissed the top of her head.

She knew he was holding back. "Tell me what you think. I have so much spinning around in my head. I need a straight answer. Tell me, and I'll make my own ideas."

"Well, she made her own choices. We don't know how many chances she was given."

She felt a rise of . . . what? Defense? Truth?

He continued gently. "But she died saving me and protecting you. She gave Shiloh up for something better after things got too desperate. And I can't help but think—"

"What?"

"I don't want to dredge up stuff, Jill. You're so understandably vulnerable right now."

She lifted her face to his. "Tell me."

He sighed and brushed her face with his fingers. "I can't help but think your mother will be held accountable."

Jill lowered her eyes. She knew it would be something like that. But it surprised her when the new thought came. *Who will be held accountable for my mother?* "Maybe . . . maybe grace doesn't just happen here in this life." She wanted to believe it was more infinite than that, that God's grace would give Evie—would give her mother—another chance.

"Jill," he rested his head on hers, "the only thing I know for sure is that Heavenly Father is a just God. He loves us, and He'll take everything into account in review of our lives here. And Christ, He . . . He knows how all this feels. He knows this." He lifted her chin and wiped a tear. "He knows Evie's pain. He knows your mom's suffering." His eyes filled with tears. "Just like He knows my mother's and mine. He knows why we make the choices we do. It will be accounted for, stacked up with all the rest. All this living. All this *fight*." He touched her nose.

She leaned into him, absorbing his words. She whispered, "Grace is not always painless."

"Hm?" He rubbed her arm.

"Nothing." She sighed. "I'm tired of fighting."

He nodded. "We'll go home. We'll love Shiloh. We'll take what's good."

A smile came to her lips. "You sound like my dad."

"He's a good man. Raised the woman I'm going to spend the rest of my life with."

Her heart pounded steadily, and she knew she was alive. She breathed. "She's a lucky girl."

"And rich, from what I hear."

She nudged him in the shoulder without thinking, and he winced. She sat up. "Oh, Scott, I'm sorry."

"No, I deserved that."

"No, you didn't." She carefully smoothed his shirt over his bandages, shaking her head. "And I can't keep that money. The police can figure out what to do with it."

"While I figure out what to do with you."

Her eyes widened, and he watched her, amused.

He leaned closer and whispered, "I love you, Jillian Parish from Lebanon, Oregon."

She swallowed. *Truth.* "I love you, Scott Gentry. I never stopped loving you." They watched each other, then she kissed him to let him know she meant it. As she drew away, his eyes opened slowly, following hers. She whispered, "You read me like a book."

He shook his head. "I'll never get enough of that."

She smiled and pushed the forms back into his reach. "Let's get out of here."

He picked up the pen. "Speaking of reading . . . I have some questions about *your* book."

She groaned softly. "I knew this would come up."

"The one character at the beginning . . . He's kind of a jerk."

"Yeah."

"And insincere."

"Yeah."

"And his name is Scout Landry."

"Too subtle?"

"It actually took me a while."

"You mean you didn't notice until you knew who I was and started really paying attention."

"That might have been it, yes."

"Well, I couldn't just come out and name him Scott Gentry. If it became a bestseller, your life would be ruined, and I'm not *that* cruel."

"Hm," was all he said.

She watched him, his tired eyes, the smile behind them for her. "Don't worry. I'm going to rewrite."

"But you haven't heard what Brasher thinks yet."

"Even if they like it, they'll say rewrite. I'll just get a head start. I need to write. My fingers are itching." She sighed.

He nodded, taking her fingers and holding them up to his lips. He whispered to them, "Change the name too."

Then she laughed, and his eyes lit up like he'd won a prize at the fair.

CHAPTER 16

"Shiloh, do you want to go see Grandpa J?"

Shiloh nodded, her curls bouncing on her forehead as she looked down at her baby doll on her lap. "Yes."

"Should we bring him some cookies for his new apartment?"

She stuck a bottle in the baby's mouth. "Yes."

"Should we go to the beach and chase seagulls?"

The little girl shook her head, puckering her lips. "No no no no no."

Jill smiled, wondering that she could love such a tiny thing so fervently.

Fourteen months old. Jill watched her daughter stuff her doll into a stroller. Shiloh hadn't spoken for so long—not real words anyway—that Jill had begun to worry she was doing something wrong. But not anymore. Shiloh now repeated almost everything.

"Does Grandpa J love cookies?"

"Yes."

"Grandpa J loves you too."

Her little girl smiled. She hadn't quite mastered his name yet.

"And Grandma loves you."

"Gamma."

"That's right, Gamma." Jill crouched down and adjusted the doll to sit a little straighter. "And Daddy too."

"Dada."

"Yes, Dada." She pulled Shiloh close. "So many people love you. And I love you too. Do you know that?"

Shiloh leaned and gave her a soft kiss. "Luh loo." Jill held her a moment, pressing her cheek against the soft curls and thought, *little drops of heaven.* She stood as Shiloh pushed the stroller around the dining table.

"Bee bee. Bee bee."

Jill breathed deeply and smiled. "That's right. Baby." She glanced down and rubbed her barely expanding belly, a bump only big enough for her to tell the difference, and a shiver of joy rushed through her, accompanied by a touch of sorrow and not a little anxiety. Still, she was happy.

She heard the keys in the front door. Shiloh stopped what she was doing and turned to her mommy, her eyes wide, her little mouth in an *O*.

Jill's heartbeat picked up speed. "Is that Daddy?"

Shiloh left the stroller and bounced toward the front door on her toes. "Dada dada dada . . ."

Scott was inside the front door by the time they got there. He set his keys down and swooped Shiloh up, and she squealed. "How's my sweetie?"

After planting a kiss on him and giving a jabbery rundown of the day, Shiloh toddled off after Hobbes.

"How's my other sweetie? Making chocolate chip cookies?"

Jill nodded, watching him. He was tired but wasn't going to say so.

He asked, "Do I get a cookie?"

She grinned, holding a cookie up in answer. He took the cookie and kissed her at the same time. He leaned in again, and she thought she'd get another kiss, but he turned at the last moment, eating half the cookie in one bite.

"Mmm," he said. "My favorite."

He kept his eyes on her, and she couldn't miss his meaning. She spread her hand over her belly. "Scott?"

He stopped chewing.

"If it's a girl, I'd like to name her Everlisse. But not Evie. We'd call her Ever. Ever Grace Gentry." There, she'd said it. Without a tremor in her voice. Without breaking down.

He gazed at her as he resumed chewing, and she held her breath. After weeks of avoiding looking for names, going back and forth, and telling him they needed to wait to decide, this morning it had come to her, and she *knew*.

He swallowed the cookie and smiled. "I love it."

She let out her breath.

He lifted his brows. "What if it's a boy?"

She frowned. "I hadn't thought that far."

He laughed. It was a good sound.

Carefully, she reached for the small white envelope on the entry table and handed it to him. "Trey stopped by with this. He made one for each of the family members."

Scott turned it over, and she watched him read the label. *In Memory of Roger Shawn Gentry.* No doubt he knew it held the slide show from the funeral, but Trey had also added footage from the dinner they'd held after. So many people had shared stories and laughter and tears, people who really knew Scott's father. As she'd helped with the final edits, Jill couldn't help wishing she had something like that for Evie. Something to highlight the fragments of good.

Scott set the envelope back down on the table. He swallowed. "We'll watch it later."

"Whenever you're ready."

He pulled her close again, searching her eyes. She wanted to be strong for him. "I like the name Shawn," she offered.

He smiled. "I don't deserve you."

She smiled back. "You deserve so much better. But fortunately, you seemed to be willing to lower yourself—"

He stopped her words with a finger to her lips, shaking his head. Then, as if he'd just remembered her looming deadline, he asked, "Did you get to write today?"

"A little, during nap time."

"Let's make sure you get time to write at the beach house."

She nodded, longing for her desk up in the captain's loft. "Are you up to proofing it again?"

"Can't wait." He took her hand, leading her toward the kitchen.

She felt herself grow quiet as he stopped in front of a collage of frames on the wall. A honeymoon picture of the two of them in front of a white stucco bungalow surrounded by giant ferns and palm leaves. Her dad with his new dory crew, Shiloh on his shoulders. Evie on her baptism day, her shy smile evoking the same little joy it had on the day Jill had found the photo while helping her dad move. Another of Jill, Hope, and Shiloh grinning on the beach. And Scott's father, so frail, smiling, thinking who-knows-what up at the blue sky. Hope had snapped the picture. His last story.

Scott brought his arms around her, his eyes on his father's portrait. Jill turned to face him.

"I miss him too, Scott." She felt his grief as he tightened his embrace.

"Thank you," he whispered. He pulled back, caressing her face with his fingers.

And she felt it. She was stronger. Ready for the waves, holding steady in the sea, eyes to the sun. She was not alone. She mattered.

Scott gazed down at her, his voice rough against his emotions. "You're my miracle, Jill."

She gave her head the slight shake she always did—the one that said she wasn't really anyone's miracle—but as he kissed her gently, she felt the strength of his embrace, the truth in his breath.

And inside, she almost dared to believe him.

ABOUT THE AUTHOR

Krista Lynne Jensen grew up in Washington State, lived in Oregon for many years, and now lives in northwestern Wyoming with her husband and four children, surrounded by mountains, rivers, and deer eating her garden. She loves to travel and explore the inspiring beauties of the country with her family and friends, and her laptop comes along too.

Krista began writing seriously after her youngest child started school full-time, and she joined a writing group, where she quickly rediscovered her passion for words. She places her characters in the settings she loves and challenges them to dig deeper and fight for what they want. Though her family keeps her busy, she tries to keep up with the stories playing out in her head—while trying to ignore the dishes and laundry.

Of Grace and Chocolate was inspired by Krista's family trips to the Oregon coast and her mother's fight to overcome a childhood overshadowed by the illness of alcoholism. Krista's love of chocolate had something to do with it as well.